Electric Life

Electric Life

RACHEL DELAHAYE

SCHOLASTIC

Scholastic Australia
PO Box 579 Gosford NSW 2250
ABN 11 000 614 577
www.scholastic.com.au

Part of the Scholastic Group
Sydney • Auckland • New York • Toronto • London • Mexico City
New Delhi • Hong Kong • Buenos Aires • Puerto Rico

First published in the UK by Troika Books in 2023.
This edition published by Scholastic Australia in 2024.

ISBN 978-1-76152-203-1

Printed in China by Hang Tai Printing Company Limited.

MIX
Paper | Supporting responsible forestry
FSC® C023121

This product is made of material from well-managed FSC®-certified forests,
recycled materials, and other controlled sources.

24 25 26 27 28 / 2

To my daughter, Matilda.

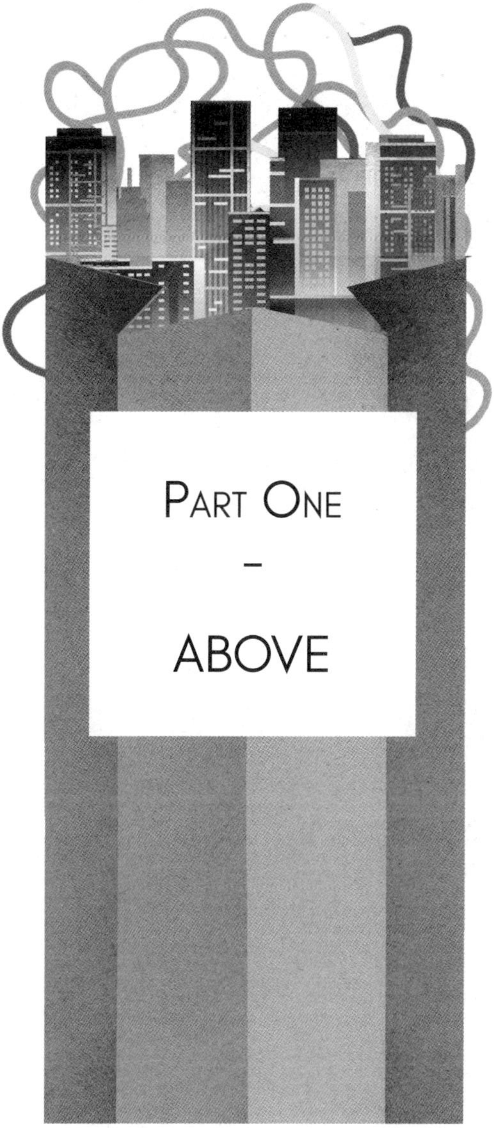

Part One

–

ABOVE

Chapter 1

I killed three people to get here. Unhooked their karabiners and watched them fall. I fended off five attacks – one from a giant who slammed into me head-on, squeezing the air from my lungs. His hands were too chunky to unclip me first go, and I was too fast to let him try again.

Now I stand at the top alone. Below me, our skyscraper city glitters like a snowflake picked out in a million lights.

I'd never imagined Estrella was this big, this breath-taking, from above. But now I can see the symmetry of it all. The city's skyscrapers radiate from a central tower in eight perfect rows like spokes on a wheel, like the compass points they're named after. They reach into the distance, one hundred towers in every direction, connected by concentric tunnels for trains and pedestrians. And from up here, on top of Central – the midpoint and the tallest building of all – the whole thing looks more like a giant, frosted web than a star.

Star is a prettier image to sell, I guess. Estrella: the star city. Though most of us call it London Star. Because that's what this place is. Or was. London.

A voice crackles in my earpiece. 'Red 2, you're the last Red in the game. Get your token and get back down to the finish line.'

I don't want to leave – not yet. I need longer to take it all in: the space, the lights, the skyscrapers we call scrapers or towers, and the penthouses that perch on their tops, private pools glistening beneath domed glass roofs. Somewhere there's a penthouse sitting empty: the prize. A Level 1 apartment. Imagine that as an address!

I turn to look at one of the most famous addresses in London Star. The penthouse of the first skyscraper in the South arm: S1/1, the home of my hero, Hoppi Burbeck. Beneath the dome, his huge swimming pool shimmers green and blue, and a large stargazer telescope points down. I'd hoped to see him, but I knew I wouldn't. He doesn't appear in public, and on screen he wears filters for privacy; few people know what he really looks like.

My gaze sweeps over the rows of apartments below Burbeck's home, and I notice how the décor becomes increasingly ordinary as the wealth decreases. Increasingly bland and not as bright. Everything below Level 80 is swallowed by gloom, and the ground at the very bottom is so black it could be nothingness. Toxic oblivion: a wasteland where no human should go.

'Red 2. Time is running out.'

The warning voice jolts me into action. I quickly collect the Red token and tug at my abseil rope, tied to Central's mast. When I'm certain it's secure, I shuffle backwards and climb over the edge of the roof. Above me, there's a spray of stars, like a reflection of the city on a black velvet ceiling.

Then *slam!* A Blue has done a running abseil round the underside of the scraper's lip. They careen into me, sending me spinning out into space then crashing back into the wall. The Red token slips from my grasp, but I manage to catch it, just, and I jam it into my mouth so my hands are free. The Blue is waiting for me to come to a standstill, so he – or she – can unclip me and send me to my death. I don't stop. Instead, I keep spinning, pushing my feet off the scraper and twisting myself round, feeding out my rope, freefalling through the air.

Through my earpiece, I hear the Blue – a female voice – tell me that I'm in critical danger, that she will help to steady me, and maybe we can do a deal. Become an undercover Blue, she suggests. I don't trust her. So I keep on falling, out of control, swaying side to side, descending fast. I plummet past windows of warmth and safety – families in their living rooms, gym fanatics in exercise pods, kids in social hubs. My eyes are blurring, but my ears are trained on the Blues' conversation: they're discussing tactics. They're discussing me, and only me.

So I'm the last Red, and my token really counts. If I don't deliver it, the Blues will win.

With uneven teams, I'm easy to pick off – if not here, then down at the finish line on Level 100 – and my guess is they'll be gathered there, watching me descend, ready to attack. The only way to get to the finish line un-ambushed is to come up from underneath. But to do that, I'd have to swing into the danger zone: the mile-high space between the last habitable level of the skyscrapers and the sea of junk below. Level 100 to the ground, known as the Drop.

It's not the greatest idea – and how will I do it without them seeing?

I catch sight of a Bolt Train pipe below – an enclosed train track heading out to Cardiff Grid, or maybe Birmingham Wheel. No matter. This is my only chance.

When my feet next make contact with Central, I push off at a sharp angle, letting the rope stream through my fingers so I'm flying – wild and frightening. I can see them now: three Blues spaced out in a line, just above Level 100. And they're looking up, waiting to catch me in their net. My rope loops around the beam of the Bolt Train pipe and I swing under it like a pendulum, below the last level of city lights and through the darkness. I pray I haven't misjudged it. That I'm not about to hit the rubbish tips.

A warning beep sounds in my ear. That's not good.

I grip the rope hard, lifting my legs. Then I'm on the upswing, and ahead is the end point: a band of green light. All I have to do is touch it. Touch it and I'm through. The Blues spot me and scramble down as fast as they can. But it's too late. I'm there, I'm flying towards the finish line, slamming into it, pressing my token against the beam. It flashes red. It's over.

'You made it, Red 2. Just in time.'

The floor rises, the lights flicker on and the cityscape vanishes, taking my exhilaration with it. Dullness returns, like fog. With a sigh, I unbuckle my harness and exit the game pod. Outside, other players are emerging from theirs, blinking and looking at their unscathed hands, which a minute ago were sore from rope burns.

A young man in a suit appears. He's not one of the big officials, although he'd like to be. His badge says *Damar, StarQuest Marshall.* He flicks open the blades of his razor pad with one hand, fanning out his work screens.

'Good semi-final, everyone?'

Some murmur. Some cheer.

'I'm going to read out four team identifications. Could those who are *not* called please make your way to the changing rooms, as you have not been successful.'

Elimination lights are lit on the helmets of every other person in my team. As the only Red left standing, I know I'm through.

'So, here it is: those going through to the finals are...' Damar drags the relevant details out from his pad, one by one, and the pages hang in the air. 'Red 2, Blue 2, Blue 4, Blue 10. Well done, you four. You're StarQuest finalists.' Damar nods approvingly at us and claps his hands, folding his razor pad in the same movement.

The rejects clap dutifully and slink away, muttering about how unfair the game was, how it wasn't thought through, how someone else should have been eliminated instead of them. And when they've gone there is a collective release of tension – spontaneous laughter – and the four of us turn to each other and shake hands. I can't see much through my gaming helmet but, judging from the height differences, I figure three of us are female. Blue 10 is big – he's the one who nearly got me; he shakes my hand like he wants to break my bones. I see it for what it is – intimidation, not a greeting. The only reason I'd want to find out who he is, is so I could keep away.

Our identities have been kept secret until now. We've played all the other rounds in private heats, sworn to silence to prevent match fixing. But now that we've reached the finals, everyone will know our names. Everyone will want to know everything.

'Will there be media?' Blue 10. Definitely male.

'There'll be coverage. But don't expect red carpets and designer clothes.' Damar laughs. 'This isn't *The Hunger Games*, you know.'

Chapter 2

I wait a while in the doorway, watching Mum and Gavi leaping around and Dad blowing up balloons. They've paused the TV. It's an image of me, with my profile details:

StarQuest finalist Alara Tripp, age 16
Quest game most played: Wilderness

'She's here!' Mum cries. 'Oh, well done, Alara. Well done!' She flies towards me and hugs me tightly, rocking me side to side so hard we fall off balance.

'Congratulations, Banana.' Dad beams, peeling Mum away, and takes me in his arms.

'How did they do it?' Gavi says, tugging my top. 'Were you really *outside*?'

'Later, Gavi!' Mum scolds. She pushes me onto the sofa and her eyes roam my face. 'You could try to look nicer. You know, now that you're famous.' She picks up a lock of my limp hair. 'You should make more of an effort.'

'Mum,' I warn.

'I know, I know.' She stands up, her eyes twinkling. 'We are so, so proud of you, Alara. The finals. *The finals*!'

'So what's next, Banana? Are you heading to a hub to celebrate? Fancy clothes? A bit of dancing?' Dad wiggles his hips.

'Er, definitely not any dancing that looks like that! No, I'm going to stay in.'

'You are a funny thing,' Mum says, stroking my cheek. 'Never known a kid who doesn't want attention.'

'I want attention!' Gavi says eagerly.

I grab his arm and pull him down onto the sofa next to me. I'll happily talk about gaming, if it means we don't have to talk about me.

'You want to know how it's done? We were in game pods, all here inside London Star. It was like the rock-climbing game, *Scar Face,* but more real somehow. So advanced. There was wind, like the breeze you get from flying and sea-simulation games. And emptiness, open space. It *felt* like we were out there. It really did, Gavi.'

Gavi shakes his head like he can't believe it, and skips across the room to the Ent. The entertainment room is Gavi's personal cave, although it's supposed to be for all of us.

'So!' Mum says. 'My daughter. A champion festa...'

‘Not festa! It’s questa, as in “person who likes quest games”, and please can we not talk about it anymore? Why don’t you tell me what you’ve been doing today?’

‘If you like.’

Mum’s so passionate about her work. I love hearing her talk about it. She’s an assistant food technician at the meat-growing lab. Not handling the tissue science or anything. Making flavours. And the head technician *always* takes credit for her creations. Mum’s been trying to get a promotion for years, but Etti Lorn is an evil bot. Guess she wants to keep people in their place.

At the kitchen table, Mum pulls up a work screen on the carousel: an old-style computer with rotating air screens. She spins through to one showing colourful pie charts. ‘I’ve been coming up with winter flavours.’

‘What are these?’ I point to spaces in the chart.

‘Stabilisers and emulsifiers, mainly, to ensure the meat tissue doesn’t react with the flavours. I’m setting up the presentation for Etti first thing tomorrow.’

‘You might want to close your shopping windows, then,’ I say with a wink.

She blushes and fiddles with the other screens that are sitting behind her work tab. There’s one for skin-polishing, another for a kitchen design company. It’s nothing we could ever afford. We live down in the Quarters, in social housing, and that kind of luxury is way out of reach.

‘Is this all daydreaming for if I win? I might not, you

know. I could come away with nothing.'

'I know, I know. I'm sorry,' she stammers. I'm embarrassed for her transparency. Her desperation to move up. Up in prosperity, up in location. It's the only reason I'm doing StarQuest. It's all for her.

'I'll do my best, I promise.' I give her a reassuring smile, and spin through some of the remaining screens. 'Hey, what's this page?'

'Nothing.' Mum tries to close it, but I knock her hand away and stare in disbelief at the catalogue of rubber-faced robots.

'Mum! I can't believe you!'

'There's no shame in RoboPals. Sami at work's daughter has one. '

'I'd look like a total bot.'

'You can't even tell –'

'No.'

'But you don't have any friends,' she pleads. 'A girl should have friends to hang out with.'

'I've got Moles.'

'Moles.' She shakes her head. 'What use is Moles.' It's a statement, not a question.

I check the Flip on my wrist. The smart-band is waiting to tell me a thousand things, like my heart rate and what events are happening in the city, but a message from Moles isn't among them. Not a *well done, champ.* Not even a choice piece of sarcasm. Did he even bother to watch?

'Alara! Look what I'm doing!'

'Coming, Gavi!'

I enter the Ent room, expecting him to be playing a cheap Level-Up game. I can't stand Level-Ups; you collect points, try not to die, that's it. Quest games, on the other hand, are experiences. The good ones take years to make. PlayBeck Games creates most of them. Hoppi Burbeck's mind is insanely imaginative. I've tried to get Gavi into questing, but like most people in this place he has a five-second attention span.

But Gavi's not playing a mindless Level-Up this time; he's embroiled in a combat game. I play them occasionally to keep fit, but I don't seem to feel the pain as much as others; my opponents' punches land on me like dull thuds. There's something wrong with that, with *me*. I *know* there is.

'Look who I'm fighting,' Gavi says with bravado.

He's in the gaming ring, and even without my gamelens I can see the warrior he's up against. I instantly recognise the plaited beard and broken front teeth of Kagu Mactua, the most aggressive fighter from *Warlords*.

'Kagu? He's way above your level.'

The warrior doesn't know that my brother's only ten. The sensation chip in Gavi's arm won't take that into consideration either, not since he paid some guy to hack the info-connection with his Flip so he can play games meant for older kids.

He darts backwards and forwards to confuse his

opponent, just like I taught him. But you need to land strikes to weaken Kagu – and big ones. When Gavi stops to catch his breath, Kagu attacks; he spins, whipping out a side kick, and Gavi cries out, gripping his stomach. Another kick and he screams, like his bones are broken. Then he's panicky, throwing punches in the air, aimless, tiring. My wrist beeps. Gavi's Flip has picked up his elevated heart rate and is alerting mine, for assistance. Oh, yeah, Gavi needs help alright. Kagu has struck again, and kicks once more while Gavi is doubled over. He gets Gavi's throat. Gavi gargles. I yank him out of the ring before the medics come knocking.

'That's enough, Gavi. I've told you before, you're not ready for Kagu.'

'But I want to be like you.'

'Take a rest. Stop rushing things.'

But Gavi is loading another game. *Scar Face.* In the beams of the ring, the section of mountain rockface appears. He reaches for a handhold.

'You really need to get a life,' I mutter.

'Still got all my lives – and a power pack.'

I pick up a game-lens and watch him a while – although I'm more drawn to the surrounding ambience screen, with its crisp scenery of flowing rivers and lush forests from old times.

I love green. Real green.

Real green is the Botanical Gardens, the pea shoots, the broccoli in our food deliveries. But there's never enough green in London Star. Only our games show green in healthy swathes. But it's fake. It's all fabricated. The time of natural green has gone. Along with robots, the ancient pyramids, and living on the land.

Chapter 3

I've had a free morning, and spent most of it trying to ignore Mum's suggestions to do something normal, like hang out in a social hub or gaming arcade. I don't do that, ever.

It's not the money – or lack of it. All that stuff is free in the Quarters, just shoddier, with hand-me-down equipment. London Star looks after us, from people in social housing right up to those in the penthouses. It's the opposite of what happens when you have the powerful rich and an underclass that suffers. It's not *The Hunger Games*. We read that in primary school – a fiction text to study alongside history books about the dangers of neoliberalism and forcing people to fend for themselves. We learn how, by contrast, Estrella is built on fairness for all. We don't have poverty. We don't have illness. We don't do unrest.

But I am restless. In a fidgety way, not a rebellious

way. It's probably medical. I mean, in a city packed with entertainment, how can I possibly be discontent, uninterested, stuck for something to do? And yet, I am. All the time. Right this moment.

There's always questing, of course. I've yet to tire of that. But Gavi's using the Ent room, and gaming arenas are all Level-Ups and tedious bragging. Hell is point-scoring with an audience.

My Flip beeps. A message from Mum: *Do something, Alara!*

Alright, alright.

I clap a set pattern. The Synthetic Intelligence Animation – Synthia – appears on my bedroom screen dressed like a cowgirl. The things you'll do when you're desperate for amusement!

Hello, Alara. How can I help?

'Synthia, I'm –'

I don't use the word 'bored' outside my own head – not since the time Synthia alerted Medico and I was stuck for hours doing tests and talk therapy.

'I'm looking for something to do.'

You can do a puzzle.

'I don't want to do a puzzle.'

You can go for a walk.

'Been for a walk.'

You can go to the gym.

'Next.'

You can go to a social hub.

'No, thanks.'

You can play a game. The newest game on the market is Devil's Island. *It has a rating of five stars and –*

'Next.'

Those sneaky advertisements drive me crazy. I never listen to them on principle, and anyway, I couldn't afford *Devil's Island* even if I wanted to.

Call coming in. Caller is Moles.

'Accept.'

The screen is filled with Moles. My friend. He tries to push his shaggy hair off his face but it falls right back like a stubborn curtain, covering his big, dark eyes.

'Hey!' I try not to sound annoyed. 'So, to what do I owe this delight?'

'Just wanted to say well done for getting through.'

'Oh, do you mean the StarQuest competition? I'd nearly forgotten all about that, seeing as it was a *week* ago.'

'Time flies.'

'At least you don't forget the important things, like my birthday.'

'I was only three weeks late.'

'Try nine.'

I met Moles working a Saturday job at Rapidos health wrap stall in a scraper out East. I was doing it for extra money; for him it was social rehabilitation after losing his brother. Being sociable is London Star's cure-all. Moles' real name is Nate, but I've always called him

Moles, because he has more than a few – they're spaced out across his wide face like a constellation. His family's rich enough to afford skin-refining, but he says he can't be bothered. He can't be bothered to do much, to be honest. It's a wonder he bothers to wake up.

'Stop being needy, Trippy.'

'Don't call me Trippy.'

'Tripp-me-up, then. Alara Tripp-me-up, please do tell me about the semi-finals.' He drums his fingers.

'It's hard to explain if you didn't actually bother to *see* it.' I take a big breath. I feel like I've told the story so many times. 'It was a capture-the-flag game. We were climbing the skyscrapers. Inside game pods, of course; it was all simulation. But I saw the outside of the city, Moles. *Everything.* The whole of Star was lit up. It was beautiful. Seriously. Beautiful.'

I've thought about it a lot since that day. It *was* beautiful. It was also an epiphany. Only when you're outside it, vulnerable and exposed above the grey, jagged wasteland, do you realise how protected we are. How safe we all are inside these walls. It may have been a simulation, but the fear – of not returning, somehow – was real.

'So how did you win?'

'I just went into a spin – not entirely planned, I'll be honest. But it got me out of an ambush. Thought for one horrible moment I was going to crash and burn in the Void!'

Moles' gaze slides away, and I realise I've been tactless. The Void is the ground. The Void is death, and I've only gone and reminded him of Peron. He hardly talks about his dead big brother, and he doesn't express emotion when he does. But I know he suffers. He stuffs the pain deep down, smothers it with displacement activities like Sensii trips, hating his parents and obsessing about germs.

'So, when's the finals?' he says, still not making eye contact.

'Two weeks' time. Hey, do you want to meet up?'

'Er…' Moles is fiddling with something. 'You know what, I'm a bit tired. I don't think…'

'Don't do a trip, Moles,' I beg. 'I'll call Medico.'

'You wouldn't.'

'No, I wouldn't. Look, I'll be getting a yiros after Media class.'

'Mmm, yiros.'

I knew that would tempt him. Wraps with fillings and sauces. The spicy one can blow your head off. We're the only ones in Star that ask for it, I reckon.

'Great. That gives you a couple of hours to do whatever you're doing. See you there, okay?'

Our Media Studies teacher has called us to meet for a face-to-face. Intriguing. Face-to-face classes are rare, and Mr Leppito has scheduled this one at Central, of all places. Central's the home of official stuff. No one gets to enter unless they work there or have parents with connections. All the entry points are password-protected. But we were sent the code that morning, and we've been told to head on over and meet in the Tourism Department, which is basically a show-off for visiting diplomats, foreign executives and trade tycoons.

From my home in W38/100, the easiest way there is by East–West Compass train, which runs backwards and forwards through all the skyscrapers in the East and West arms, passing through Central. But when you sit on trains, people check you out. They always do. They'll unsubtly scan you with their Flips and find out your name and age in a heartbeat. It can tell them your heartbeat too, if they want it. They can even send the reading straight to Medico.

Fully Linked Information Platforms. Flips. They're mandatory, because it's connectivity that keeps us safe. No one falls through the cracks in Estrella. Not even if they want to.

But now that I've been on TV, this integration will work against my wish to be invisible, and I'll be a sitting duck in a train. Within seconds, my face will be all over social media... Stuff that. I prefer going by foot, anyway – the tubes are long and straight, and if there's no one around you can build up a sprint. Running in the tubes is not allowed, but I do it.

I've barely broken into a skip when I hear voices.

'Hey, you. Stop.'

Three boys. Aged seventeen, maybe. Lanky and confident. The leader shakes his head and tuts. 'Oh dear, oh dear.' He holds his wrist towards me, then checks his Flip. 'Let's see. Oh! It's Alara Tripp.'

The boys look at each other and grin. They know who I am.

'Alara Tripp, StarQuest finalist, are you aware that running in the tubes is not advised?'

'Yes.'

He taps his lips. 'Are you aware that I could make a citizen's arrest right now?'

I hope this is a joke. If it escalates, there'll be delays. I can't be late. Media is my favourite, and I don't want to get kicked off the course. Looking for stories is pretty much the only thing I'm passionate about.

'I'm really sorry.'

One of the boys snaps a photo and they saunter away. 'She's such a bot,' one says.

So, within seconds, I'll be plastered across media screens after all. Great.

But if I'm going to win this thing, I'd better get used to it.

Chapter 4

We circle the glass case. In it is a 3D-printed model of Estrella.

'So, what's this all about, you ask?' Mr Leppito says. None of us asks.

It's funny how we're all a bit shy. We're not used to seeing each other or our teacher in the flesh. We shrug a lot, suddenly lacking confidence now we're not behind a screen.

'Come on!' he shouts. 'Ideas? You lot are supposed to be full of them.'

'Our end-of-year project?'

'Yes!' Mr Leppito hisses the 's', swinging round and pointing to Dew, I think it is. I recognise him as the student who sits in the top left corner of my schooling screen. I've seen him pick his nose, like he's oblivious to the multi-way cameras.

'Yes!' Mr Leppito declares again. 'That's right. The

end-of-year project.' He rubs his hands together with relish.

'What – are we making miniature cities?' a girl quizzes.

Mr Leppito wafts away her words with disgust. 'It's really quite straightforward.'

'Estrella?' I venture.

'Yes! Estrella!' He paces in front of us. 'Designed by architect Esther Gallows-Bigg and one hundred years old this year. *One hundred* years old. It seems fitting that this miracle of construction should be our end-of-year topic. So, what is there to say that's media-worthy about Estrella?'

'The shape?'

'Dew...' Mr Leppito moans, placing his hands on the boy's shoulders. Dew flinches. 'The award for exceptional journalism is somewhat out of reach for you, I fear. Dear me. Anyone else?'

We stare at the model again, at its eight arms of miniature scrapers. Each tower's hundred storeys are marked in the tiniest detail, from the penthouses at the top to the mid-budget apartments in the middle to the Quarters at the bottom. Like layers of wealth. *Social strata,* Dad says. Layers. *Stratum,* singular. *Strata,* plural. It's Latin, a language even more ancient and more dead than Old London.

But the structural strata don't end at the Quarters. Beneath that, there's the scrapers' hollow supports, piercing the space known as the Drop – five thousand feet of metal and composite, encasing rubbish chutes and lift shafts. Like legs holding our civilisation up off the wasteland, where the old city lies rusting and where we dump all our trash. A toxic mix of old and new. Dad works there as a Refuse Manager. The model city even has tiny sweeper trucks, just like his, made of tin, balanced on polystyrene rubble.

'Estrella is alive with innovation,' Mr Leppito bellows. 'But what is going to be your subject of choice? What's your perspective? Shock me, surprise me, tell me something *I don't know.* Give me a story. Look around at the displays and see what inspires you.'

The walls of the tourist centre are panelled with screens, all projecting the brilliance of Estrella. There's a history section, explaining how we turned tragedy into fortune: how disaster was the catalyst that made us the cleanest, happiest country on Earth. A magnificent map shows Estrella's place in the world as the capital of New Anglia, renamed when Old Britain broke apart. The city's star-shaped motif sits in the bottom right-hand corner of what was once England, and just across the sea is New Europe, greyed out because of its pollution. Above us, Scotland is also coloured grey.

There are video tours of Estrella's magnificence: the solar-harvesting glass, the waste-to-water plant, the cruelty-free food production, the eugenics department that adapts genes and eradicates disease, and Advice – the progressive policing unit.

That's where I see my academic rival, Landi, loitering. Perhaps she'll do something about the legal system. *Advice combined with self-policing makes Estrella a society of self-aware equals.* Advice's words for visiting officials, not mine.

Cheeks burning at the memory of narrowly dodging a citizen's arrest, I avoid that section, drawn instead by the 3D architecture display, where sketches are drawing themselves in mid-air: Flip city designs that we sell to countries desperate for safe, clean citadels like ours. They're popping up all over New Europe, we're told: Paris, Rome, Amsterdam, Lisbon. Flip is probably our second-best export. But to make it a media-worthy story, I'd need to interview architects, and I don't have access to those kinds of people. And who wants to write an advert, anyway? Because that's what it will be. Where, in Estrella, is the hidden story?

'Alara.' Mr Leppito appears at my side. He carefully steers me towards the entertainment section. 'Your name might be in one of these displays in future. It's one week until the finals, am I right?'

'Yep. Seven days.'

'Do you think you'll be able to find time for your studies?'

'Of course.' I smile. 'It's only a game.'

'Good. Well, they say you should write what you know,' he adds with a wink. 'Find me a mind-blowing story about questing.'

The biggest industry naturally has the biggest display. Holograms and ambience screens illustrate the worlds within worlds that we all have access to right under our skin. London Star's integrated sensation technology – Sensii – is sold across the globe, but for anyone born in Estrella it's a birthright. Rich or poor, we all get it, just like an old-time vaccination. A chip inserted into the left armpit that can be paired with simulation games, adjusting and stimulating hormones so we can feel what it's like to fly, dive, or to be within a whisker of an extinct Bengal tiger. And it does so much more than gaming. It maps our body systems, sending updates and alerts to our Flips, or direct to Medico if it's bad. And the skyscrapers' walls are packed with sensors to monitor us and keep us safe. Maybe there's a story here. A new angle. Perhaps something that integrates all aspects of Sensii, from gaming to health to connectivity.

Mr Leppito calls time. 'Those applying for the Third Teach Media course, step forward.'

I step up alongside Landi, Felice, Wilt and Karem. We're all well aware of each other. We're hoping to make media a career, not just a school module.

'This assignment might be just another end-of-year project for some, but for you it will be a step towards getting on the higher course. Your assignment will go straight to the selection panel as your sample piece. There may only be one place available on the course this year, so, to put it bluntly, this is not really a project: it's a competition.'

Another competition. StarQuest is for my family. This is for my sanity.

After class, I head to the yiros place in a social hub in South-West. I message Moles. He says he'll come, and I wait. But of course, he doesn't come.

Moles is flaky at the best of times. Relying on him to help you out is about as ridiculous as his addiction to Sensii tripping. His late techy brother kind of invented it. He found a way to isolate a game's sensory output so you can plug yourself into the sensation, freefalling into whatever emotive state it offers without going through the gaming part. I doubt Peron would have done it if he thought for a second Moles would get addicted. But I gather that Moles isn't the person he was when Peron was alive; perhaps back then, he was stable and self-regulating, able to trip just for fun. Now, it makes him useless, just like Mum said.

But I can't let it get to me. There's too much on my mind and too much to lose if I let myself surrender to despair. I head off, walking aimlessly, changing tubes, zigzagging my way around London Star until I find myself in a social hub. I don't even know which scraper I'm in or what level I'm on, but I grab a slushie and perch on a sofa and try very hard not to be bored. All the screens are on their advertising cycle and I watch, bemused yet transfixed, as people around me hold up their Flips, spot-buying all sorts of stuff they don't need. And then, to add insult to injury, there's an ad for RoboPals. New, improved, more lifelike than ever. RoboPals, so bottish, how sad. But is it any sadder than clinging to a so-called friend who can hardly be bothered to talk to me? Should I at least try to make new friends? The hub is full of people being friends. How hard can it be?

I look at the group of girls on the next sofa along. They pick at mini-doughnuts, sip hot chocolate and shriek at someone SpyLogged with bad make-up. Why is that funny? They laugh and laugh, and I give up trying to understand. It really doesn't look as if I'll be making any meaningful connections today. Then Landi walks in.

She's alone, carrying a cup, a digipad under her arm. She's hard to fathom. Always been a bit enigmatic, wearing shades in online class, her dyed purple fringe hanging over one eye. We might be competing for a media place, but maybe we could be friends? She's not like the others. That might be what we have in common.

She makes her way across the hub, unselfconscious, in long, bouncing strides, and takes a seat with her back to the social media screens. That's a good sign. She sips from her cup with birdlike delicacy and flicks at her digipad. I take a big breath, gather my things and head over.

'Hi Landi, can I sit with you?'

She nods.

'I've been meaning to ask if you wanted to grab a drink sometime,' I say casually, noticing her coffee cup. I wish I wasn't drinking a slushie. I don't even like slushies.

'Why? What did you want to talk about?' Landi pushes back her fringe with a slow sweep of her hand.

'I don't know. Stuff.'

'Stuff? Really?' Her tone is patronising. I'm being too childish.

'Or we could talk about the media project, perhaps?'

Pointedly, Landi flips her digipad over, as if I might be trying to look at it. Then she slumps back in her chair and whips off her shades, eyeballing me before closing her eyes. 'Is this what it's all about? You want help with the project?'

'What? No. I just wanted to hang out with you.'

'And why me?'

'Because it would be nice to get to know you more.' I smile and shrug.

'Look. As far as I'm concerned, this isn't something to get friendly over. I'm not saying you'd steal my idea on purpose, but if I did happen to mention something and you happened to do something similar … so awkward.'

'We can chat about something different, then.'

'Take that away, and we actually have nothing in common.' She drains her coffee. 'No offence.'

It's my cue to go, which I do in awkward silence. Thankfully, no one around me has noticed her snub. They're watching the rolling reels of live apps, gossip and comments. I'm walking towards the exit when a lady – middle-aged, maybe seventy – approaches me.

'I've picked up that your serotonin levels are low,' she says, tapping at her Flip. 'Can I help? Would you like me to call someone?'

'No, I'm fine. Really. Thank you.'

'They all say that, dear. But if you don't get it sorted, then one day you'll be down the Drop.'

'Well, thanks for that. I'll take my chances.'

'Very well. But I'm going to log a concern with Medico, none the less.'

Before I can protest, she turns away and heads for a smoothie bar, where I see her do the same to someone else. She noticed their iron was low, or their heart rate was high. Do-gooders. However irritating she is, I have to admit that she's what London Star is all about – community and safety. A cocoon of care. Otherwise, it's like she said: *you'll be down the Drop.*

Chapter 5

Jogging through a pedestrian tube from South-West to South, I'm stopped again. I've committed so many minor offences already, a grumpy Advisor could stick me in a correction cell for a day. But it's usually ordinary people who make a fuss, hoping to earn good citizen bonuses to cash in for luxuries. Advisors don't get bonuses, so they tend to be more relaxed.

Like this one, who scans my Flip and wags his finger playfully. 'Where are you in such a hurry to get to, young questa?' he says. 'Let me guess – the new games pods in South 50?'

'The Botanical Gardens, actually.'

'Well, that's different. How old are you – ninety-five?' He laughs heartily and shakes his head, and as soon as he's gone, I run again.

I guess it's not normal for someone of my age to hang out at the Botanical Gardens. It's a cavernous space filled with specimen tanks. Not a slushie bar or gossip screen in sight.

There's a bench opposite a giant golden pothos – a jungle vine with heart-shaped leaves in green and yellow. I sit and gaze at it, following its snaking stem up into the canopy. Like all the plants, they're inside glass for safety. Theirs and ours. They're the last remaining samples of the old land, and they harbour toxins and diseases in their cells. They are beautiful dangers. Apart from me, the viewing gallery is empty, and I can hear the ambient sounds clearly – the squawks of parrots, the chimes of bell birds. I close my eyes and imagine the exotic birdsong is not a recording piped through speakers, but actual calls, bouncing off the canopy of an endless jungle, like in *Wilderness*.

But I'm not decompressing as quickly as I'd hoped. Landi rattled me and I need to laugh it off. *Moles, please, please step up.*

I press my Flip, and it sends purrs across my skin as it dials.

He picks up.

'I waited for you,' I say.

'Yeah, sorry. Where are you now?' he asks dozily.

'Botanical Gardens, South.'

'I'd rather eat my own head than go to the Botanical Gardens.'

'But I need to see you.' I hold up my hand. 'Listen. Can you hear the birds? They're calling you. *Come, Nate, come…*'

'Just not my thing, Alara.'

'I know, but do it for me. I need some company.' There is silence. 'I haven't seen you for ages. You don't even have to pay your entrance. *I'll* pay. Listen to how desperate this is. I'm offering to pay for your friendship. Come on. *Please*. Mum's threatened to buy me a RoboPal if I don't start hanging out more with friends!'

Moles laughs huskily. 'That's hilarious.'

I pause, turning serious. 'Moles, I just tried to make conversation with this girl from class and she basically told me she hates me.'

'How did she do it? I've been trying for months.'

'Oh ha ha … please, Moles.'

'But I've just started something…'

'Another trip? You bot.'

Exasperated, I cut him off. We have a friendship based on the ability to make and take cutting remarks. But sometimes it's not enough. A simple hug would do today, but I suppose that would be asking too much of him. I head back to my home in West. It's a fair distance, but it gives me a chance to walk off my annoyance.

Through the window panels, I see blazing sunshine. On days like this, the city looks its very best, like it does in all the brochures, its gleaming, solar-harvesting skyscrapers puncturing a bright blue sky. And it's on days like this that I could do with rich penthouse friends, with private pools and sun domes.

We don't have those kinds of friends. My parents don't

know gene therapy scientists, architects or programmers. They don't socialise with money. My parents work long hours, late into the night, and still we're in the Quarters – an okay apartment on Level 100. It doesn't seem fair that we're on the bottom when Mum works hard all day to give those rich people good flavours, and Dad risks his life as a Refuse Manager. He should be compensated for that, not held down: until the day he dies, he'll be facing the same miserable view, day in, day out. The Void. Abandoned metals, plastics and bricks, the ruins of toxic Old London.

Our Civilisation teacher, Miss Luvic, talks about the Void as being the legacy of 'a stupid civilisation that poisoned its own doorstep'. That's a bit unfair, I think. They were trying hard to make things better, before the incident. The Centre for CO2 Solutions had been working on a formula for a carbon dioxide absorber using lithium and potassium, when an untested gas was released by mistake – in massive quantities, from every storage facility in every city. The corrosive poison leached across the whole of New Anglia.

They said it was robot malfunction. Stupid bots.

That's why all robots are banned – apart from surgery bots and the ridiculous RoboPals. Hang out with one of them, and you may as well have *bot* tattooed on your forehead.

It's sad, what happened, but sometimes you need to raze the old to start something new. And they say it was for the best. We learned all about life before: the dirty streets, the fumes, the failing health system, and the intensive farming of real animals. Who would *do* that? Who would raise animals and then send them down a conveyor belt to death? It's like a horror story. By comparison, the new shiny London Star is paradise. Humane meat, clean air, no sickness, no poverty. No 'nothing to do'. Apparently, that was also a problem long ago. 'Nothing to do' led to vandalism, violence, unrest.

Estrella eradicated all that cruelty, pollution and boredom.

So what I feel – the weird emptiness that sometimes washes over me – can't really be boredom, can it? One therapist said I lacked the right chemicals in my body. Another said I lacked purpose. That's why I've been on a diet of sugar pills and quest games since I was five years old. Quests work, sometimes. Sugar pills, not so much. They just give me energy so I'm more aware of how not entertained I am.

Moles calls. I click 'answer' but say nothing.

'Alara? Alara? I know you're mad. I just wanted to say sorry. For being distant. And for not being there after that girl said she didn't like you.'

Oh, Moles. How can I stay angry with my only friend? I soften. 'I might have been a bit over-dramatic about that.'

'Well, I hope she dies a horrible death, anyway.'

'Thanks. I think.'

'Good, I'm glad that's sorted. See you soon, Nana.'

'It's Banana. Nickname's Banana.'

'I'm not calling you that. It's ridiculous.'

'Bye, Moles.'

Yeah, bye Moles. You make me laugh, but you're still not here for me, are you? Lost in your world of messed-up sensations, never knowing what's real and what's not.

I can be guilty of that. If there's nothing else going on, then I'll retreat to that place, too. Any normal kid would think I'm mad for spending so long in *Wilderness*, but it's not just a game to me. It's a place. The home of the only other character I could call a friend – Vim. Moles won't let me talk about Vim. Ever. It sends him into a rage that I like to think is jealousy. But that's ridiculous, considering he introduced us.

That's the advantage of Vim. He doesn't do complicated.

'Are you ready?'

Vim's jaw is clenched, his eyes intense. He smiles reassuringly and takes my hand.

'What are we waiting for?'

I feel his fingers fold tightly round mine, and we run down the dirt track, weaving between tree trunks and mossy boulders. And then, the noise. We knew it would come: the sound of the forest waking in anger at the vibration of our footsteps.

'Keep going!' I shout.

But the forest is fighting us, hurling trees in our path. Vim lets go of my hand.

'Follow me.' He leaps ahead of me, over the fallen trunks, turning back to check I'm okay. He always looks after me, and I him.

'What are we looking for?' I call.

'The last clue said to find the Gamug Tree.'

'What's a Gamug Tree?'

'I don't know.'

Running and leaping, we search the forest around us for something that might be the Gamug Tree. We are surrounded by thickets and trunks and trees in a thousand shades of black, grey, brown and green. It's like an ambience screen of repeat patterns, only everything is falling, designed to confuse us, make us panic. I spot a vine untwisting itself from the canopy above in the 3D ring. It streams down towards Vim.

'Vim!'

He stops. Sees it. Grabs the vine as if it was a snake, and yanks it to the ground. Ten more descend in its place. He runs forward to protect me, but it's not the answer. You have to *think outside the box*. Vim told me that himself.

'Climb them!' I shout, pointing upwards.

We can't see where the vines lead, but if we get higher up the canopy, we'll avoid their strangling tentacles and have a better vantage point.

A thick vine drops and curls around my neck. I prise it off, tie a loop in its end and hook my foot through it. Vim copies, and I watch his arms as they take the strain, easily handling the tension while my own begin to ache a little. Suddenly, the vines stop fighting us and rise back up toward the canopy, taking us with them. Vim looks over at me and winks, and I feel a warmth in my chest. We laugh as the tendrils pull us to the top and then we fall silent as we emerge into a previously unseen world of treetop bridges and walks. We scan the new panorama, looking for a stand-alone tree.

'Tell me again what the clue said,' I say.

'The hidden room is back around the split Gamug Tree,' he recites. 'We should start by looking for a broken tree, then. One that's been hit by lightning.'

'Maybe.' There's something in the wording that reminds me of the crosswords my dad does. The fiddly clues, each containing the code to its own cracking. *Back*. Indicates a word backwards. Gamug. Mugam? The *split*... Break it into two words first, perhaps.

'Vim. It's a ga gum tree. No, wait. Ga... Backwards, it's Ag. Ag, the symbol for silver. It's a silver gum!'

I whisper it into my Flip and it returns a flickering image that I present it to Vim. A silver gum tree. We look up and see it shining in the distance, ghost-like. Treetop walkways lead right to it.

'Yes!' I clap my hands. Vim moves in for a high-five and then slips his arm around my waist. It's not appropriate, but I allow it. I made it happen. 'Are you getting soppy?' I laugh.

'I'm allowed to,' Vim replies. 'You said I was the only one.'

'And if you complete the sentence...'

'You said I was the only one crazy enough to be your quest partner.'

'That's more like it.'

'I knew deep down it was a hidden message.'

'You kid yourself,' I mock. But I know that it's me who's kidding herself. This is not as real as I wish it was. 'Hey, you're not going anywhere yet, are you?'

'And leave my favourite human? You must be kidding.'

My name is shouted. It sounds distant, but I know it's near. 'I have to go. Bye, Vim.'

Mum enters the Ent as the game is folding back down into its virtual box, taking with it the forest, the quest, the boy.

'Mum?' I pull away my game-lens.

'What's that look in your eye? Have you been playing with Vim again? You spend too much time with that Pixel. Pixels and trip-heads. Why don't you get some real friends?'

'Leave it out, will you?' I laugh incredulously. 'I'm practising. For the competition. It's a quest.'

'If you say so, Alara. Dinner's on the table.'

She's right, though. The way I feel about Vim is a bit

weird. Vim is just a Pixel. And yet when we're together I feel like he accesses a part of me that's been caged and unfed. Crazy, I know. I've wondered if this is what love is supposed to be like, but it's a stupid thought. Love doesn't happen to teenagers, and the reality is, from his beautiful eyes to his smooth talk, Vim is just an expensive toy.

Pixels come with a face and a blank identity, over timc growing a personality based on their gamers' tastes and desires. They're top technology, and I couldn't afford one in a million years. Vim was originally a gift to Moles from his dads. In disgust, Moles passed it straight to me. Moles' loss is my gain.

After dinner I go to my room and switch my window to one-way glass. It's hard enough to find privacy in London Star without being spied on in my own home. Not that anyone would be looking at the Quarters. People generally look up, trying to catch glimpses of the high life. But I don't long for luxury. That's where me and Moles are similar. He's way up there, but he says it doesn't make him happy. His place is in N14/12. Level 12! That's super-rich. One of his dads is something in architecture and the other is big in health and fitness equipment. They're big on flaunting their success and throwing show-offy dinner parties. Moles can't stand them. To him, Peron was his only family. And now Peron's somewhere in the Void. Probably in pieces.

I try to see the Void through binoculars that Dad

gave me – cast-offs from work – but it's night-time and there's just a whole lot of darkness. More than a mile of it. Down there, that's where Dad and his team take their sweeper trucks, riding the waves of junk on their huge caterpillar wheels and shovelling our rubbish into the wasteland beyond. Sometimes they tip-turn: scoop up the Old London junk and flip it over to stop gases from building up. If they didn't, the gas could cause explosions. Estrella is like a finely tuned instrument, they say. Can't risk explosions here.

My Flip warns me it's late, and that for optimum health I should sleep. And I do feel kind of sleepy. I resist it, blinking through tired eyes, and switch the binoculars to night vision. The green filter makes the Void look like a spooky swamp, lapping at the legs of the towers. An endless jumble of waste. I'm about to turn away when I spot flickers amid the rubble. Dots of pale light. It's not the first time I've seen them – little specks that suddenly appear, then disappear just as quickly. Eyes of wild animals, maybe. Bits of broken glass.

The front door slams. Dad's back. I run to the kitchen.

'Hey, Banana!' He takes me in his strong arms and squeezes me. 'What are you still doing up? It's a weekday.'

'Dad, anything?'

He shakes his head and strokes my cheek. One day I hope he'll say yes, they've found a body. If I could give Moles one thing, it would be Peron's body. It would be closure. Then, perhaps, he could wake up and move on.

Chapter 6

Mum's gone to work and left her carousel screens up. Again, they're for stuff that's way beyond our means. A page for KeepSakes store – an interior design company that decorates your apartment based on psychometric testing of your personality and needs. I mean, seriously? Some people have *way* too much money, if you ask me. She's hoping I win StarQuest so we can slot into that demographic. Like we could waltz in there and people wouldn't treat us differently. They'd know we were just Quarters dwellers who got lucky. I guess we'll find out. First I need to win. And to win, I need to train.

I clap for Synthia.

Good morning. How can I help you?

'Tell me where the least busy gaming arcade is.'

The current data suggests South-East 88/40 is the least populated gaming arcade.

That's a pain to get to. Too far to walk.

'Next.'

The current data suggests that the second least populated gaming arcade is in North 10/40.

'Call Moles.'

Calling Moles.

He appears on my screen wearing a hoodie and dark glasses.

'Moles, are you okay? Or are you a visiting diplomat from the Kingdom of What the –?'

'Yeah, let's just say that,' he says. He takes off his shades and looks up sheepishly. His brown eyes are bloodshot.

'Oh, you didn't!' He's been up all night, gaming. 'What did you play?'

'*Cruel Sands*.'

'I've never even heard of it.'

'It just puts you in a desert, with no map, and you have to survive. That's it.'

I scoff. 'Well, I'm glad I called. You might have died out there!'

'I'd just spotted an oasis, actually,' Moles grumps.

'Probably a mirage.'

'I guess we'll never know. So, what's up?'

'I thought we could go to an arcade. I could use some practice gaming in public. You know, for the finals.'

'I don't know, Alara. I need to lie down.'

I'm not surprised. I'm not even angry any more. 'If you change your mind, come and find me.'

Moles is vanishing from my life. We used to have fun, proper laugh-until-you-cry stuff. Sometimes serious conversations, too, like when I needed to let off steam about my illicit boredom, or when he wanted to complain about his arrogant, neglectful dads. And rarely, but sometimes, he opened up about Peron.

Peron was a technology prodigy. A proper genius. Messed-up, just like Moles; he'd been having chemical and talking therapies for years, but they didn't do him any good. Didn't stop him. They looked for him everywhere, of course. But London Star sees everything, so if you're not in London Star then the only other place you can be is down the Drop. It's an unusual method of un-lifing – to throw yourself down a rubbish chute – but you're guaranteed not to survive. Even if a dropper did survive the one-mile tumble inside the scraper leg, they'd quickly drown under the mounds of trash, shovelled out into the wasteland with the rest of the rubbish. And if they survived that? Well, the toxicity or wild animals would get them. Imagine how desperate you'd need to be.

But Peron wasn't the first, and he won't be the last. Every once in a while, someone goes. It's not made public, but Dad tells me in confidence. *I've been told to look out for another body, Alara.* Not that there's any point in looking for bodies. To date, not a single one has ever been brought home. Not even a bone.

Moles never introduced me to Peron when he was

alive, and he has never showed me a picture of him. There's no media about him either – believe me, I've looked; I guess his powerful dads embargoed images and comments to avoid gossip and save Moles pain. But I have a vision of Peron as this illuminated figure, radiating warmth. A warmth that Moles misses. I see it every day in his strained eyes. And yes, I worry. I worry that Moles might crack, too. He's already testing the limits of his brain and body with his all-night games and Sensii trips. When you have nothing to live for, then what's the point of being safe?

At the arcade there's probably fifty people. Not bad. Only once have I ever managed to get a gaming arcade to myself. It was a rubbish, understocked place way out South-East – but in the days when I didn't care about train rides and being noticed, I would go to the end of the line for an empty place. Games can bring out the worst in people, and I've seen what an audience can do to fragile egos. Unfortunately, arcades are the only place I can train for StarQuest. At home I've got *Wilderness* and a couple of other old free-to-play games, but I need to get familiar with the newer stuff, because who knows what they'll throw at us? I certainly wasn't expecting our capture-the-flag game around the scraper tops, and you don't walk into a free penthouse without a challenge.

There's no one on it, so I take *Sky Jump*. I press my Flip against the panel for payment and health check and step inside the pod. The floor is divided into panels that move independently, forwards and backwards, up and down. The walls are 3D visuals and the objective is to leap from mountain ledges to broken bridges and tall buildings without your heart exploding. It's all monitored, broadcast on a screen outside for onlookers to see. I really wish it didn't have that feature.

After the game has paired my Sensii chip, the lights dim and the floor starts to move beneath me. I am on a railway track, walled in on either side by rock, jogging at an even pace, glancing left and right to see if anything is rolling down the escarpment at me. Something will be programmed to make me jump. I see it! A train coming full speed towards me. There is a low ledge to the left, but it's too close and the train might hit me as it passes. It has to be the right. Higher, but safer. I leap right, my feet making contact with the floor, which has raised; on screen it's depicted as a narrow ridge on the side of the rock. I am allowed to walk a little now, but I mustn't relax. At any moment the floor might speed up, throwing me off. The train is below me, carriage after carriage rumbling past. An eagle above. A dot at first, but now huge. Its claws are spreading, flaring razor talons. I leap down onto the train and run as fast as I can along the carriage roofs to keep from flying backwards into the pod door. My pulse has escalated, but it's okay. I just need to focus and breathe. The train is running out of carriages. I could jump to the ground, but that would be too easy – way too easy.

Probably a trick. On my left there is an opening in the rock face. High, but I can make it. I run and jump, looking down in time to see that the ground beneath the train is razor-sharp with broken glass. I knew it! The 3D wall spins round so I am running into the tunnel carved out of the rock. The light fades, and it is up to my other senses to detect changes in the environment. I hear scuffling ahead – a monster, maybe – and feel to my right with my foot. The floor isn't raised, so I shift across and hope I have judged the movement of the creature right. It shuffles past but I continue on the right at a walk. There is a glimmer above me. I see it, but too late. The sharp icicles fall and the Sensii reacts, sending a sensation, cold and sharp like blades, across my skull. I shrug it off. There is daylight ahead. And a rolling boulder. The centre panel drops. I leap down onto it and crouch so the boulder rolls safely above me. And then *GAME OVER*.

It's because I haven't put enough money in. Not because I got hit or my heart rate exploded, which I'm pleased about. On StarQuest I will need to keep my cool.

The pod doors open. Outside there's a crowd of spectators who have been drawn to the broadcast. There are backslaps, questions about tactics. Embarrassing.

'Alara Tripp!'

I turn to see some beefed-up guy swaggering towards me.

'Blaze.' He says his name like I should know him. The arrogance of some people is insane.

'Blaze? Is that your real name?'

'It's Duggin,' I hear someone shout.

'Yeah, but it's Blaze for StarQuest,' Blaze snaps.

'Right.' I try not to laugh. Duggin – or Blaze – doesn't look like the kind of guy who can laugh at himself. And he's the male StarQuest finalist I got crushed by. Great.

'So, what would you say your strengths are?' He folds his arms across his chest. I'm perplexed. Why does he assume I want to talk to him?

'My strength is not caring.'

'Sure you care. You live down in the Quarters, don't you?'

'Yes. But I think you care about that more than I do. Bye.'

I walk away, my hate of arcades reaffirmed. Although, dammit, now I want to win more than anything. It's not just about what I'm working for, it's also what I'm working against.

We are all sitting down to eat together. That's rare because of Dad's shifts, and also because it's hard to coordinate a family meal when we've all been picking at food throughout the day. I have already had a breakfast muffin, a veggie wrap, some sushi and two protein bars from the free canteen. But Mum has insisted that it's a special occasion. She puts a stew on the table in front of us.

'What do you think?' She stands back and looks at it like it's a piece of art.

'It looks like puke.'

'Gavi…' Dad warns.

'Thank you, Gavi.' Mum winks. She is soft on him, she really is. 'Alara? Any ideas?'

'Looks pretty, Mum.' I smile encouragingly.

'But what do you think it is?' she pushes.

I shrug.

'It's turkey … with cranberry, juniper and cream!' She claps her hands.

'Your winter concept, Mum!'

'Yes! Accepted, produced and ready to serve. This is the first batch. Have a taste.'

Spooning stew direct from the dish into my mouth, I detect the sweetness from the fruits and the savoury from the meat, binding together with cream to create a velvety sauce – not crazy flavoursome, but nice. However, Dad and Gavi are moaning like it's the most delicious thing they've ever tasted. They dip their spoons in again and again. Maybe over time chilli has warped my taste buds. I'm always asking for extra chilli. I don't dare, tonight.

'Marvellous,' Dad says through a mouthful. Gavi just grunts, which is as much as can be expected.

'It is good, isn't it?' Mum says, blushing. She has a right to be proud of herself. All things considered, it's as good as it gets.

'Will you get credit for it?'

Blood rushes to Mum's cheeks and she shakes her head. Her shoulders slump.

'Oh Mum, I'm sorry. We need to talk to someone

about this. It's not fair.'

'It's fine,' she mumbles, looking up with a brave smile. 'You know, so long as *you* know it's me, I'm happy.'

'You deserve so much more,' Dad says.

She does deserve more. More even than a penthouse. That's just decoration.

'If I win StarQuest, the first thing I'm going to do with the money is –'

'No, no, no,' she interrupts, still blushing. 'Don't be silly. Money doesn't solve anything.'

But we both know about the shopping screens, and right now I'd accept a RoboPal if it made her happy.

After food, we watch news hour. The first half is not really my bag – it's hard to care about trade deals with the southern hemisphere or whatever. Where money moves to doesn't make a difference to those who have none. But we watch anyway, in case there's something about food technology for Mum, or something about the Void. Dad takes his job very seriously. When there's a report of a minor tremor or explosion, he sees it as his fault for not rotating the tips properly; he sits, chewing his nails, waiting to hear if there's been damage to any of the scrapers. It's always alright. He's really good at his job.

The second half of news hour is better. It's the Entertainment slot: the games that are selling best, here and abroad, and what's in development. Gavi and I like this bit best, because they sometimes ask for testers to try out new stuff. Every kid in the whole of London Star wants that. Testers get to meet programming teams and maybe spend time at their laboratories and penthouses. The penthouses are a thing of mystery for bottom-dwellers who can never see that high up. It's a good thing they're out of sight. The envy would kill.

Most of tonight's news has been about a fighting game that's had complaints about being too rough.

'That's you, Gavi.' I laugh, shoving him off the sofa. 'If I hadn't stopped you, Kagu Mactua would have given you a heart attack.'

'Shut up, Alara. If you hadn't butted in, I'd have kicked his backside.'

'Shush, shush.' Dad stands up abruptly. 'There's an update on StarQuest.'

StarQuest is news. That's amazing in itself. Questas are few and far between, and there's never been an official questing competition. There are Level-Up jousts every hour, and plenty of small contests run by individual arcades or entrepreneurial spectators, and it's a great way to top up your bank account with credits. But quest games? Never. Games like *Wilderness* take weeks to complete, with no guarantee of winning, and most people give up before they've even really started – too much reading, puzzling, exploring. I love quests for all of those things. There's a purpose to them.

Now, for some reason, questing has finally been recognised and given its own big tournament by the Entertainment Board. Is anyone apart from questa geeks even interested? I guess they must be. Right now the viewer counter on the news-hour screen is in the thousands. It must be the prize – the cash, the penthouse.

'Woah, was that you?' Gavi points to footage taken from the semi-finals.

The film is of London Star – brilliant, bright Estrella, floating like a phosphorescent crystal in a black ocean – with gamers dangling on ropes from the top of Central. A brilliant avatar re-enactment of the experience. The viewer counter is going up.

The word *FINALS* flashes on the screen, along with the faces of the four finalists. Everyone's seen this line-up already, the night of the semi-finals. Why do they have to go and milk it? I burn red.

'Look at you!' Mum says proudly.

There's another word. *UPDATE*. My face alone on the screen. Serious-looking. Ridiculous. We were made to pose like old-time squaddies, standing sideways on, saluting. Gavi, rightly, is laughing his head off, and I get up to leave. But my brother's annoying laughter stops suddenly, as if someone's pulled a cord. Mum gasps and Dad grabs my sleeve and yanks me back down.

'What? What is it?'

'What does *that* mean?' Gavi winces as he tries to read the word that is now stamped in red across my squaddie face. Mum and Dad are silent.

DISQUALIFIED.

Chapter 7

What do you wear to a formal disqualification? I have no idea, so I'm wearing a second-skin suit to regulate my temperature and on top I'm wearing loose trousers, T-shirt and trainers. Next to the snappy suits in the Central travel hub, I'm seriously out of place. They look at me with raised eyebrows, and I just know they think I'm trying to get into Central illegally. Lots of people try, for the free restaurants that serve mad good stuff, like sushi meat with the best flavourings. Some go to butter up Advice workers to up their career chances. Maybe the two guys walking either side of me think that's what I'm doing – planning to bustle into an open lift after someone else has opened it. Not me. Because I have today's code.

Central Code: PLH78.

The message was pinged to me, just as it's pinged to all Central workers at one minute past midnight every day. New day, new code. Me, a girl from the Quarters!

It should make me feel special. Maybe if I were coming to collect a big fat prize I'd get a flutter of good feelings, the boost of serotonin that I apparently need. But I'm not excited. I'm confused. What's the point of a meeting to tell me I'm disqualified when it's already been plastered over the TV? I got the message. And I'm over it now. Don't need the glory or the attention. Don't even care how Blaze will gloat – I just care about Mum and her shopping screens. And the return of boredom.

It's something only Moles could even begin to understand. But I'm learning to face the fact that Moles is a lost cause. He simply doesn't care. Not a word – not a choice, sarcastic, slap-in-the-face word – since the whole of London Star found out I was disqualified. *What use is Moles?* Yeah, Mum. Maybe you're right.

Level 70. The doors slide open. To the shock of the suits, I'm met by Welt Eldon in person. The top guy. Advice's commander-in-chief. His end-of-year televised report is unmissable. It always ends with *Go, Estrella!* Everyone says it with him.

Welt smiles broadly and encircles my shoulders with his arm, guiding me along the corridor. It's awkward because he's so tall. It's awkward, full stop. I am so glad I'm wearing my second-skin; I'd be sweating buckets without it.

We move through the crowds, and he's slow and careful with his words as he makes conversation. It's like he's never spoken to a young person before and reckons we're all a bit simple; he asks if I've managed to get some sleep and whether I'm in a good mood. I say yes to both, although what the actual hell? I've been disqualified, right?

Welt's small talk stops once we're out of the public eye. We're in his office and I'm sitting across a table from him, with four other people who are wearing white coats and unreadable expressions. This is weird, so out-of-proportion serious. Like I'm being disqualified from the whole of Estrella.

'Alara.' Welt leans forward. 'I'd like you to tell me about yourself.'

'Um, the Entertainment Board should have all my details, scores and stats.' And what has he got to do with this, anyway? He's not a programmer, he's Advice. 'Is this about running in the tubes? If so, I'm really sorry.'

I'm interrupted by laughter. Welt's fatherly boom and strange muffled giggles from the whitecoats.

'It's not about running in the tubes, Alara.'

'Well, anything else you need to know you already have. Advice holds all Flip data, right? And the Medico records. Is it about my sugar pills?'

He shakes his head.

'O-kay... You're going to have to tell me what you want to know, then, because I seriously don't have a clue.'

'Let's start with quest games. Why do you like them?'

'I don't know.' I try to guess what he wants to hear. 'They're fun.'

'Fun,' he repeats. 'Maybe.' He pulls a razor-pad stick

from his top pocket – of course his has gold blades – and fans it out on the table in front of us. 'Let's look at it from another angle. The angle of purpose.'

From the main page, he selects a sub-page and drags it up. It hangs in the air like a guillotine blade. I'm rock-still. Petrified. The man can read minds.

'Records show me you've been to the doctors several times over the last couple of years. Comments include' – he expands the paragraph – '*lack of purpose* and *restlessness*. What do you think they mean by *restless*?'

So this *is* about my medical records. That would explain the whitecoats. They wear those in Medico. Sweat prickles under my second-skin. This is turning weird.

Don't say the 'bored' word, don't say the 'bored' word.

'I just sometimes feel like I could be doing more.' I smile, but he waits for more, not blinking. 'Quest games give me a mission.'

'One doctor has written that she thinks you're *dulled*.'

Ouch.

'No, no. I'm not dulled.' The heat rushes to my cheeks.

Admit to being dulled, bored, and it's like admitting you have a terrible disease. There's serious medical intervention for that, that's the rumour: weird pills or brain adjustment. Painless, of course. And hey, maybe I'd be happier if I gave myself up. But instead I shake my head and deliberately look confused.

'It's okay, Alara. It doesn't matter to us if you're dulled or restless or just inexplicably discontent with your life. We're here to help.'

Everyone in the room looks at each other and nods. Is that good or bad? I've got a feeling it's bad.

'Look, I'm sure that whatever my data says about me, it's just a passing phase.' I gaze imploringly from one person to another. Sweat has broken out on my forehead. And in my armpits. It should be impossible with a second-skin suit, but I'm betting they've never been stress-tested this much before.

One of the whitecoats springs to Welt's side and whispers in his ear. Welt nods, and leans back in his chair. They chuckle.

'Cole here tells me there are some terrifying rumours about treatment for dulling, and you're probably nervous about that. You can relax. We don't want to make you medically content; we want to make you incredibly useful. Alara, we have a confession. You didn't do anything wrong in StarQuest. We disqualified you from the competition so you could work for us. We need you. If you'd gone ahead and won, which I'm told was a big possibility, you'd be too famous for too long. This way, you'll soon be forgotten about – and that's better for all of us.'

'Well, that's one silver lining.' I roll my eyes.

'StarQuest was not the Entertainment Board's idea, it was ours. We wanted to find someone mission-driven, with curiosity, intelligence, free thought. It's harder than you think to find someone with free thought in Estrella.' As if to demonstrate, he flicks on a wall screen and brings up a webcam of a hub, where everyone is staring at Flips and digipads and social media screens. 'Everyone is just too … content.'

We all laugh. It is kind of funny, but my knee is jigging. What's coming next?

'Contentment and connectivity. Two things that are very important to us. That was Esther Gallows-Bigg's vision when she designed Estrella: an easy existence, a community on a grand scale. That's why we have provided so many things to entertain everyone, running alongside a web of support. Who in their right mind could get bored in London Star?' He stops and gives me a conspiratorial wink. I'm starting to like him. 'But contented people aren't a lot of help when there's trouble. And there is trouble, Alara.'

'Trouble?'

'We have a mission for you – a simple case of information-gathering so we can keep our city safe. It's a quest game, if you like. Will you help us?'

Like I have to think twice. 'Of course.'

'It's a big ask. There may be danger.'

'No problem.'

'And we will require you to be loyal and to obey orders, for the sake of your own safety and for Estrella's. Can you follow orders without question?'

'Absolutely. Yes. I can do all that.' My heart is thumping like crazy, and a whitecoat checks his Flip and gestures to me to calm down.

'Learn to control that heart of yours, Alara. We don't want Medico telling us you're not fit.'

'But I am fit. I'm the fittest person I know!'

'Yes, and you can prove it to us now. Apparently, you've managed to beat Kagu Mactua in *Warlords*. That's impressive. Can we see you in action? Would you mind?'

'That's absolutely fine.' More than fine. I need an outlet for the excited energy ripping through my body.

A whitecoat passes me a game blade styled like a scimitar. The weight is good in my hand. I've never had such a sweet piece of weaponry before. The 3D ring comes down from the ceiling, circling me in its stripy, moody light.

'Alright, Alara. Kill anyone you meet. That's an order.'

The fighters come – small-fry characters from the simpler fighter games – and I dispatch them quickly, my Sensii forcing my arm to feel the resistance as the blade slices through their bodies. Then bigger combatants arrive. Still nothing too challenging. Welt and the whitecoats are clapping. Someone cheers as I send a grotty berserker flying. I suppress a triumphant smile and fight on. I'm pumped and ready for anything. Even Kagu wouldn't stand a chance. And then a new character arrives, unarmed, and kills my heart dead.

Are they serious?

'It's an order,' Welt repeats softly.

But why? Why on earth would they do this?

Vim stands before me, his arms open, his lips forming a sad smile.

'Do what you have to do, Alara.'

'But Vim...' My heart sticks in my throat, and I want to be sick. For a Pixel, dying on screen means dying for real. He'll be wiped and refurbished and reissued. A blank canvas. All that life, gone. All that friendship, erased.

'I'm just data,' he says. He steps forward and strokes my cheek.

I cup my hand against his ear and whisper the truth. 'I think I love you.'

He shuts his eyes, as if he's waited a lifetime to hear those words. My blade arm dangles by my side as I take a step back. He is still, calm. He's ready for the end. Biting my lip so hard it hurts, I grip the blade with both hands and rest its tip against his heart. And push. I feel every bit of resistance as it slides slowly through his chest.

Vim makes no sound as he dies.

When it's done, he fragments into a thousand scraps. They swirl around me, pieces of a friend. Then they evaporate. There is a silence in the room for I don't know how long.

There's pressure behind my eyes but I refuse to let the tears fall. He was just a Pixel, after all – a gaming element, a piece of my imagination. I breathe slowly, forcing my heart rate down.

'Good control.' It's one whitecoat to another. Of course – this was a test.

Welt vanishes the screen, taking with it the last cubic crumbs of Vim.

'If it makes it any easier, Alara, that Pixel was about to be retired.' Welt's hand is on my shoulder. 'You'd had it for far too long already. Entertainment was worried you'd developed it way beyond their control. Imagine if it grew resistant. What *would* happen if it grew resistant?'

I look up, but he's not talking to me, but to a whitecoat with a digipad.

'If it became too synchronised to one human, it could be under that human's control *and* be able to access the programming systems. A rogue. A threat.'

'So, you see, Alara, it's not personal. Take a seat.'

Nodding numbly is all I can do, because it feels personal as hell. With Moles like a ghost, Vim was the closest thing I had to a friend. More than that – he made me feel something. With him, I wasn't dulled. There's no time to dwell on that, though. Welt has brought up footage from the semi-finals, from my helmet cam as I swing across the Drop and above the Void. The lights dim and we're all in the dark, watching the spectacle. We've seen all this before – they played it yesterday during my disqualification broadcast – and besides, I thought StarQuest had nothing to do with this. No one says anything, and we're watching and watching, and we dive with my avatar, down and down into the gloom, into the danger zone, leaving the million lights above and behind, plunging deeper into the one-mile murk that hangs above the Void.

'How did you feel at this point?' Welt's voice is probing.

'It felt like the best tactic at the time to defeat the Blues.'

'Were you scared, so close to the Void?'

'No.'

'Good.' He turns the lights back on. 'Because that's where we're sending you.'

Chapter 8

They told me the mission. Went over it again and again, wanting to be sure I was on board. They shared Advice secrets – security secrets. My head is reeling, my brain so occupied, it barely remembers to tell my legs to walk. My slow pace makes me look even more out of place in Central, among the focused business people, snapping their razor pads, tapping their Flips.

'Are you okay?' A do-gooder. 'Are you lost? Do you want me to check your levels?'

'No, I'm fine. Thanks.'

And I remember what Welt said just before I left the room. *Act normal*. Alara Tripp must do what Alara Tripp always does. Well, Alara Tripp does not usually hang out in arcades for fun, so he got that wrong. But Welt says I must, so people get their fix of gawking – they all need a good look at the questa who was disqualified. *The sooner you're noticed, the sooner you'll be forgotten*. He's right, of course. And he did look suitably apologetic.

It's also an opportunity to train my heart rate. When you lie, your rate automatically speeds up – and between now and the mission, I'm going to be doing a lot of lying.

Welt suggested an arcade in South, where there are big crowds. Big crowds attract beakers – people who stick their noses into everything – and it's them we need to exhaust. Once they've done all the beaking and gossiping they can possibly do, they'll move on to someone else, like the other questas still in the game, or even just someone who's done their hair funny. Seriously, beakers are blank between the ears.

Once that's done and I'm forgotten, I can slip off the social radar and get to work. As a security operative. I say it over and over in my head. *A security operative for Estrella.* Even if I were allowed to tell anyone, who would believe it? Me, a nobody from the Quarters? If he were still around, I'd tell Vim. Vim kept secrets. But he's gone. Out of play.

On the train I share a carriage with a group of girls comparing thin-skin tattoos and talking about the latest SpyLogs. They are loud and unashamed, talking about going to the gaming arcade in South because video stars will be there – social media influencers with heaps of followers. I bet these girls do their homework. It sounds like they know the names, faces and statistics of every vlogger in every hub.

I shrink low in my seat to avoid their attention, even

though the only reason I'm here is to attract it. This space is too enclosed – the proximity plus the fuss would be stifling. This is harder than I thought.

When we arrive at the hub, I hang back, trying to build up my heart control before facing the crowds. The reality is, as soon as the lift doors open, panic kicks my heart into a canter. I freeze and stare despairingly at the huge groups that stand around simulators and 3D rings and gaming pods. Everyone's laughing, swigging bright drinks, moving from one attraction to the other, shouting at the tops of their voices. Right in front of me, there's a swell of jeering as a small kid in a 3D ring gets pummelled by a beast of a wrestler in *Fight Club*. Big bully kids push him back in the ring for more, when all he wants to do is get out and go home. Everyone is ignoring his heart rate, but that's the cool thing about our fully linked information platform – if it goes on too much longer, Medico will be alerted automatically. The only thing that'll be hurt is his pride. He starts to whimper and I remember what Vim once said to me. *You have to stand up* for *people – and stand up* to *people.* Or maybe that came from me. Maybe those were my principles. Either way.

'Leave him alone.' The words spring from my mouth before I've had a chance to think of the repercussions. Welt said I had to get noticed, but I'm not sure this is what he had in mind.

People stand back. The boy stumbles out of the ring

and runs, leaving the *Fight Club* wrestler pulsing on the balls of his feet, waiting for a challenger.

'It's that disqualified questa,' someone shouts. I want to run, but no. Bring it on. Let's do this properly.

'Why d'you get disqualified?' a voice shouts.

There's a nugget of pride in me that wants to tell them the truth – *I've been chosen* – but this exercise is to make them forget me. I'll have to take pride in being successful at that, instead.

'I went out of the designated zone. I cheated.'

'Well, if it makes you feel better, we'll let you replace the kid you just let go.' It's the bully. He's tall, and he walks right into me on purpose. He's either been working out or he's wearing a tough-skin suit. Either way, it hurts. I'm rubbing at the sore bridge of my nose when he lifts me by the shoulders and raises me off my feet so we're eye to eye. He nods to a friend, who steps forward and grabs my arm and presses my Flip. He waits for my Sensii to connect to *Fight Club* then throws me into the ring.

I pass right through the wrestler hologram. The body shock registers, and I'm winded. While I'm on the floor, the wrestler stamps on my back. It doesn't really hurt, but the boys erupt in laughter. Behind the hollers, there are gasps from new onlookers. I roll my head to the side. Faces fuzz in front of my eyes, Flips blink as they snap pictures, and it makes me mad enough to leap to my feet. I'm enmeshed with the hologram and the protracted contact creates shuddering thuds through my body, and then I jump free of him and adopt a fighting position: one foot forward, shifting my weight onto my right thigh, protecting my face with my raised elbow, my other hand balled in a fist, tucked into my side.

I'm lucky. Unlike *Warlords,* where there are no rules, *Fight Club* is all about the rule book. The wrestler sticks to his programmed moves – pulling, grabbing, throwing, stomping. I dance round him, lashing out with a fist to his neck and a straight-legged kick to his knees, cracking his kneecaps. The red 'illegal' light flashes at my every hit. But I'm not after game points. I just want to inflict enough pain points on the wrestler to call game over. Eventually, after an outer roundhouse kick to his kidneys, the wrestler sinks onto all fours and raises a hand in surrender. The game says I'm disqualified. It's a gift to some bigmouth.

'Disqualified again? Alara Tripp, it might be better if you just gave up gaming.'

When I step out of the ring, they form a circle round me. I'm not worried about getting hurt. Physical fights don't happen here – there are too many people standing by, ready to rack up those good citizen bonuses. But they are crowding me, taking up my personal space, and it's basically my nightmare. If I ever have a bad dream, you can bet it's about being caged or suffocated or trapped. I even sleep with one leg outside my duvet for fear of being engulfed. Here, right now, there are legs, knees, arms, jackets and bags, Flips, and cutting laughs ringing in my eyes and ears. They sway before me. They lean into me.

'Her heart is about to burst!' Someone laughs.

'Hip hip hooray! Medico is on the way!' Another idiot.

I shut my eyes tight and imagine that it's a dense forest and Vim's there, just ahead of me, like he was in *Caves of the Kraken* and *Trembler*, telling me it's make-believe and it's all going to be okay. *Chill out, Alara – just breathe.* But if Vim is me, my bravest side, then I can say it to myself, can't I? I stand, immovable as a rock, and eventually they get bored.

People begin to peel away, drawn by a commotion elsewhere in the arcade, but not before snapping me a million times. Any second now, my face will be reeling across the media screens in the social hubs with captions galore. I hope Welt's happy.

As I jog through the pedestrian tubes, the stress melts away. I don't have to make myself a target for idiots ever again. If I were still a contestant, I'd have weeks of that to come. Television, interviews, public competitions. At least this was short and sharp and over with. And, of course, there's the bright side – the reason it was all necessary. I'm going on a mission.

Don't think I'm not scared. I'm petrified. But if I dwell on the Void, my guts twist – and there'll be plenty of time for gut-twisting when I'm down there. Right now, I have to focus on the positives. On the feeling of purpose – something is actually *happening* in my life – and on the deal I struck with Welt. Mum gets a promotion immediately. Right now. No more of this credit-stealing crap that is keeping her down. If I complete the mission, my family gets cash, a new apartment, a shopping spree, whatever they want. Just as if I'd won StarQuest. Although there's a downside: I might be dead.

'Alara!' Landi is standing in front of me. 'I've been trying to catch up with you.'

I stop and stare at her. 'Why? What's up?'

'Thought we could have a nice chat, after all. Get to know each other. We're a lot alike, you and I.'

'Oh. Right. Well, maybe later, because –'

'Or how about now?' She grabs my arm and pulls me to a bench. 'Tell me about your disqualification.'

'What? I thought you just wanted to chat.'

'I do. But first, let's talk about StarQuest. Or your not being in StarQuest. You've been to Central, haven't you? What did Advice talk to you about?'

Her Flip is lit. She's recording. This isn't a 'nice chat' at all.

'Landi, I'm busy.'

She grips my elbow. 'Look, you do me a favour and maybe I can do you one. Put in a good word with my parents, get you invited to a party, maybe even get you access to somewhere interesting for your project. Look, I've chosen to do a feature on aspiration in Estrella, and you could really, really help me with it.'

'I don't know how. I got disqualified.'

'Yeah, but I've seen you play. I know how good you

are. And Central doesn't just have cosy chats with cheats. Something's up. Tell me.'

Her ice eyes could squeeze the truth out of anyone, given time.

'You're off the mark, Landi. It was a formal dismissal, not a secret meeting.' I feel my cheeks burn, and walk on before I give anything away.

'I'm on to you!' she shouts as I start to jog. 'You're up to something in Central. You're cosying up to the suits, aren't you? Aspiring to rise above your dirt-poor existence.'

How much can one person take in a day? Missions, humiliations, ambush. I'm relieved to finally reach my 'dirt-poor' Quarters. Home is usually a place of calm, but Dad's home, Mum's home, Gavi's playing with a new toy. Everything is a merry-go-round. What is going on?

'Alara!' Mum shouts my name as if I've been gone years, and wraps her arms around me.

'What's happening?'

Gavi zaps me with his toy – but it's not a toy, as such. It's an Echo-Pen! Catch a moving scene and you can replicate it as a 3D hologram anywhere. He's already reproduced holograms of Mum and is making them pop up all over the room. Twenty Mums doing a dance. My head is spinning.

'Turn it off, Gavi,' Dad says, snatching it away, but his tone is playful.

Mum hands round glasses of fizz. Champagne?

'To our lucky mascot,' she says, raising her glass. To me.

I don't know what's happening here. Surely Welt hasn't told them. No, it's a state secret, and my family wouldn't be *happy* to find out where I'm heading. Especially Dad.

'Yay to me!' I cheer. 'And could someone tell me why?'

Mum pulls me close. 'Because today, my darling, a mere day after you were talking about it, I was given a promotion.'

'A promotion? Mum, that's incredible. Then this is to you!' I raise my glass, and Dad and Gavi follow. Four glasses in the air.

'To me!' she says.

'To you!' We toast her again, then Gavi sneezes as the bubbles go up his nose.

'So? Tell us what happened,' Dad says.

Mum prepares her face for the story, trying to tame her huge smile. It makes me want to grin like crazy, seeing her so happy.

'There was an information leak, and the Food Technology Board found out exactly who had been creating all these wonderful flavours. Ta-da! Me, and not Etti Lorn, after all.'

'A leak? Wow, someone's going to be in trouble. They're bound to catch them,' Dad says.

Mum pauses. 'Yes, I hadn't thought of that. Oh dear.'

'Don't worry, Mum. You didn't ask for it to happen,

and whoever leaked it probably knows how to get around the Flip system. Maybe they just wrote it on a piece of paper.' I squeeze her hand.

Or maybe they told Welt Eldon in person.

'Will we have loads more money?' Gavi, subtle as ever. He's got Ent upgrades in his eyes.

'Actually, yes.' Mum can't hide her excitement. 'It's not just a one-tier promotion. They looked back through my work history and did some knowledge tests and – well, it turns out there's a directorial position that's opened up, and they'd like me to take it.'

Mum's face is bright. She's standing taller, too. She looks like a director, not the hunched, resigned tech assistant she was just a few hours earlier.

'That's incredible!' That *is* incredible. I did not expect them to go that far. Right now I could hug Welt Eldon and his weird bunch of whitecoats.

'What can we buy?' Gavi's table manners have been atrocious, but he's now sitting straight in his chair like a golden child. 'Anything we want? Can we get a new 3D ring?'

'Well, we'll have to do some maths and see what we –'

'What about a new Ent room?'

'Gavi...' Dad says, exasperated.

I tap his head. 'Go on, Gavi. Go to the Ent and I'll join you there in a minute.'

'Now.'

'No, in a minute. I need to talk to Mum and Dad.'

'What about?'

'None of your business. Shoo!'

Mum and Dad look at me expectantly. I realise I've launched into the hard bit without being prepared. I gesture to the sofa, to buy me some time. I'm still not sure what to say. Well, I know the story – Welt gave me that – but it's not the real story, and I'm pretty bad at lying. I can blame the champagne for my flushed cheeks and my words, if I trip up.

'What is it, Banana? All okay?'

'Oh yeah. Totally fine. Everything.'

'Are you upset because of the disqualification? Do you want some talk therapy?'

'What happened in your meeting at Central? We didn't even ask...' Mum's hand shoots to cover her mouth. 'Were they mad about it? Is there a punishment – community service?'

You could say that.

'Shush, both of you. Stop worrying. The meeting was fine. In fact, it was more than fine. Yes, I was disqualified for flying in the danger zone.' I slap my wrist. 'But I've also been noticed by a big gaming company, and they've asked if I can work with them for a while.'

Mum and Dad blink as if they're on standby. I take a sip and wait for them to turn back on.

'What will you be doing?' Mum says.

'Testing out some new technology.'

It's not a lie, exactly.

Chapter 9

I'm being plunged into a tank of something slimy. They tell me it's a solution called Santiens Dip. It should be called Satan's Dip, because it's freezing and I have to keep my eyes open. The thin membranes covering our eyes are an easy entry point for diseases, and apparently, a full-body coating of this will stop me picking up anything horrible from the destination.

The destination. The Void. A place ravaged by industrial tragedy, poisonous and deadly.

I'm only in the tank a few seconds, but it feels like a lifetime before I'm lifted out of it again. I've been told to stand and drip-dry to allow my skin to absorb as much of the Santiens as possible. Naked and shivering, eyes blinking and sore, I wait. The excess slime drips off my body onto the platform floor, seeping through holes back into the tank. Being a real-life questa is less glamorous than I imagined. And there's not going to be any aircraft, hover-gear or weapons. No cool Pixel partners to watch my back. No Vim Mark II. Just me. Oh, and they're about to put a chip in my head.

Try not to think about that. Think about the task, and following orders; think about the unthinkable. Think about what's beneath the feet of Estrella's towers. Deep beneath, buried under a century of trash and waste. No, don't think about that, either. Think of the thrill, the heartbeat. Of no longer being dulled.

Boredom is a thing of the past. Something is actually *happening.*

My skin is smooth and dry, the Santiens fully absorbed. I climb a ladder back down to ground level and slip into a gown, imagining for a moment that I'm about to dine at a spa-side restaurant in some luxury development. It's a funny parallel, the bathing and the fluffy gowns. In one reality it might be for deep-cleanse relaxation and nutrition, but in mine it's preparing for dirt and – well, who knows what I'll be eating. It won't be good, they warned me. In the briefings, they've warned me about lots of things. But there'll be time to dread-run the scenario plenty between now and tomorrow morning.

I push the call button on the door to tell them I'm done, and three women enter. They lead me out carefully, holding my elbows like I'm an ancient lady who's forgotten to put on her tender-skin suit. Or someone being taken to the clinics. There's a seed of doubt – after all, they know I'm dulled. But if they wanted to commit me, they could have done it a long time ago. They wouldn't go to all this trouble for someone who was no use.

I'm led past the white doors of the clinics and experimentation rooms, down corridors and into a lift. Not one of the ones that services Central. This is small and round, and from the speed it moves, I reckon it's for private use only. Maybe it's an escape route for the rich if there's an emergency, or perhaps it's just so they don't have to walk alongside ordinary people. We arrive at a private platform where a train is waiting. It's only two seats wide. More like a bullet. The whitecoats smile efficiently, but there are no explanations, no talking. I'm clearly being delivered somewhere, and who talks to a package? Looking around, I reckon it's an extra train tunnel built above the regular tunnel but within the same outer casing, undetectable from the outside. Top secret. It's beginning to feel more like a mission now. More serious.

We arrive at another scraper – I don't know which one – and then we're in another lift, going up. There are no clues as to whether I'm in North or South, or even if I'm still in London Star. There are rooms with internal windows. Computers, rotating holograms, light beams criss-crossing – the workers inside the rooms are still, rigid, apart from their fingers, which fly across keyboards, turning dials on either side.

We move through double white doors, and behind them there's a medical room. Unmistakable. Metal arms hang above a bed, gripping super-fine needles; it's kind of brutal-looking, like something out of *Mad Lab* – a pretty nasty horror-quest game set in a derelict medical unit. There's a panic in my chest, but I know this won't hurt. Chip implantation is a procedure, and there's no pain in procedures. There's never real pain in London Star – not the kind you see people in old movies experience, with their writhing and screaming. The worst is a synthetic boot from your Sensii chip during a game. And I can handle that easily – maybe too easily.

The whitecoats seem to know what to do. They're gentle with me, helping me onto the bed, explaining in just a few words how the chip implantation will work. It's already been explained, and I'm ready. They shave narrow lines along the sides of my head – one side for the chip, the other to balance out my hairstyle so it doesn't look like I've just had a chip planted in my head. They can make skin heal, but there's no such thing as a hair-growth accelerator, so a random patch would be a giveaway. Mum will be horrified. It'll look like I have a maverick's style, they say.

'What's a maverick?' I ask.

'Someone like you, Alara, who likes running in the tubes.'

We all laugh. They say they'll wipe my record clean.

When the buzz of the hair clippers stops, there's some bustling, talking, and my head is held still by two hands. A line is traced onto the side of my head – marking out the path of an incision. Someone holds my hand. A robot arm whirrs and moves above me. I try not to flinch, because robots – faces or no faces – freak me out. And then there's a prick in the back of my hand. Everything distorts – faces and walls, melting together in waves. The white lights contract to nothing. And I'm out.

Waking up in my own time, blinking away sleep, it feels like a normal morning. I'm still on the bed. The robot arms have been stood down. A nurse places her hand on my forehead. Whitecoats arrive and give me the full-body examination – eyes, ears, mouth, reflexes – and I'm declared a success, but I'm not allowed to move yet. *Don't move your head too much. Don't sit up.* I reach up to touch my shaven head and feel a thread, a strand thin as a hair, leading from a pore-hole behind my ear to a machine at my side. Another wire connects that to an old-fashioned video screen hanging in front of me. The nurse angles the cantilever holder for me to see.

The screen shows exactly what I'm looking at – the video screen. And the video screen shows a video screen: the image is repeated to infinity. When I try to prop myself up on my elbows, I'm quickly eased back down.

'Gen-Tech,' a voice says. 'It's going to open up a whole new era for gaming.'

It's Welt. He crouches by my side, his elbows resting on the bed, looking at me like I'm his miracle child.

'I thought the questing tech thing was a cover. I thought I was going on a mission,' I say, my voice husky. A nurse sprays water on my lips.

'You are. Every technology has a use beyond its original purpose.'

'What does it do?'

'In a minute, someone will explain. But no mention of the mission, Alara. Outside of this small group' – he gestures to the whitecoats and himself – 'no one is to know. As far as anyone else is concerned, you are testing out new game tech. You're just a girl who likes gaming, a guinea pig.' He puts his finger to his mouth. I nod and he pats my arm. 'In a way, your mission starts right this moment. Not a word.'

He smiles warmly and disappears through the doors, returning two seconds later with a man who he introduces to me as Hoppi Burbeck. Right. I don't believe it, but then I notice PlayBeck logos on the clinic walls. I'm not in Medico at all. I'm in Burbeck's development centre! I stare at my hero: the man who created *Wilderness* and a thousand other brilliant quest games. The original inventor of Pixels. I've rehearsed a thousand times what I'd say if I ever met him, but now my tongue is frozen.

He exchanges words with Welt, whose manner is relaxed. The hand-shaking goes on for ages, before their attention finally turns to me.

'Here she is, Hoppi. The girl who's going to get this

technology up and running for you. She's had a record of being, er, *dulled*, you know. So impress her, and you're on to a winner.'

Hoppi slides his gaze towards me and nods. My cheeks burn. The way Welt's described me, I sound like a demanding princess. Probably not the best introduction. I stare at this man, who is the only reason I ever watch the news – the man whose penthouse I spied on, hoping for a sighting of him. What did I imagine? Not this.

Without his face filters, I thought he'd look younger than his years, not older. He has the money for skin-resurfacing and all manner of cosmetic stuff, if he wants it. But he looks elderly. Maybe the oldest-looking person I've ever seen. His skin sags in so many places that his wrinkles are deep ravines. He has heavy bags that tug at the lower rims of his eyes, making them look large and bloodshot. I'm ashamed to say that I'm disappointed. I expected charisma. But he doesn't smile and his wet eyes don't blink. He's not the warm, wonderful – or the mad, exuberant – inventor I pictured. There is no golden aura.

There's an *aaaah*, and I turn back to see the whitecoats pointing to the screen above my head.

'Are you seeing what I'm seeing on the screen?'

'Yes.'

'How's this going to be good for … gaming?'

'The idea is that you'll be able to game using nothing but your mind.' Burbeck's gravelly voice sounds calm and patient, but I detect a hint of annoyance; he's not happy at being forced to explain his technology to a kid. I've just allowed his untested gadget to be stuffed in my head, but of course, I say nothing.

'Gen-Tech will build monsters based on your fears. Heroes based on your loves. It'll create worlds based on your memories or on your wants. Gen-Tech will know you better than you know yourself.'

Gaming using nothing but your mind? I think of Moles. It would be devastating for someone like him, because he's got monsters, alright. They torment him day and night. He really doesn't need extra help.

'The proposed catchline is *fight your demons, free your dreams*,' Welt adds. 'That's right, isn't it?'

Burbeck's looking at me in a way I don't understand. He's probably disappointed that his technology guinea pig is not someone meatier and media-hungry like Blaze. Perhaps he thinks Welt's wrong about me. Maybe he thinks it's all a waste of time, or I'll break his prototype.

'When will it be ready for use?'

Burbeck and I are still locked into some kind of staring competition.

'When we're sure it won't explode your eyeballs.'

I gasp, and Burbeck frowns. 'It's hooked up to your optic nerves, Miss Tripp, and I do hope that was explained to you. You knew what you were signing up for?'

I catch Welt's eye and he blinks slowly. 'Yes, yes. I just forgot. Don't know biological terms, that's all.'

'Right. We'll leave it for a couple of weeks so it settles in, then we'll do some tests, quest trials. It'll take time. Perhaps months. But you're not in a hurry to go anywhere, are you?'

'No. Not at all.'

'Good. Because it's now a permanent part of your head.'

I didn't know that, either. But I suppress my surprise. Don't want to raise suspicion, even if I'm alarmed that Welt didn't fill me in on the fact that I'm now part-machine.

'I can't wait to explore it.' I try a smile. Then it strikes me – this is new, this is a story. *The story.* I've been given a special pass to a whole new era of gaming. Mr Leppito's 'new perspective'. Media winner. 'Mr Burbeck, what inspired you to create Gen-Tech?'

'When you reach the top, you quickly realise there's nowhere else to go.' He looks at me again that way, and I worry I've got the questioning angle wrong. But will I ever have another chance to speak to him, the genius recluse?

'Sorry if I'm asking too many questions, but can you explain why going somewhere in your head is any different to your other quest games, like *Wilderness*?'

He looks around. Welt and the whitecoats are facing the other way. He suddenly leans close to my ear and hisses, 'Because it's *real*.'

What do I make of that? Maybe he hates children. Maybe he's mad.

'Well, I think it sounds exciting.'

'Yes, it is. Originally, Advice blocked development, but now they've changed their minds, it is rather exciting.' His voice is flat, but loaded with something – bitterness or cynicism? Maybe he's just not Welt's biggest fan. Or vice versa. If so, I'd get it – I don't think I've ever met such a weird person as Hoppi, but perhaps that's what the super-rich are like. Intellectual brains, with the social skills of bots.

'Now, if I could have my laboratory back?' Burbeck says it with some force.

Welt spins round. 'Of course. Of course. If you could give us a moment while Miss Tripp gets dressed.'

Burbeck and his team pause in the doorway. Burbeck raises a hand to speak. 'Miss Tripp. If you have any questions or feel any strange sensations, I want to know right away. I'll set your birthday as your password for my lab. You'll be able to walk straight in.'

'I think it would be better if she came to us,' Welt says, placing a hand on my head. Kind of possessive. 'We wouldn't want to waste your time if it's something that Medico or our clinics could deal with.'

Burbeck's jowls wobble as he clenches his teeth. 'She comes to me. Only my people understand the calibration. If your whitecoats fiddle around, they won't only break my tech, they'll break her brain.'

'Of course,' Welt says, with a little bow.

Great. If I wasn't scared before, I am now. Welt holds

me quiet with warning eyes while Burbeck and his people shuffle out. Then his whitecoats pack up their things.

To think that meeting Hoppi Burbeck was a dream of mine. I've just had the dream and the nightmare all in one go. And now there's something in my head that'll be in there forever, and I still don't know why it's even necessary.

'Mr Eldon, how's Gen-Tech going to help my mission?'

Welt helps me sit up and checks my head, gently, as if I'm made of eggshell. 'We won't be activating the gaming element, just the base software, which will track and map-build. It means you won't have to remember routes or take notes or do anything that might arouse suspicion and put you in danger. Your journey will be downloaded when you get back, and we can overlay your map onto the ones we already have and fill in the missing pieces. Your job is to cover as much ground as possible.'

'Watch that heart rate of yours,' a whitecoat advises, staring at his pad. 'We can't afford Medico to get involved.' He says that to Welt, rather than me. Welt nods.

'Alara, you're bound to be nervous, but what we're asking you to do is treat this like any other quest game. Your mission objective is actually simple – there are no puzzles or traps. You just go down, look around, return. The challenging bits are keeping calm and keeping to the story. Do you think you can do that?'

I'm not sure. I'm really not sure. If only Vim was with me.

'Yes.'

'While you get dressed, we'll go over it one more time.'

A screen is drawn around me so I can slip out of the gown and back into my clothes. The shadows of the others move across it, just on the other side. And it's suddenly so real – the pressure to remember everything, do everything, not mess up… Although it's a wonder my mind hasn't already exploded, with the revelation of what's waiting for me.

Welt tells me that the Void is contaminated, and will remain that way for thousands of years. I knew that. But what I didn't know – what nobody but this small group knows – is that below the deadly surface, in the buried tunnels of Old London, lives a community. When Estrella was born, a few crazies decided that a paradise city wasn't for them. They opted to live like rats, exposed to poison, suffering early death. Protestors existed even before Star's construction: objectors to connectivity. We learned about them in History. They fought against advancements in health and improvements in the structure of society, just because they didn't like change. And now, beneath our scrapers, having managed to exist, undignified as nematodes, there is a whole lot of them – an *uncivilised* civilisation – living in the dark, scrabbling around in the dirt.

When he told me this, Welt had laughed at my reaction. My face must have been a picture. I mean, who can blame me for looking shocked? Who the hell would give up a comfortable long life for a short life of poverty and pollution, and in the dark?

'Some people can't be saved from themselves,' Welt had said. And it made me think of Peron, who had wanted to self-destruct so badly that he threw himself down the Drop.

So if some people can't be saved, then what was my mission?

'We have a symbiotic relationship with Under,' Welt explained. 'We don't make them join us in Estrella, even though our doors are wide open. But at the same time, they live in tunnels that weave around the foundations of our towers, and we need to keep an eye on that. As you can imagine, these tunnel-dwellers haven't exactly evolved to keep up with the technologies we have now. And if they dig too close to a skyscraper or in any way interfere with one, then both of our societies are going to come crashing down. Ours on top of theirs. It would be a catastrophe. We've felt some tremors recently, and so we need you to see if everything is in order. See if they're being careful.'

'Can't you just ask them?'

Welt shook his head, sadly. 'Most of Under's civilians don't know we're even aware of them; they think they're safe in their secrecy. Similarly, most people in Estrella don't know they exist either.'

'But you said we had a symbiotic relationship.'

'Hmm, well, I suppose you could say it was more *charity* than symbiosis. We leave them in peace, despite knowing that some paranoid groups down there consider us a threat. They think we want to force them into Estrella. We really don't, and we don't want any trouble. Sending officials down there might cause unrest, and we see no reason to upset them. We just need to know that our structures are secure. If not...'

Welt did an impression of a falling tower with his hand, and that was enough to convince me that my mission was super-important. In a single tower there could be thousands of people. London, in any incarnation, did not need another catastrophe.

'But you said the mission was dangerous. Why?'

He pins me with a look. 'Because they might be hostile. No, there's no point in treating you like a child, Alara. Some *will* be hostile. If they think for one minute you're nosing about on behalf of Estrella, then you'll be outnumbered and alone... Stick to your story and you'll be fine.'

My story is that I'm the survivor of a terrible accident. But for the story to work, there first has to be a terrible accident. How else would a teenage girl find herself in the Void, all alone? That's the bit we haven't yet discussed.

Now the Gen-Tech chip is implanted in my head, there's

nothing to delay the mission, and with a whitecoat updating us with a report of two more tremors recorded that morning, there's no time to lose. After I dress, we head back to Central, to a secret room in the Advice offices. I try not to scratch my shaven head. Plates of the finest sushi are brought in for us while we discuss the final details – how I'm going to get onto the ground and into Under. It's what they call the 'delivery'. No one can know. No one. Welt says that London Star residents will freak out if they discover there are people beneath our feet, and I can imagine that, totally. I'm trying not to freak out, myself. A community of dehumanised people running between our scrapers, bug-ridden and vicious... It's creepy as hell. The whole operation has to be secret. But it's hard to have a terrible accident in secret, though.

'We have come up with an idea for the delivery aspect of the mission,' Welt says. 'Kit here...' – he points to a whitecoat – 'was tasked with searching through your history to see if it threw up any ideas. Kit?'

The whitecoat leans forward. 'We've learned that Mr Leppito, your Media teacher, has recently set you a task – to discover something fascinating about Estrella. Is that right? And of course, your father is a Refuse Manager. It's a match made in heaven.'

'How?'

'You ask your father if you can go tip-turning with him because you're doing refuse management for your journalism piece on Estrella. He'll object, of course.

No kid is allowed anywhere out there, not even with a thousand hazard suits on. But if you can be persuasive enough for him to at least ask Advice, then he'll find that Advice, on this occasion, will be cooperative. Especially for a student hoping to get on to Third Teach Media.'

'Why don't you just dump me down there? Wouldn't that be easier?'

'Because the story – that you are an innocent girl caught up in an accident – needs to stand up to scrutiny. If one of the people from Under sees sweeper trucks at the time you said you got lost, it'll be more believable.'

'Okay.' I nod. 'How's it going to work – the accident bit?'

'You'll go to work with your dad, and at some point during your journey we'll arrange a distraction. We'll radio in a problem, something that means the sweeper will stop and the workers have to get out to investigate. That's not decided yet. All you need to know is, when there's a chance to go, you go.'

'Go where?'

'Anywhere away from the sweeper, into the night. Hide. Do what you have to until they give up. Then you can look for openings into Under.'

I've always visualised stuff as if it were a film playing out in front of my eyes, and I can see it so clearly now – the sweeping, the excitement, the interruption ... and my escape. But the trouble with being the director of a movie is that I get to see all the perspectives. And now I see my dad, worried sick, screaming my name until his voice is gone, returning home, broken and desperate and telling Mum that he lost their daughter in the Void.

Welt puts his arm around me. 'Is it scaring you?'

'No, it's not the mission. It's my father, my family. They'll be...'

'They'll be fine. We'll give them something. Something to help them stay calm. And before they know it, you'll be discovered safe and sound and delivered right back to them. All's well that ends well.'

If it ends well.

'And how will I get back? Will you give me instructions through my Flip or this thing?' I tap my head, imagining Welt's steady voice telling me what to do and when to go. The idea of voices that aren't mine kicking around in my skull is weird, but in this situation I suppose it might actually be comforting. A connection to home.

Kit leans forward again. 'Gen-Tech isn't a telecoms system, and your Flip won't work. The Unders are primitive people. There's no connectivity down there. Estrella is a closed circuit. If you get into trouble, we won't know a thing about it. But we've done our homework and watched hours of your gameplay: we know that you're resourceful enough to cope, you think on your feet. We've done the algorithms, and there's a near-zero chance that you'll run into trouble, but if you do, you'll figure it out. You've figured out nearly every puzzle thrown at you during questa games. We can honestly say that you're the right person for this job.' She smiles warmly. Welt does too. And I know I never want to let them or Estrella down. Suddenly I miss the warmth of London Star, and I haven't even left it.

'What about coming home? When?'

'We need you to do whatever you can in three days. We'll keep our search cameras pointed at the ground, with guards watching 24/7, and we'll scoop you up the minute we see you. But until then, you're on your own.'

Unconnected?

'And Alara?' Welt searches my face with his kind eyes. 'We can extend the mission for a few hours if you hit a problem, but nobody from Star can survive the environment down there for much longer – disease, animals, violence. If you're not picked up by then, we'll presume you've failed.'

'And what would you tell Mum and Dad?'

'I'm afraid we could never tell them the truth about the mission. You understand that?'

'Of course. It's for the security of Estrella. But what if I wasn't dead?'

'If you're not dead, you'll get back in time. If you don't get back in time, you're dead. Come now. We've talked enough.'

'I won't fail,' I add quickly. 'I'll come back. Three days, I'll be back.'

My stomach dives at the thought of it. Living without

connectivity is like doing trapeze without a net. A high-wire without a crash mat. An intensity game without a heart rate alarm. If I fail in this mission, there's nothing to catch me. Nothing at all. But alongside the thud of my heart, there's a flutter in my stomach. A flurry of excitement. *Oh Vim, I wish I could tell you!*

Chapter 10

We are standing on a platform in a narrow metal tube streaked with grease, being transported down the Drop. Like the others, I'm wearing a hazard suit – full-body and made of thick black rubber. There's a transparent hood with an inbuilt air-supply – fed by air sacs sewn into the shoulders. The suit is totally flexible, apart from the feet and hands, where the rubber hardens to form boots and gloves. I feel like a total bot. Dad winks at me through his visor, but only quickly.

Dad is in charge of a team of ten – all men. They tower over me, kind of serious-looking. Dad warned me about that: their humour will return once the shift is done, but keeping focused on the job is what keeps them alive. It's pure poison out there.

A doorway appears in the tube in front of us, and the lift comes to a halt with a shudder and a clunk. We step out onto the ground floor of the giant scraper. The workers dutifully circle Dad and he gives orders – how far out to go, what formation to sweep in. He goes through the light signals on his lead sweeper truck, although the men must have heard them a thousand times before.

I get a small buzz from the intensity of everyone's expression and a thrill from the clanging of metal – the internal workings of the scraper. The residential levels are soundproofed; we are literally sealed off from everything but the sounds of our own existence, in a world of soft furnishings and smooth surfaces. Industrial clatter isn't something I'm used to. It feels alien. It vibrates through my bones.

The men peel away in pairs and head for their trucks. Dad leads me to his. It's bigger than the others, a yellow base with caterpillar tyres and sweeper arms that jut out at right angles, snarling with hundreds of curved metal teeth. The driver's pod is an inverted glass bowl on top with an exterior light display, and inside there is a single long front seat, with two seats behind. I assume I'll be in one of those, but Dad pulls me up onto the front bench and I find myself squashed between him and his teammate, Luk.

There's a lot of settling in, with flasks of coffee needing to be placed in cup-holders, the satellite mapping device in the satellite mapping device holder, phones in phone holders. Dad apologises, but I'm not bored. How could I be? I'm charged with so many emotions, my body feels electric. I love seeing Dad respected and revered by the workers. I don't get a chance to see that at home, where he acts like his job is filthy and lowly; it's almost as if he hates himself for it, like it's eating him up. Of course, we tell him that tip-turning is *necessary* – he's an essential worker. I know that even more now, having discovered more about the vulnerabilities of Star and its precious towers. But you can't cure someone of insecurity. He probably thinks if he was an architect or a gaming programmer, we'd be prouder.

He could barely believe it when I said I wanted to base my project on his work. It took a lot of pleading, of pulling out all the emotional stuff: he must *know* how much I want to be a journalist; after the disappointment of StarQuest, this would mean *so* much. I'm not proud of myself, but I had no choice – and neither did he, if he ever wanted to see me happy again. He approached Advice with the request. And here we are.

Dad made me agree to follow the rules and told me to prepare for a long, boring trip into the wilderness of the Void. We'd be gone from dawn until dusk. I've just got a pad to take notes for my Media project – that's my only prop. There's nothing else I need. At some point, I'll be gone. No idea when. I just have to wait for the 'incident'.

We're first in the queue to exit the foot of the tower and roll out into the open.

My stomach flips when I see the true scale of it all – metals, plastics, twisted corpses of machines, stacked high, ugly and precarious. Some piles are higher than the sweeper trucks. It's like *War Zone* for real. It's awful; it's mind-blowing.

'So what do you want to know?' Luk says, his head jerking with the motion of the sweeper. I freeze. For a moment, I had forgotten my cover story. I tap my pad, as if I have prepared questions.

'Um, so why isn't all this stuff being recycled?'

'It's contaminated,' Dad says. He looks ahead, concentrating on navigating the ground. The sweeper dips and sways over the hills.

'Can't it be cleaned?'

'Yes, but then it needs to be quarantined for months. It's a long process, and there's a lot of junk out here. Everything that existed before London Star – it's all right here. And the population was once fifty times bigger. Just imagine. Considering the danger and the effort needed, there doesn't seem much point in recycling this lot. Eventually, the toxicity levels will drop and we'll be able to do something about it. Maybe not in our lifetime, though.'

'Why is there still junk here, so close to the towers? Why haven't they cleaned it up and cleared the ground?'

'No one ever comes out here. It's not worth it. And it offers the bases of the skyscrapers protection from the weather.'

'Why do you turn it? What's tip-turning all about?'

'To release any build-up of trapped gases. We don't

want an explosion. Look!' Luk says, pointing at the windscreen.

'Oh! What is *that*?' I shriek, then cover my mouth with embarrassment. Dad and Luk laugh.

'A trash crab. Once you see one, you'll see thousands. Take a look.'

'He never gets bored by the job, do you, Luk?' Dad laughs. 'Luk the Keen, we call him.'

'And we call your dad Mikal the Master.'

They chuckle. The grey trash crab, the size of my palm, runs off the truck windscreen and back down to the ground. Luk is right. I pick out more of them scuttling sideways across the rubbish, darting down cracks as the shadows of the sweepers loom over them. Some are like stones, camouflaged and totally still apart from their claws, busily feeding crumbs of noxious waste into their mouths.

'They are seriously weird,' I muse.

'Certainly are, Alara,' Luk says. He's clearly enjoying his role, despite Dad's teasing. 'But not as weird as some of the wild things we've seen out here.'

'Like what?'

'Can't say for sure. We never got close enough. Mutant wolves. Evolved laboratory monkeys. Nobody knows.' Luk does a ghostly 'woooo' sound to add intrigue.

'But if it's poisonous out here, how do these animals survive?'

'Well, we don't know that. Or how long they live

for. They might live very short lives, or they might have mutated to withstand the poison… It's all speculation until someone catches one and gets to work on it.'

'Gets to work on it?'

'Examines. Dissects.' Luk nods seriously at my repulsed expression.

'Poor animals,' I say. He laughs and shakes his head, like I'm crazy.

Every week Dad's team clears rubbish from a different skyscraper. This time we are doing the final one in our row. It takes three hours to reach 100. Like all the final towers in every row of London Star, it's dedicated to food production. Insects are intensely farmed and harvested, and hydroponics is practised here – that's food grown in water, under lights. In just one scraper there are a hundred levels of foodstuffs, like crickets, mealworms, herbs, legumes and fruits, grown by expert farmers. A crop can be planted and reaped within a week. Mum says they are injected with quick-grow genes, colours, vitamins and extra flavour, but I'm not sure if I'm supposed to know that. On the packets they only ever advertise 'Fresh Peas' or 'Fresh Grub Flour'. There's no mention of extras. I wonder, briefly, what I'll be eating in this underworld; Welt didn't fill me in much on that. I force it out of my head before it affects my heart rate.

A mountain of garbage is waiting for us when we arrive, heaped up around the scraper foot, puked out from the chute inside. Most of it is recyclable: imperfect foodstuffs and biodegradable wrappers. Although I do make out a desk lamp that someone has lazily thrown out instead of sending to the recycling plant. And a keyboard.

'Hey, Banana, do you want to do some sweeping?'

Dad nods encouragingly at me through his visor. He positions the sweeper next to an enormous pile and points to a blue button. Should I be doing this? I want to, but then, I need to be ready to bolt when the incident happens.

'Am I allowed?'

He holds his finger to his mouth and grins. There's something about his smile. He wants to treat me, and I can't say no. I reach forward and press the blue button.

There is a groan as the sweeper arms lower, the points of their teeth just millimetres from the ground. He gestures to the black button next to it. Looking out of the window, I watch the sweeper jaws angle themselves backwards. Then Dad takes my hand and places it on the central lever and together we push the sweeper truck forward. We drive right into the dirty pile, the sweeper's arms gathering trash, which starts to build up in front of us like a tidal wave. I look behind to see others in the sweeper fleet, lining up behind us to take their share. When I turn around again, the rubbish is at windscreen height and I can see, close up, the gunk that the farmers have thrown down the chute: slime – algae, perhaps, worms, strange-coloured pellets, corn on the cob, squished tomatoes. It begins to smear against the glass. Dad points at the central lever and tells me to tug it to the left. The vehicle slowly turns, pushing the load in front of it. We move away, out into the land beyond the skyscrapers. The sweepers behind us do the same, catching up with us until we are all in convoy.

'Are we heading out to a landfill hole?'

'No, this is just biological matter from the food producers,' Dad says. I decide not to say anything about the lamp and the keyboard. 'We just spread it. Hey, look!'

Dad has told me about the little birds that flock around the sweepers, waiting to sort through the waste, looking for food and nesting material. He smiles at me, and I beam back. They are beautiful. Red-breasted balls of feathers with twiggy feet, bouncing along the ground alongside us.

'You might think they're cute, Alara, but they're probably diseased,' Luk says.

I've come to realise that Luk always has something to say.

When we have been driving for half an hour, Dad angles the jaws of the sweeper further backwards, letting a small tide of rubbish fall free. The other sweeper trucks pull alongside us. We are a horizontal army of muck spreaders. Trails of dirt and food fly out behind us, bits and pieces dancing in the air.

We return to the tip and drive out to the distant Void ten more times before the sweep is complete. The light is fading when we embark on our final return journey. The multitudes of trash crabs dissolve into the gloom. There's still been no sign for me to start the mission. Something must have happened. Welt must have changed his mind. Relief and disappointment hit me in a wave, and my heart doesn't know what speed to beat at.

Dad and Luk are getting tired. Their banter is dying and they put music on, settling in for the long, boring ride home. Dad is driving while Luk browses a manual called *Refuse: Management Protocol*. How do they do this day after day? My dad is a hero.

He's also a parent with psychic skills. He picks up my unease and suggests I hop into the back seat and grab some sleep. I move to the back, but there's no sleep for me. Instead, I look despairingly out of the window, trying to make sense of everything. All that preparation – the implant, the Santiens Dip – for nothing. Staring out at the dark, I imagine where I'd be now if the mission hadn't been aborted: alone, frightened, stumbling around in hazardous waste with the weird crab things. Instead I'm headed back home, where, after a day's discomfort, I'll cherish my soft, temperature-controlled bedroom more than ever.

'Mikal!'

My daydream is broken by Luk's voice.

'Mikal, Mikal!'

He's yelling now. The sweeper crunches to a halt. Other sweepers continue to pass us on the way back to the tower, but Dad is frozen in his seat, clutching at his chest.

'Dad? Luk, what's happening?'

Luk checks Dad's Flip. 'His heart. He's fine, Alara. It's just skipping beats. We need to get him back to Medico quickly. Mayday, mayday!' Luk repeats it over and over into the radio but there's not even a crackle in return. 'The comms system is down. Help me move him across the seat, Alara. I need to drive.'

'Dad? Dad, are you okay?'

Dad grunts and nods. His hand is still spread out over his chest and he gasps as if his breath has been taken away.

'You need to move now, Dad.' I leap into the front of the pod. Dad's heavy, really heavy. Everything is more difficult because of the hazard suits. But somehow Luk and I manage to pull him across to the passenger seat, and Luk tries to get the sweeper going. But it won't go. He slams the controls in frustration.

This is not good. 'What's the matter with it?' I beg, like he's keeping the answer from me.

'It's stuck. Maybe the track has come off.' Luk looks at me, panicked, and we both look at Dad. His breathing is more regular, less wheezy – he's going to be okay. But we need to get him up to Medico as soon as we can.

'Stay here. I'll run ahead to one of the sweepers and get them to come back.'

Luk opens the pod and lowers himself down into the

Void. In the gloom I see him leaping gingerly across the rubble towards the nearest sweeper. Its lights cast an eerie fog all around. Next to me, Dad seems a lot better, but he looks exhausted.

'Dad, can you hear me?'

'Yes … it's okay, Alara. It's okay…' His eyes flicker and then close as he gives in to sleep. I can't see Luk any more, but the sweeper he was aiming for has stopped. It begins to turn, clumsily, bucking against the uneven ground. It's coming back for Dad. My worry disappears. If the comms system is working on the incoming sweeper, Medico will be able to give advice over the radio. Dad's going to be fine.

But. What if this is it?

It can't be, can it? They couldn't plan Dad's heart trouble – could they? But they could have planned for the sweeper to break down, and the comms system to go offline. Dad has moaned about work, but he's never mentioned a problem like that before. This is it. This has to be it. Dad's heart was just coincidence, and he's going to be fine. As he sleeps, his chest rises and falls evenly. The sweeper trundles towards us. I have to go. Now. There's not much time. I plant a kiss on his cheek and slip out into the night.

And so it starts – the biggest quest game I've ever played. But this game has a time limit. Three days. Three days or dead.

It's getting darker. I've got a torch, but it's too risky

to use it, and it won't be long before Luk realises I've disappeared. Only a matter of time before they come looking.

The terrain is treacherous. Sheets of metal, bricks and asphalt shift under my weight, and I skid and slip and stumble. Everything feels awkward. I'm used to the smooth, horizontal floors of London Star. It's alien how everything rocks and dips, and I imagine I'm playing *Sky Jump* with the moving floors, testing the ground ahead of me with my toes before stepping forward, wary of the cracks and crevasses. If I break my ankle, I'll be in trouble. It would be way easier and faster to move like a four-legged animal. With the tough gloves of my protective suit, I confidently grip hard edges and swing my body over boulders, swiftly and quietly. Sheets of glass and metal snap and bend under my weight, but I can afford to be reckless. The hazard suit isn't built to tear.

Calls, hoots, shouts. I look up to see tiny beams frantically criss-crossing in the distance. They're looking for me. And if Dad's gained consciousness, he won't stop looking for me – not ever. Still not daring to use my torch, I stand and watch – for an hour, maybe more – until their beams disappear and the tiny lights of the sweepers have vanished. I try not to think of the pain that is about to be unleashed on my family. Welt said Medico would give them something to make it easier – a sedative or emotion-blocker or something. But that doesn't help *me*. Right now I'm buzzing with emotions. Frying inside.

The climbing is tiring, but my mind is like a boxer in a ring, bouncing around, waiting for the next punch. I am questing with Kagu on my tail. If I think like that, it keeps me alert. Because if I stop for just one second, fear squeezes my heart and strangles my throat.

Finding a way in, that's the next step, but my legs are crying out for rest. They buckle under my weight and I skid down a rubble-strewn bank. It's becoming more dangerous to continue than to stop. I spot a gap between giant fallen breeze blocks and crawl inside, wriggling around until I find an area that doesn't have spikes and lumps that dig into my back. And then I listen.

I always thought the Void at night would be still and silent, but there are creaks and snaps as rubbish contracts in the night air, shifting and sliding as it settles. It makes me uneasy. A trash crab sidles into my hidey-hole, dangling upside-down above me before dropping onto my lap. I have never been this close to a living thing that's not human. Part petrified, part curious, I let the creature crawl up my chest and onto my visor. Its underbelly of moving plates, robot-like, fascinates me. Its calcified feet tap-dance across my face and its claws scrape around, looking for miniscule particles which it shovels greedily into its little slit of a mouth. I have never seen anything like it.

I'm feeling almost relaxed in my protected nook with my new pet. But then there's a crunch outside on the rubbish heap. And a voice.

'Who's that?' it says. 'Who's that?' A girl's voice. Husky. Stern.

I freeze, the pulse in my neck leaping so hard I'm sure it can be heard.

'I know you're in there. So why don't you just come out?' the voice hisses.

'Ok-ay!' I stammer.

I have already worked out what to say. I've practised the story a thousand times. But the time to say it is right here, right now, and suddenly I'm scared I'll forget it all. Not knowing what I'm about to meet, I reach forward and pull myself out of the darkness into a bright beam of light. As if it senses trouble, the trash crab scuttles away. I try to shield my face from the flashlight, but my hands are knocked aside and hands grip my wrists and upper arms, fingers digging through the suit and into my skin. There's more than one person; they don't speak. I am marched, stumbling awkwardly over the broken ground, my shins banging against solid objects, making bruises on top of bruises. My legs are not used to navigating the jagged terrain. I'm not used to it, I tell them. I ask to slow down, but they don't. They just shove harder. And we walk. We keep walking, and I curse myself for accepting this mission.

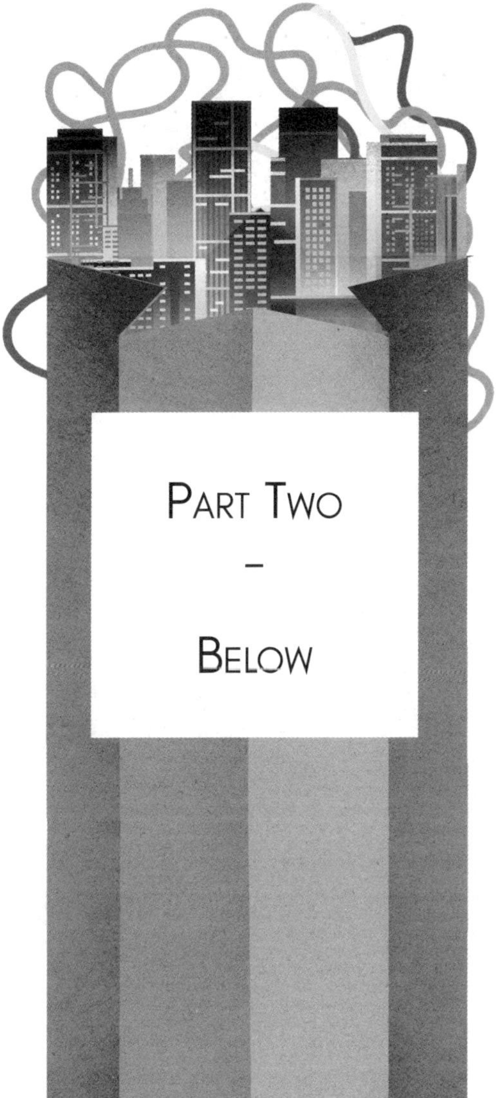

Part Two

–

Below

Chapter 11

The torturous journey lasts for what feels like hours – up and over the mountains of trash, my legs battered and aching, my arms sore from being yanked and tugged and bent backwards. I don't understand. Even the grumpiest Advisors are never rough. When I get caught running in the pedestrian tunnels, it's a gentle warning, a fine at most. But maybe that's not how these people work. I can't say I wasn't warned.

We start descending, steeply, into the darkness of the earth. There's a change in air pressure. We are in a tunnel. It's definitely a tunnel. I reach out my arms to test the width of it, but they're slapped down. My captors are in front, behind, on either side of me. Everything is so uncomfortably close, so crowded. My breathing starts to quicken; I can't take in enough air. The walls feel like they're closing in. My worst nightmare. Beneath me, the floor begins to even out, as if smoothed with use, and it's immediately easier to walk on, but my jelly legs still give way. Strong hands haul me back up and push me forward, and I trip and stagger the length of the tunnel. My heart drums and I gasp for air. This is panic. I coach myself, as I do in quests, tell myself it's a Sensii trip – nothing is real – and it seems to work, although everything inside me burns, and I feel like I might throw up.

Some way into the tunnel, the flashlights come back on. Their glow reveals clay walls pitted with stones. I have absolutely no point of reference. Nothing that I've ever read or experienced in a game has suggested that an environment like this exists.

We stop and I'm released. I rub my upper arms where they gripped me so hard, and ask where I am. No one talks. Instead, they push me against the wall, pinning me there with hands pressed against my chest and legs. With a blinding flashlight they take a good look at their catch. Then the lights go off again, and I hear shuffling footsteps as some walk off, their whispers floating back my way. I can't make out the words, but there's questioning and uncertainty.

Then, without warning, I am spun around and my suit is unzipped and peeled off me. My hood is ripped free of my head. I shout in panic. 'Don't! I need –'

'Shut up.'

They tug my suit downwards and slap the back of my calves to make me step out of the boots. I try to hold my breath to stop the poison, until I can't hold it any more and involuntarily draw in a lungful of stale, poisoned air.

'Please...' I beg. 'I need protection.'

'No, you don't.' The voice is efficient.

A different voice suggests a blindfold.

'I can't see anyway,' I protest, but hands are fussing around my face and a piece of cloth is stretched across my eyes.

We're walking again. I'm in socked feet, able to feel the atmosphere through my thin second-skin suit. If I'd worn more underneath my hazard suit, I'd be less vulnerable and embarrassed. But so far, my lungs aren't burning, my skin isn't blistering on my face. Perhaps this place has toxin extractors, or something. I don't know, but it's one less worry. Although there are plenty more concerns queueing up, like diners in the Quarters kitchens.

Eventually the tunnel levels out and I can put one foot in front of the other without skidding or tripping. The atmosphere changes again. We are in an open area now. I can sense space above my head, but there's no breeze. The air is still. Blind, I search for logic. We can't be above ground; we were walking downhill for so long. And it's cool, but not cold, as it should be on the surface at night in early summer – I've seen how the towers' external barometers and thermometers drop. Underground maintains its temperature. I learned that in both Engineering and Geography. So we must be beneath the trash. I must be in Under.

I register footsteps, doors shutting, chatting – it sounds like there are a few people, a crowd. I call up memories of working at Rapidos, the noise of the food hall. There must be twenty or thirty people here. They quieten as I pass.

'Can someone tell me what's going on?'

I'm dragged away and forced down another path, my shoulders banging against the walls. And then I sense space again. My captors' footsteps echo. My dusty coughs echo back to me from the walls and the ceiling. This place must be vast. We turn left and there is a knocking. Another door.

There is talking in the room beyond and I'm moved in. It's stuffier here. No echo. Softness underfoot. Carpet. Suddenly a hand pushes down on my head and a chair is forced against the back of my knees, making me sit. There is a tugging at the blindfold, but it doesn't fall; it tightens. Silence. Breathing. I am being circled, peered at. I whip my head from side to side.

'What's your name?' A deep voice. Female.

'Alara.'

Silence again. 'Alara,' the voice says. There's a faint mocking ring to it. 'Alara, where are you from?'

'Estrella.'

'And what were you doing out there in the open?'

'There was an accident. I – I was in a sweeper. There was a crash.'

Silence. They want me to say more. But I have to

keep details to a minimum. Safer that way. Less likely to slip up.

'Or were you spying?' It's a male voice now.

'No. No, I got lost.' People are circling me again. I can hear the shuffle of their feet. One of them touches my head. I am acutely aware of how exposed I am in my second-skin. It might keep me at an ambient temperature, but it reveals every line and curve of my body. 'Can I get some clothes?'

'Why would you be out on a waste dump?' says the man again, ignoring my request.

'I was going to work with my dad. He was sweeping. And I was wearing protection,' I say.

There's shuffling, murmuring. People leave the room again. Or maybe they're coming in. Someone starts feeling me, frisking my arms, under my armpits, the back of my neck. Then I can feel lips against my ear, breath on my cheek.

I try not to squirm.

'Just say you're here to start a new life.' It's a male voice, quiet and urgent. He covers it with a cough.

'What?' I swing my head around, but he coughs again, grabs my wrist. My Flip is unstrapped.

He's close to my ear again. 'If you want to live.'

'Got everything you need?' a voice says. Female this time.

'Yes,' says my whisperer. 'Checked for tech. Nothing on the upper body. Wristband removed.'

'Excellent.'

There is silence again as someone leaves. If it's him, I'm sorry he's gone. I don't know why I should trust anyone, but it sounded like he wanted to help me. I lock his words into my head, hoping they'll be all I need to get through this.

'What are you doing here?' It's the woman's voice. Calm but firm.

'I told you, I was in an accident.' I'm using my sweetest voice, trying to be friendly. But they don't soften.

'And no one took you back to Estrella? Why not?' she says.

'They searched, but they didn't find me. They gave up. They think I'm dead.'

'Did you call for help?'

'No.'

'How did you see us?' The man.

'I didn't see you. You saw me.'

There's a silence. I hear pacing. More murmuring. 'Would you like someone to take you back? Would you like to go home?' It's a different voice. Not one I heard before. *Go home? Yes. Take me home. Get me out of here...*

'No, I'll never get another chance to escape Estrella. I'm looking for a new life.'

If you want to live, the voice had said. I hope I have said enough to save myself. I hope it's coming out right.

'Where were you looking for a new life?'

'I am looking for a new life.' I hold my hands still in

my lap to stop them trembling. I don't want to say the wrong thing, but I don't know how much longer I can get away with that one line.

'Did you think you'd find one here?'

'I am. Looking. For. A. New. Life,' I growl. I'm running out of ideas, hoping that shoving hostility back at them will give them the impression I'm serious.

There is a brief pause and my blindfold is taken off, roughly. I blink to adjust to the light, which flickers from a strip on the ceiling. I can't help looking at it. It's as if my eyes are craving it. But after so long in the darkness, it's also painful. All of me is painful. I wince.

'Too bright?' It's the woman, softer now. 'Someone light some candles.'

The horrible light is replaced by a warm radiance. I look around the room. There are candles in ornate metal holders, creating a flickering glow against walls made of stone. Old, dimpled walls. The room's window is shaped like an arch, the glass inside it made of coloured see-through pieces, arranged to form a picture. Figures in a scene, but I can't make it out.

'Alara.' The woman speaks again. Plump, with a wide face and shaggy mouse-brown hair, she sits behind a desk. She slowly places her hands on the table between us and smiles. 'I am Diana.' Everyone else has gone. 'There's no need to panic. We're just going to have a little talk.'

'You're not going to kill me, are you?' The question leaps from my mouth before I have a chance.

Diana leans back in her chair and laughs. 'Why would you think that? What have you heard about us?'

'Nothing.' *Come on, brain.* 'I didn't even know you existed.'

'Well, we definitely do exist, and we don't kill people for no reason.' She smiles warmly and I try to make my shoulders relax but they won't, because what if they find a reason?

'I don't know why I said that. Forget it.' I smile.

'That's good. So tell me what you were doing on the rubbish tip.'

We're here again. 'There was an accident. But now … now I'm looking for a new life.'

'So you say,' she repeats, raising an eyebrow. 'And why would that be?'

'Because I don't like my life.'

'You live in London Star, yes?'

'Yes.'

'So let me get this straight. You didn't know we existed and you believed the ground to be uninhabitable, yes?' She leans forward. I nod. 'So why would you think there was any future for you here in the Void?' Her tone is warm but challenging.

I shift uncomfortably and rub at a bruise on my knee. 'I once saw shapes. Creatures. Lights.'

'Lights?'

'Yes. I was looking down with my binoculars and –'

'Why were you looking down? You knew there was

nothing to see on the ground. That's what they tell you, isn't it? Or have they changed their story?'

'I was bored, that's all.'

'Bored,' she repeats. 'And when you're bored, you look out of the window instead of, say, watching a film or playing a game? You seem very hard to please. I mean, I hear London Star has some amazing entertainment.'

'I'm not ungrateful,' I say in a rush, thinking that she reminds me of Mum. 'I get distracted easily. Games don't hook me like they hook other people. My brother, he's totally hooked. He never gets bored. I'm jealous, in a way...' I'm talking too much.

'Have you told anyone you get bored?'

'My family knows I get bored, and so does my best friend, but he just tells me to...'

'To what?'

'Do a Sensii trip or something.' I shrug. 'It's this system –'

'I know about Sensii,' Diana says sternly. Instinctively, I tuck my fingers under my armpits. 'Who knows you left London Star?'

What do I say? I wasn't prepared for this questioning. When we'd discussed the mission in detail, Welt had told me to act injured, to make the accident story believable, and to provide a reason to stay until I had everything stored in the chip. But that plan is out the window. I followed the voice instead – adopted the motive of looking for a new life, and completely forgot about faking an injury.

I've let Welt down. But he let me down, too. He never prepared me for all the questions, and I guess he doesn't know these people like he thinks he does – they're not as primitive as he made out. I need to think on my feet. And Diana is staring, waiting for me to slip up.

'Just my family.'

'No one else?' she says, disbelievingly.

'No.'

'Why is that?'

'Because my dad let me come on his sweeper with him. It's not allowed. So we didn't tell anyone. And now he thinks I'm dead.'

'That's terrible. You can live with that, can you?'

'Yes. It's my life.'

'How long before someone notices?'

I think about the Flip, which would know instantly. You don't go missing in Star. Down here, clearly you do.

'Dad will probably report it right away, although he'll get in trouble. They'll search but they won't find me. But no one will suspect I'm alive. People do vanish from London Star, you know. People who have had enough and want to die.'

'Who are these people?'

'People with a genetic malfunction.'

'Like you, then?'

I think of the Gen-Tech chip and how it's mapping, not recording conversation. It's kind of liberating; I can say what I want about myself, the truth of my dissatisfaction.

'Maybe. Maybe that's why I get bored. Not bored enough to kill myself, though.'

Diana squints and looks at me as if I'm an interesting specimen. She clicks her tongue.

'But let's go back to your new life. At what point in your accident did this cross your mind?'

'After the accident, I was going to return to London Star. But when you found me and I heard voices, I knew that there was an alternative. Please don't make me go back.'

Diana moves towards me and places a hand on my shoulder. She is silent and I don't know if I'm supposed to say something. I open my mouth, hoping conversation will come to me, but she walks away and calls a name through the doorway.

'Alara, this is David.'

Diana returns to her desk and a man arrives at my side. He's middle-aged, serious. He and Diana exchange a look, and she nods. David then puts his hand on my shoulder, like Diana did. I notice he's carrying a needle in his other hand, and he quickly pushes it through my suit and into my upper arm. It scratches. And then darkness.

There is dry spittle at the corner of my mouth, and my eyelids are heavy. I've been drugged; I don't know how long I've been out. I'm still in the room with the candles and the window, but I am on my own, slouched in my chair. Voices float from the other side of the open door. I hear Diana's low tones. I don't know who the others are, but I know they are discussing me. I can make out a few sentences.

'Was she invited?'

'There's no record...'

'She's a child.'

'Hardly a child...'

'So she could be a problem, then?'

'Possibly.'

'We could just see.'

'Let's not jump to conclusions.'

'Shhh.'

Eventually, the voices stop and someone comes to check on me. I shut my eyes and allow my mouth to hang open. My eyelid is peeled back. I roll my eye back into my head. The footsteps fade and the conversation starts up again.

'So what do we do with her?'

'David?'

David talks, but his voice is irritatingly soft and I can pick out only cadences, not words. I don't have a clue what his suggestion might be. They talk for another ten minutes or so, and I feel myself drifting back to sleep. It's just easier to be asleep.

'Alara.'

I am being shaken. I blink myself awake and wipe at the corner of my mouth. Diana is back behind her desk, flanked by two men. I rub my shoulder, which is sore from the injection.

'Sorry about that.' Diana nods. 'Precautions.'

'Precautions?' I sound lispy from the sedative. 'But I'm not armed.'

She ignores me, drumming her fingers on the table. 'Alara, we've found somewhere for you to stay tonight. And a little longer, if things work out. One day at a time. David's sister has room, and a niece your age. Fifteen?'

'Sixteen.' I smile meekly.

'Perfect. Mark, if you could just double-check her, then we can show Alara around.'

I'm guessing Mark is around twenty. He's tall, angular, fair. Not friendly. He pats my stomach, arms and legs.

'Anyone else checked her for tech?' he snarls. There's no warmth there.

'A wrist device was taken,' Diana says. 'Is there anything else on you, Alara? Anything that can be tracked? We wouldn't want them catching up with you.' She points to the ceiling.

Feeling as if the Gen-Tech chip is flashing red lights and giving me away, I shake my head slowly.

'Good. Alara, your wristband has been taken down to the workshop to be dismantled. It's just for quarantine. You can have it back when you leave.'

The last words hang in the air. I circle them with my mind. *I can leave*. But the notion of it is a trap.

'I don't plan to leave.'

'We'll speak again very soon. In the meantime, I hope that you settle in well with David's family.'

Settle. The opposite of leave.

I'm confused. No one has explained how this place works, but I don't have time to ask and I don't want to, in case it invites more sedatives. My head is already full of fog. David leads me out of the stuffy room and into the large chamber I passed through before, when blindfolded. I can see it now. It's a huge stone room, its high ceiling carved with figures and words I can't read. And I know what it is. I've read about it in Civilisation class. It's a place of worship, from a time when people had religion and believed in a higher power.

There are old buildings; nothing is clean; the people have outdated names, like Mark, David and Diana... Perhaps Welt was right about them being primitive. Why wouldn't he be? A civilisation that lives in conditions that even pre-date Old London.

I am suddenly dizzy. David catches me as I stumble backwards; he slips his arm behind my knees and picks me up.

Chapter 12

I wake in a creaking bed. Outside the window there's no infinite blackness of night-time, nor the blaze of daylight. Just a murky light, like the skies you get in warm winters, when the clouds are muddy.

Struggling for details. I remember, vaguely, meeting the strict but motherly Diana. And David. Who drugged me. And then carried me when I passed out. Or maybe I was sedated again. Either way, they must have put me straight to bed, and I don't know whose house I'm in. There's another bed opposite, empty, clothes laid out on it. Guessing they're for me, I slip them on over my second-skin – baggy shorts and top, and a pair of ancient-looking trainers. They smell musty. I probably smell musty, too.

Outside the bedroom door I hear noises from down the stairs – a steady low chatter, a clatter, scraping – and smells. Such good smells. My stomach emits a long groan, as if it's being wrung. Clutching my middle, led by hunger, I descend the wooden stairs to a kitchen area. There's a table in the middle, and a girl with an elfin face is sitting at it. She jumps up when I approach, her face cracking into a wide smile. She has really crooked teeth. Why are her teeth wonky?

'Alara!'

'Hi.' I wave awkwardly.

'I'm Martha.' She jumps up and comes to hug me, like an old friend. She smells earthy. Her coarse short hair brushes against my skin. There are freckles on her nose and cheeks. Her arms tighten around my waist. It's weird behaviour. A bit suffocating, though not intended to be.

'Martha, give our guest some personal space!' A woman with blonde hair bundled on top of her head brings food to the table. She's wearing a baggy blue dress. 'Alara, we welcome you into our home. Come and eat something. You must be starving.'

What is this place? Somewhere in the back of my mind is the thought that I could be in a quest game – paralysed and trapped, in a deep comatose state somewhere in Burbeck's laboratory.

'Thank you. I've been made to feel very welcome.' Unthinkingly I rub at my sore shoulder. It doesn't go unnoticed.

'Yes, David filled me in on all of that. Sorry. It's not hostile, just... Anyway, never mind now. They've decided you'll stay with us, and that's wonderful. Our family is your family. Ellie's my name.'

There's an awkward silence. I'm not sure what the etiquette is here.

'Sit. Sit.' She pats the tabletop and disappears to the back of the kitchen.

Martha's still grinning at me as I sit waiting for … I don't know what. Then Ellie brings me a bowl of what looks like mashed potato. Not exactly my favourite stodge, but it's been hours since I ate, so I tuck in, not knowing if this is breakfast, lunch or dinner. Or poisonous. But the potato is delicious – like *extraordinary* delicious. Not like 'Farm Fresh Potato' at home. It's so good, it has to be bad. I look up, and I guess my face says it all.

'She likes it,' the girl calls to her mother. She grins at me. 'I bet it's the butter,' she says. Then she clocks my confusion. 'Don't you know butter?'

We do have butter at home, but it doesn't taste like this. My mouth is flooded with creaminess, texture and flavour, and all from a simple potato. It's like a miracle. Martha and Ellie watch me with a mix of amusement and fascination, as if I'm an exotic animal. I'm behaving like an animal, it's true, but I can't stop scoffing. It's so incredibly good. My stomach feels hugged and my tongue tingles. That's the salt – but it's different salt. Ten times saltier than salt. Butter and salt. Bigger and bolder-tasting than I've ever had before. I scrape the bowl clean.

'There's more if you want it,' Ellie says in her

gentle voice. But now I've stopped I can feel the meal solidifying, forming a rock in the pit of my stomach. It's uncomfortable. I shake my head and push the bowl away.

Martha takes it back into the kitchen. It gives me a chance to look around – at the floor, the table, the chairs. Everything is old. All these edges and blocky squares; there's nothing ergonomic. No white melamine surfaces, like home. Definitely no self-cleaning glaze. The microbes that must be embedded into the creases and cracks…

'It's not in the best of shape,' Ellie says, apologetically, following my stare.

She seems kind. Perhaps I could ask her what's happening, and why I'm being treated so nicely by them after having been handled so roughly by the others. But I'm not sure if I can trust her. Only hours ago I was plucked from the Void. I have to remember that. I don't get a chance, anyhow, as the girl is in my face again.

'We're going to hang out together today. It's so exciting!'

'Okay.' I smile. Although I can't get excited about 'hanging out'. I'm too confused. I don't know what I was expecting from Under, but a forced friendship didn't feature in the briefing. On the positive side, hanging out might mean walking around – and it would give my Gen-Tech a chance to map. And maybe I can meet that guy again, the one who whispered to me. I didn't see his face, but I got the impression he saw right through me. Which means he's either a friend or a threat, and it would be good to know which.

'It would be nice if we could offer Alara something more substantial to eat this evening, so why don't you two go up to Crouch Farm and get eggs? In fact, get a whole chicken, too. And some root vegetables. I have greens.'

'Okay, Mum.'

Ellie kisses Martha on the head and leaves the house, and through the doorway I get another glimpse of that weird light I saw through the window. And I realise this house, windows and all, is underground. And these people live in rags in the dark, in tunnels like moles. My lungs seize at the sudden thought of being buried alive. I long for London Star's glass and light.

Three days. I just have to make it through three days. Although keeping track of time down here seems impossible.

'Martha, what time of day is it?'

'Morning, dopey!'

'Right...'

If I hadn't been told her age, I'd say she was two or three years younger. It's the sparkling eyes, full of excitement, looking at me as if I were a present waiting to be unwrapped. I compare her with the dead-eyed gamers in London Star.

'Martha, where are we, exactly?'

'Here? We call it London Under. Good, you've got

your shoes on. Sorry, they were old ones of mine, but they looked the right size. Are they comfortable enough? We might be doing a lot of walking.' She is bustling around, fetching a bag and bottles of water.

'Yesterday I heard people talking. They said I wasn't *invited*. Do you know what they meant?'

Martha paces around some more, then crouches in front of me and places her hands on my knees. There's dirt under her fingernails.

'I'll tell you as much as I know, okay? I'm not even sure if I'm allowed to say anything at this point –'

'At this point? Why? When *can* you tell me?'

'I don't know.' Her hazel eyes are huge and serious.

'You're from the Spikes, aren't you?'

'London Star. Estrella.'

'Right. We call it the Spikes. Anyway, you decided to come down to the ground on your own, right?'

I nod again. We're getting somewhere. But then there's a beeping sound. Martha looks flustered. She pats herself down until she finds the noisy object in her pocket. 'They gave me this,' she says, kind of apologetically, retrieving a metal slab from her trousers. She clumsily puts it to her ear and steps outside.

While I'm waiting for Martha to return, I run my fingers across the wall. It's old brick, rough to the touch, divided by criss-crossing beams. It reminds me of the photos and videos we have at home of the great-great-great-grandparents Tripp having family meals in their house. Before the disasters, before Estrella.

Those were the days when not everyone lived stacked on top of each other. Some houses were side by side, with upside-down V-shaped roofs to stop rain and snow settling on top. They had a lot of wood in those days, too. It was a major material and so much more interesting than moulded eco-plastic, like we have. More variation, texture, character. Although, apparently, wood was terrible for harbouring dirt and bacteria. It wouldn't be allowed in London Star. Not without a special coating; not looking this rough, like it's just been hacked off a tree.

Martha returns. 'We just need to pop by the town hall. They want to see you again.'

'Who? Diana?'

She smiles apologetically. 'After that we'll go to Mum's shop to pick up some chits.'

'What are chits?'

'Chits. You know, for exchanging.'

'Like money?'

'I guess.' She shrugs.

The front door to Martha's house leads onto a 'street' – a strip of ground as wide as a pedestrian tube – and on the other side of the street another row of houses faces this one. A roof of solid soil and concrete arches like a rainbow between them, and I understand now that Old London was literally buried and built on top of, and then excavated from underneath. But while we may be underground, and it may be gloomy here and there, it's not dark. Little lights are strung along the walls and ceilings, heading in all directions, following the 'streets' and alleys that branch away, creating a twinkly map of the underground city.

'Come on, Alara!' Martha beckons to me.

She looks expectant, like I should be racing along by her side. But as well as being slowed by curiosity, I'm held back by my worry about this place and the people in it. It hasn't yet been twenty-four hours since I was dragged down here, blindfolded, interrogated, injected.

But I have to pull myself together, because Martha's my stroke of luck. Of all the possible outcomes of finding myself here, this was a good one – good for me, good for the mission. If she wants to show me stuff, I'll let her. If I win her trust, she might take me to all corners of this place. Imagine being so good at my mission that I get some kind of recognition from Central – not public recognition, but maybe the password every day, and free sushi… Without thinking, I scratch where the Gen-Tech chip was implanted. Oops, mustn't do that. Especially in front of Diana and David.

'What's Diana?' I ask, catching up with Martha. 'Is she the Chief Advisor?'

Martha looks at me oddly. 'I suppose you could call her that. Yeah, I guess she's going to advise us. This is a situation we haven't had before.'

'Me? Am I the situation?'

'Yes.'

We come to a stop outside the place of worship: the

place where it's not so friendly. But I should be okay if I stick with Martha and my excuse of 'looking for a new life', which I am now sure is some kind of password for London Under, just like Vim and I worked out that 'I like suckers' was the way to get into the caves in *Caves of the Kraken*.

Chapter 13

'Good morning, Alara. Did you sleep well?' Diana's voice rings off the stone walls. 'Come this way. Martha, you too.'

The three of us walk back through the giant prayer hall and into the room I already know, with its carpet, candles and picture window. Diana disappears into a back room. We take a seat and sit in silence until she returns with a pot in one hand and mugs in the other. They dangle from her fingers and clank together. It reminds me of kitchen noises at home. My heart skips a beat at the thought.

'Tea,' she states, pouring from a large vessel. 'Bit hot, so let it cool down.' Diana sits in the chair behind the desk, crosses her legs and smooths her tunic over her knees. She looks at me and cocks her head to the side. 'I'm going to ask you some questions, and I want you to answer them honestly. Okay?'

'Okay.'

'First, your full name and age.'

'Alara Tripp. I'm sixteen.'

'Alara, do you know where you are?'

'Not really. Under the ground somewhere.'

Diana's expression doesn't change. 'Now tell me – how did you get here?'

Again? 'I went to work with my dad and the sweeper crashed into a hole. I...' What? I hadn't thought of the details. 'I think I must have hit my head and blacked out. Maybe we all did. I don't know.'

'Hit your head?'

I nod.

'And now, what do you see happening?'

'A new –'

'A new life. Yes. Still, it's quite sudden and daring of you to decide on a new life without any planning. And now you're here, do you know what you want to do next?'

'Not really. But I heard someone saying I wasn't invited. And I'm really sorry about that.'

'What happens if you decide you'd like to reclaim your life in London Star?'

'I'll stay, but if for some reason you don't want me to, I won't tell anyone about this place when I go back. Cross my heart,' I add, spotting a cross on the wall and wondering if she's religious.

'I'm not sure we can take that risk.' Diana puts her

hands on the armrests of the chair and pushes herself up. 'Wait here.'

When Diana leaves the room, I'm out of my chair and at her side. 'Martha, tell me what's going on. Why is everything so serious all the time?'

'Because you're not expected. You're uninvited.'

'So you keep telling me,' I mutter. 'It's a good job I'm not too sensitive or I'd think you were being rude!'

'Stop treating this like a joke,' she begs.

'If anyone's in trouble, it's me,' I protest.

'Well, what *are* you doing here? Just tell the truth.'

Her abruptness shocks me. I don't see how this makes any sense. But I don't have time to talk to Martha because Diana is back, and behind her is a group of people – about twenty of them. They look rushed. Some are clearly hassled. Someone says something about the crowd outside. I don't know if they mean people in London Star, the Refuse Management team, or the people down here. Diana retakes her seat. So do I.

'We only have one option, Alara, and that's to tell you where you are and gauge your reaction. Only then can we look at what steps to take.'

'Okay.' I nod.

'I'll start by introducing us. You are in a city, carved out of the ancient town of London, right beneath the skyscrapers of Estrella. The streets outside are dirty and our sky is fortified trash, but for us it's home. And we're very keen to keep it that way.'

An old-world existence beneath a hi-tech one. It's not what this place is that puzzles me; it's why anyone would want to live here. But for now, I have to pretend this is a surprise.

'Do you understand what I'm telling you?' Diana's voice is stern. I snap my head up to look at her. 'Do you understand, Alara?' she repeats, as if I'm a naughty kid.

'Yes. This is a city beneath a city. You live here. In secrecy.'

'I'd say about three thousand of us live here.' She opens her hands, gestures around. 'And we don't want to be moved. So we'd like to know your intentions.'

'I don't have intentions.'

'Having no intentions can be just as dangerous as having them.' The voice comes from a short wiry man, probably forty years old, athletic-looking. 'I'm Michael,' he adds. 'And I'm in charge of surveillance. And security.' He motions to a group behind him and they circle me, four or five of them. Their hands press on my shoulders and legs, pinning me down. Michael straps a band to my ankle and tugs, so it ratchets tight against my skin.

'This is a tracker. Just to make sure we know where you are while you're here. For your own safety,' he adds with a tight smile. 'Until you decide.'

'Decide what?' I ask.

'Whether you'll stay. Staying will mean sacrifices, and you'd better be damned sure before you make them.'

Michael and his security team leave, and Diana

stands. She nods at us to stand too. 'You'll be tracked for a week to begin with. If you convince us that you're sincere about living here, we'll remove it. If you don't, then we'll discuss what to do about your return.'

Outside, Martha and I sigh heavily, as if we've been holding our breath. She loops her arm through mine, but I'm feeling far from friendly. Star is allowing these people to exist and they've got some crazy notion that, with our advanced society and hygienic ways, we might threaten their existence! Welt warned me about this.

'Sorry if I got snappy with you. We're just a bit paranoid down here,' she says, seeing my expression.

'Paranoid about what?' I growl. But she doesn't flinch. She just rubs my hand.

'Nothing,' she says, shaking her head. 'Don't worry about it.'

'Don't worry about it? About what? The weird talk or the tracker on my ankle? I'm not going to cause a war, you know. I'm not Helen of Troy.' In honesty, I'm not mad, I'm nervous. Like any moment they're going to find out what I'm here for and tear the chip out of my head with their rusty tools.

'You know about Helen of Troy?' Martha looks surprised.

'Of course. We have Civilisation class. We learn about all cultures.'

'Apart from this one,' she replies, sneakily.

I nod slowly. 'Yes, apart from this one.'

'In which case, I'd better be your teacher!'

'Okay then.'

She's looking at me with those excited eyes. It's not her fault. And not only is she on my side, she can make this mission a lot easier for me. 'Ready to learn, Teacher Martha.'

As we walk down the street, with its vaulted ceiling of compacted rubbish – maybe one hundred years of it – my eyes itch with the dust, and my nose stings with the heavy smells of things I don't recognise. I'm constantly reminded that I'm on my own here, and it's making me uncomfortably alert. I've never felt so jumpy.

We've wandered into a residential area round the corner from Diana's praying place, and everything catches my eye, from the side-by-side houses to the laundry dangling on lines between them; a washed cuddly toy hangs by its ears. People talking through open windows and doors, hollering down and across streets, their shouts clashing in the air above me and ricocheting off the muddy roof above. Old-world bicycles and toys are scattered in doorways, drooled on by babies wearing nothing but nappies. I'm inside the history of our city, walking around the beating heart of it.

Martha is pointing at stuff but I can't pick up everything she says. My growing sense of awe is muting all her explanations, my eyes catching new sights and tugging my brain in different directions. The roads have names here, like Fitzroy Street and Dobbins Road.

Martha's house is 76 Barnaby Lane, she tells me, because it was originally excavated by someone called Liam Barnaby. It's like a child's play map. She tugs my arm and leads me down an alleyway, into a bustle of people pulling bags on wheels and holding children. And there are animals.

'Wolves!'

Martha shakes her head. 'It's like you were born yesterday! Domesticated dogs. Friendly dogs.'

Without meaning to, I'm doing a good impression of someone who had no idea this place existed. Of course, I'm immediately distracted by one of these 'domesticated dogs', which has stopped to sniff my foot. Copying Martha, I tentatively offer it my hand. Its whiskers tickle. Its tongue laps my knuckles. The dog is tugged away by its owner, but not before I lay my hand on its warm flank, feeling its fur against my palm. My heart is leaping, and I look around anxiously. But of course, no one's going to check me out or send me to the clinics. Do they have clinics here? Healthcare? I visualise animal germs from the dog slobber permeating my skin. I have to try to forget this stuff. I'm protected by my Santiens Dip, and when I get back, I'll be quarantined with a full-body wash, inside and out.

'So this is the high street!' Martha stands, arms outstretched. 'We've got food stalls, clothes shops, electrical shops, hairdressers, toys. That's Mum's shop over there.'

Daley's Salvage is painted on the lintel, and the shop is nothing more than a room filled with random bits and pieces. The stuff is placed artistically on shelves; in the window area, Ellie has connected tyres and wires and poles to create a human-like figure, seated on an old sofa.

'Come on in,' Martha says, pulling me through the doorway. 'Mum!' she calls, and there's Ellie, wearing grey overalls.

'How did it go?' she asks.

'They were pretty rude, and they've strapped this thing to Alara.'

I twist my leg so she can see the tracker in its full, ugly glory.

Ellie tuts. 'I don't suppose you'll be made to wear it for long. Come here.' She steps forward and hugs Martha and then me, awkwardly. She tries to hide her uncertainty, but it's there. She's worried about me. Just like they all are.

The feeling's mutual.

'What a lovely shop,' I say politely.

Ellie wipes her hands on her overalls and picks up items on the shelves. 'That's sweet of you. I know this must look like a lot of rubbish to an Estrella girl.' She blushes, suddenly self-conscious. 'But everything has a use. Even this ancient music machine – Martha found that.'

'I had to dig down deep for that one, but it's one of my best finds. You should come raiding with us, Alara.

You'd love it.' Martha knocks me with her elbow. 'But not in that rubber suit you arrived in. It would weigh you down.'

'How do you know about that?'

'The raiders who found you aren't very discreet. They said it made you look like an idiot.'

I open my mouth to object, but Ellie's wagging her finger.

'No raiding yet. She's not fully…' She searches for the right thing to say. 'Assessed.'

I'd say that was the wrong thing to say. Words like 'assess' don't put you at ease. They make you realise that you're 'uninvited' and 'unexpected' and 'a threat'. They make you want to go home. Every moment here makes my nerves jangle, and it's exhausting. I miss the empty moments I used to be so desperate to fill, the brightly lit parcels of free time.

The investigative journalist in me is disappointed. The questa in me is wondering whether she's cut out for this, after all. But it's too late – I'm in deep, and this is far from over. I have three days, and I'm hardly into the first.

Martha recognises my discomfort. 'So, the chits?' she says, to change the subject.

Ellie reaches into a pocket and pulls out a stack of plastic squares. They make a satisfying clicking noise as she drops them into Martha's open palm.

'Drive a bargain. If there's any way to get something cheaper, take it. It's not been a good week. See you at home later!' Ellie calls as we walk to the door. 'Here, take the trolley.'

We step out onto the street, Martha pulling a bag on wheels.

'You hungry?'

Not after the mountain of mashed potato. In London Star we eat little and often – tiny bites throughout the day of ultra-healthy energy snacks; only good fats are allowed. We read about old-fashioned butter. It was blamed for causing heart problems and obesity, along with a lot of other stuff. If I stay here too long, I'll go back riddled with risk. *If I ever get back.*

'Do you have a supermarket or delivery service down here?' I ask.

Martha wrinkles her brow. 'Um, sometimes there's a street market. And we do our own delivering.' Martha rattles the trolley. Then she wraps her arm around my neck and pulls me in tight for an affectionate squeeze. I've never been touched so much. I know what Moles would think – there wouldn't be enough antibac scrub in the whole of Star to cope with Martha.

'Seriously. Let's eat. What are in you in the mood for?' she says, releasing me.

'I liked the potato.'

'We have more here than just potato, you know. Just because we live underground, that doesn't mean we only eat root vegetables.'

'I know. I just liked the potato.'

She hugs me again. 'You're crazy. Come on, I'm going to make you try something delicious. It will cheer you up.'

'Can I have it with old butter?'

'Usually we have it with chilli sauce. More butter later, I promise.'

On our way to get the food, we pass other shops. There's a hairdresser, much like the ones at home, although here there's no mock-up screen – it's just someone with a pair of scissors in front of a mirror. Another shop is full of books bound in colourful covers. I pause in the doorway to gaze at them.

'Books,' Martha says, returning to my side. 'You know what they are, right? Stories printed on paper and bound together?'

'Yes, but I've never seen so many. All our stories are on screen.'

'Doesn't it hurt your eyes, reading on a screen all the time?'

'No. But still, it's not as pretty as these...' There are bright covers, interesting lettering, strange titles. 'What's *Station Eleven?*'

'Couldn't tell you. You can borrow it if you want.'

'Borrow?'

'Yes, this is a library. Have you heard of libraries?'

I shake my head.

'Wow, that's backwards...' Martha murmurs.

Backwards. This is the past, so why is it I'm beginning

to feel as if *I'm* the one who's out of touch?

'Come on, we don't have time to read.' Martha laughs, pulling me away, and we move on again, turning into Chadwick Street, where the air changes from cool and dusty to an atmosphere thick with scent. There are fires at the side of the road: cooks are grilling, lading hot food onto customers' plates. The smoke makes me cough, and through watery eyes I notice people everywhere – they sit in groups chatting and laughing and eating. It's not usual breakfast foods, not even potato. Dollops of hot, filling food, heavily spiced: vegetable and meat stews.

'Chadwick Street. Also known as Eat Street.'

'Why are so many people here this early?' I puzzle.

'They probably just got back from serfing.'

'Surfing?' I think of *Surf the Wave,* and wonder if we're near the sea.

'Yeah, serfing. You know. Working for food or chits. This is the night shift having their dinner.'

Martha stops at a stall where a man is shaking a pan above a fire; the pan is bigger than my head and sizzles with a ferocious heat. I try to peer in, but he waves at me to stand back and tosses the contents in the air. The hunks of food fall back into the sauce, and he shakes the pan again to coat them. The smell is tangy and biting and my mouth is watering.

'We'll take two, please,' Martha says.

The chef is a guy with a little beard and two teeth missing. Wordlessly, he rests the pan back on the grill.

Flames lick up the sides, but he plucks out morsels – they look like charred stones – and flings them into a napkin, first one for me, then Martha. She hands him a chit, which he accepts without looking.

'Don't recognise you,' the man says to me, narrowing his eyes.

'That's because she's a rancher, Jim.' Martha smiles. 'With steaks for breakfast, who needs trash food like yours?'

The toothless chef wags a dirty finger at her and laughs. Martha pulls me away.

'What do you mean I'm a rancher?'

'Ranchers live way out – they rarely come into the centre. It's an easy way to explain who you are, for now.'

Ranchers, way out. I groan inwardly. How am going to see it all in three days? Although it's just the foundations Welt is worried about. Just the space below the skyscrapers, the tunnels beneath the Drop.

'Now come on, taste it. Don't bite right into it or you'll burn the inside of your mouth.' Martha blows on her food and swaps it from hand to hand.

Following her lead, I nibble the brittle edge. It cracks between my teeth and something soft oozes out. It's salty and sweet and creamy all at once.

'Oh, wow…' I mutter. Martha laughs at my wide eyes. I realised I'm nodding crazily, too, and making 'mmm' sounds. 'What is this?'

'They're litter bugs,' Martha says, spitting out some

shell. She then rips off what I now realise is a leg, and sucks the meat out. 'You must have met one of these fellows before – up on the surface? They scuttle.' She uses greasy fingers to mimic the action.

Trash crabs. I gulp. At home we eat plenty of insects, but I'm repulsed by the thought of eating these meaty little creatures. They're animals ... and we don't eat animals. Not us. Not since tissue labs came into existence, and that was a long, long time ago.

'But they're full of waste!' I object through a mouthful. 'They must be really bad for you.'

'Nah. They're clever little things. They process the waste, break it down, poo it out...'

I wrinkle my nose.

'Don't worry, they're cleaned before they're cooked. And they're cooked till they're piping hot.'

'Trash crabs? Really? Disgusting.' I bite right into it again.

We're laughing, sweating too, with all the chilli sauce the poor trash crabs have been blasted with, and juice is running down my chin. I think briefly of Moles and our yiros-eating competitions. I think of the extra chilli I always order – nowhere near as powerful as this. As I crunch into another mouthful, Martha looks up as someone approaches – probably another person wanting to know about me. I keep my head low.

'Oh, hi!' Martha's voice is bright.

'Litter bugs? I always knew you were a bit rough,

Martha, but this is the lowest of the low.'

'They're delicious!' she protests. 'You're just a snob.'

'And you are?' The owner of the voice bends forward slightly in my direction.

'That's none of your business,' Martha says.

'Nothing round here is none of my business,' he says.

And then I look up at the boy next to us, who's looking amused, his hands on his hips.

I – I can't breathe.

Is this a trick? A test, maybe?

'Is she okay?'

I'm coughing, choking, my eyes swimming. I feel hands pummelling my back. And then I'm fine. I'm alright. Their faces are worried, searching me for an explanation.

'It's you.'

Chapter 14

Vim.

Before I can look at him again, he's gone. Melted into the throng. Martha is pulling me to a water pump. It's connected to a fresh underground spring, she tells me. She pulls down on the pump and releases a flow of crystal-clear, freezing water. I rub my hands together, scrubbing at the sticky sauce. My mind is in such a jumble, I don't even stop to wonder if the water is full of microbes or poison. I pause, think, then shake my head. Over and over.

'Are you okay?' Martha looks at me with curiosity.

So much for thinking on my feet, acting normal. The only way I can pull this back is to tell the truth: he looks like a boy in a video game. They're so alike, they could be twins, I tell her. She shrugs like it's no big deal.

'So who is he, really? Because clearly he's not a video game come to life.'

'Just Jay. Quite a character, isn't he?'

'Is he a friend of yours?'

'Not really.' Martha wipes her hands on her top. 'He serfed for us a couple of years ago. Just salvaging stuff for Mum's shop. We gave him food.'

'Why doesn't he serf any more?'

'No need to. He has a special job in London Under. Super-confidential. I probably shouldn't tell you, but I will say it's important enough that they gave him his own house. Didn't even have to excavate it or buy it. And he can have anything he wants for free. Within reason.'

'Wow.'

'Yeah, wow. A boy who has everything…'

'He seems to like you.'

'He seems to like everyone. Total flirt!' She lowers her voice. 'I have to admit – I adore him. But I don't stand a chance, unfortunately. He likes older women. Come on, we'd better go to the chicken man, or Mum will kill us.'

Although I hate the stench of fatty smoke in my hair, I regret leaving Eat Street and its smells, all the people huddled around hot dishes, sharing plates, laughing, their mouths full. The vibrancy is off the scale. The colour and sound. Better than the graphics on *Grunge City* and *Graffiti Train*. Better than a social gathering at any hub back home, where so-called friends ignore each other to watch videos. I'm sorry that Vim – or Jay – won't be coming with us.

My heart is scatty with anticipation and uncertainty.

This is sensory overload and I'm probably on the edge of a breakdown. And if I am, who's to know? Not Medico – not down here.

I turn to see Jay standing by a seated group, leaning on someone's back, gesticulating in some lively conversation. He turns and catches my eye. He nods quickly. The nod doesn't come with a smile. It puzzles me.

'Do you have a boyfriend?' Martha touches my arm.

'What do you mean?'

'Go on, you can tell me.' She grins, leaning against my shoulder.

'What do you mean?'

'I *mean*…' – she rolls her eyes – 'do you have a *boyfriend*?'

'No. I'm *sixteen*. People don't fall in love until they're at least twenty-five.'

Martha looks at me as if I'm crazy. 'Twenty-five? Most people have had a couple of kids by then. I had my first boyfriend at thirteen.' She stops. Blushes. 'Just casual.'

'Is that allowed?'

'Of course it's allowed.'

'Well, either you're early starters or we're slow.' I laugh. 'Don't get me wrong, I know about relationships. We study them, too. I'm ready for when it happens. And…' It's my turn to blush. 'I have downloaded a kiss before. Illegally.'

'You did *what*?'

'Downloaded a kiss.' I grab Martha's hand and make

her feel my arm, running her finger from my wrist up to my armpit, so she can feel the lump. She pulls her hand away, disgusted.

'It's a Sensii chip. It stimulates chemicals in the body when you play games. But if you know the right people, you can download all sorts of sensations.'

'I've heard of those things.' Martha nods slowly, her eyes wide. 'I thought it was made up. They're real? What sort of stuff can you download?'

'Whatever anyone uploads, you can download. Some people even make money from it. It's a kind of pastime, really… I've tried most things in my age range I can afford, and I don't think I've rated anything more than two stars out of five. Sensii doesn't really seem to work on me. The kiss just felt like chewing sashimi – cold, raw fish. Don't think I'll be tempted to do that again.'

'Downloading *feelings* … that is freaky!'

'Not really. Not if you're used to it. We get Sensiis at birth.'

Martha's mouth drops open. 'Here we sing songs to babies, we don't send them on trips! Wow. Just, wow.' She knocks her forehead with the heel of her hand and I realise that, to her, I'm kind of super-space-age. It's like telling my great-great-great-grandparents that one day their meat will be grown in a laboratory, they'll eat bread made from insects and, thanks to tender-skin suits, they will never have to worry about falling and breaking a bone. We walk on in silence. I can tell

Martha is still digesting what I have said.

Our first stop is Sue's Food. It's a tiny shop with boxes and crates all over the floor, packed with vegetables. Martha picks out pumpkins and potatoes.

'Yeah, get more of those. In fact, buy them all!' I laugh. The owner looks taken aback.

Martha pulls a serious face. 'I must apologise, Sue. My friend here has Urgent Potato Syndrome.'

Sue blinks several times. Martha sweeps the vegetables off the counter and into the trolley, and places a couple of chits on the till. I see a smile twitching at the corner of her mouth.

'Potato, potato, potato,' I say in a zombie monotone, playing along, and the two of us burst back out into the street, laughing like crazy. 'Urgent Potato Syndrome? *Urgent Potato Syndrome?*'

'Yup. It's serious. Cured only by a generous helping of butter.'

'In which case I'm very sick indeed and I may need lots of it.'

Martha wraps her arm around my neck again. I've come to realise it means she likes me. She likes me a lot. But I'm not here to make friends. I have to focus.

We've walked such a long way that my feet hurt, but I'm glad I've got some mapping done. I try to look at everything, so no alley or street is left unregistered. It slows me down.

Martha skips most of the time. She's springy and tireless. Although I'm pretty sure I'm healthier than she is, she seems to have way more energy. Maybe it's because they get to run in their tunnels more than we do.

'How much further?'

'To the chicken man? Miles, yet. You tired? How tired?'

My face says it all.

She sighs. 'Okay, we need to go this way, then. But we'll need to do some bargaining at the other end to pay for it.'

I nod apologetically, although I don't know what 'bargaining at the other end' means. We change direction, weaving through smaller and smaller streets, all good for mapping although I don't know how important they'll be. Not all passageways are fully finished. Some come to an abrupt end, walled off by earth and trash, not yet excavated. Or too dangerous to attempt, maybe. But at least Welt can't tell me I wasn't thorough. Meeting Martha was the best thing I could have hoped for. She knows shortcuts and we slip down alleyways forged between houses, zigzagging across the primitive township, until we arrive at the mouth of a tunnel.

'Come.' Martha runs towards the gloomy opening. There are steps leading down, and people coming up from under the earth, carrying trolleys and bags. A gang of boys on bicycles judder past us down the stairs, their hands tight on the handlebars, their knees bouncing, standing on their pedals to take the shock. They whoop and cheer. One slips, and his bike skids out from beneath him.

'Watch out!' someone cries, and the people below stand to one side to make way for the boy and his bike, now tumbling independently down the staircase. When we get to the bottom, he is gripping his wrist in pain. But he's also laughing, and his friends slap him on the back and grab at his arm to check the damage. He holds it protectively against his chest, grimacing.

'Martha, he looks hurt.'

'He'll be fine.' She shrugs. 'His decision to be an idiot – no one made him.'

Just then a voice thunders up the tunnel from below. *Leaving in two minutes.* People pick up the message and pass it to others on the stairs. *Leaving in two minutes.* Everyone quickens their pace and Martha starts taking the steps two at a time, dragging the trolley behind her. I follow, jumping down the stairs, thinking of *Sky Jump.*

At the bottom we break into a run, darting through another tunnel and then into another, wider than the rest. I can almost *feel* the map growing bigger in my head. I'm turning into a living atlas of Under.

At the bottom of the staircase a row of carts, joined together with chains, waits. We clamber aboard one, squishing in alongside two elderly people who are wearing so many layers of clothes, they look like they've been inflated. It's to keep warm, I suppose. I think of the old people in London Star with their tender-skin suits

– fully protective with constant warmth. *Arctic-proof,* they say. As if that's relevant to people who'll never leave London Star.

A young man swaggers along the side of the carts, holding his hand up to collect chits. 'Where are you going?' he asks every passenger.

'Crouch End,' Martha says as he approaches.

'Two chits each.'

'But we're only little,' Martha pleads, cocking her head to the side. She elbows me and I elbow her back.

He laughs. 'One chit each.'

Martha juts out her bottom lip. I make a whimpering sound.

'I've got to eat, you know!' he grumbles. 'Go on, give us a chit, then. I'm not full.'

Martha hands over the plastic chit and gives me an appreciative nod. 'You're good at this,' she says. 'A fast learner.'

In Star, there'd be no questioning. No debate. Price is all determined by Advice and automatically paid via Flips. So strange, all this talking and touching. I lean out and look down the row of carts. The boys we saw before are in the end one, crammed together, arms looped through the frames of their bikes. The one who got hurt is still rubbing at his wrist and pulling faces. I think he's trying not to cry. With Sensii, the pain comes and then goes. But here, pain is real. It goes when it's good and ready.

'Where are those boys off to? Chicken man?'

Martha laughs. 'No. They'll be off freewheeling. Finding old chutes or tunnels to go down, or wide cracks in the earth.'

'Are they caused by the tremors?'

'What tremors?'

'London Star detected some tremors. That's why I –'

Luckily she interrupts me before I put my foot in it, and I grit my teeth, angry at my stupidity.

'If there's something shaky going on, then it's your place, not ours. It's solid as a rock down here – although it's still pretty dangerous, what those boys do. Some of the places they go are unstable. Three kids died a couple of months ago, but it doesn't stop them. Adrenalin junkies. If they're lucky, they'll just have a couple of broken bones to go with the sprained wrist. Doctors' nightmare.'

'You have doctors?'

'We're not savages. Of course we have doctors. Very good ones.' She sounds offended.

The cart jerks forward, and I turn my head the other way to see what's moving us. It's a buggy thing, hooked up to the front cart. It whines as we trundle down the tunnel.

'Is he pedalling?' I ask.

'We have electricity too, you know. Just because we live basic doesn't mean we're completely Stone Age. Solar-powered battery, if you must know.'

'You need sun for solar.' Not once have I seen the sun, the sky or anything above ground since I got here.

'We got sun.' She smiles at me. 'We got sun. You'll see.'

At various stages of the journey, people jump from the carts, sometimes in large groups. These are serfers, Martha explains. They are the day shift, being led to various areas to excavate or clean or farm in exchange for a good meal, a bed for the night, a couple of chits. Nothing so much that would make them rich, and nothing so little it would be exploitation. They're laughing, nearly all of them. I can see no resentment on their faces. It's alien to me, but it's an arrangement that seems to work.

The journey seems to take forever, and it's not fun. London Star and its smooth swoosh between travel hubs is a million miles away – our bolt trains, propelled by compressed air, that extend to other developed cities, like Liverpool Loop and Cardiff Grid, are like flying by comparison. Here, I doubt even a tender-skin suit would protect your bottom from the constant bumping and lurching on the wooden seats as the carts sway relentlessly.

Although the tunnel is lit with strings of lights, people have brought torches to read by. They flicker irregularly on the tunnel walls; it makes me feel sick. I'm used to steady light, regulated air, a shock-free environment. After all the sensations I've had to endure today, I can take no more. I lean over the side of the cart and vomit.

There are disgusted moans and cheers, and someone claps. The old lady opposite hands me a cloth.

I can't wait for it to be over.

Chapter 15

The buggy at the front slows. The boys at the back throw down their bikes and leap off before we've stopped moving, apart from the one who hurt his wrist. He's in too much pain. He has to go back. He puts on a brave face, but I can see he's feeling wretched as he watches the others vanish into the distance. I envy them, too – all that energy. I feel drained.

'Not far now.' Martha nods in the direction of another tunnel. Another? I don't know how much longer I can bear it, the hideous gloom of rabbit life. I shut my eyes and recall London Star's open spaces – the hubs, arcades and shopping centres, cool and crisp. To think I was bored with it all! Now I realise that when you're bored with safety and ease, it's a sign of a good life. Even the Quarters are luxurious compared with this. When I go back, I'll see it from a different perspective. I might even be content.

If you're not back in three days, you'll be dead.

The weight of responsibility eclipses my discomfort. How can I balance the time restriction with being sure I've done the job properly? I could go back tonight, slip out when everyone is asleep. But I'd have little in my head to show for all the planning this trip has taken. I haven't seen enough yet. No matter how real the threats to my sanity and my health, I have to keep going as long as possible. I'm a questa, and I was chosen not to fail.

'What are you thinking about?' Martha says, flashing her torch in my face.

'How I can't wait to see every corner of this place.' I smile, shutting my eyes against the glare.

We hop off at the next stop. My stomach continues to lurch, as if I'm still aboard the rickety cart. Eventually my footsteps, one in front of the other, ground me. Martha gives up teasing me about the vomit and we continue in silence.

We walk uphill through a smooth tunnel that leads to a gate. Behind it is a cluster of stone dwellings, their roofs tucked beneath the dirt canopy of the underground tunnel. Martha rattles the bars and hollers, and a young girl comes to meet us.

'It's Martha Daley. We're after eggs and a chicken.'

'Customers, Dad,' the little girl calls, not taking her eyes off us. 'It's two girls.'

'Okay,' the voice shouts back. 'Let 'em in. Lock it behind you.'

The girl fiddles with a bolt on the other side of the gate and we step through. She shuts the gate then sprints ahead of us past the buildings – I see dry twigs and grass through their gaping doorways and windows. Around the end of the last building on the left, we step into a yard area, ablaze with natural light. Instinctively, I shield my face.

'Told you we got sun,' Martha says triumphantly.

There are chickens – masses of them. Real live chickens with bronze and gold feathers and rubbery feet, clucking, pecking, scratching and running around in a circle of light that pours through a hole in the mud roof. Without thinking, I step forward into the beam, scattering chickens everywhere. Standing right beneath the light source, I look up, through a shaft that has been drilled through layers and layers of soil and waste. Up and beyond is a wide circle of blue sky, a white wisp of cloud passing overhead, and I stand there, bathed in light, wishing I could stay here a while. Unfiltered sun rays are dangerous, but they feel so good.

'What's she doing?'

The man, with a full beard and wearing a suit made of wool, is not happy. I've upset his chickens.

'Sorry,' I mumble, and turn to say it again, but Martha shakes her head at me, telling me to stop. He watches me. Suspicious. Stupid. I shouldn't be drawing attention to myself. When I'm with easy-going Martha, I forget that strangers aren't welcome here.

'So what are you after?' He talks to Martha, but his gaze keeps sliding back towards me.

'Two dozen eggs and a chicken, please.' She fumbles in her pocket for chits.

'Three chits for twenty-four eggs. Five for a plucked chicken.'

'I've got six chits in total.' Martha shrugs, handing them over. I know she's kept some back. 'Any way you can knock some off?'

The man purses his lips. 'Are you willing to work?'

'Yep. We're willing to work, aren't we?' Martha nods at me enthusiastically.

'Okay, then. You kill the chicken. And you take it home, feathers and all.'

'Done,' Martha says, holding her hand out for him to shake.

She smiles at me and does a thumbs up. I return the gesture, but my smile fades as I realise what we're about to do. This living, pecking ball of feathers is not a piece of meat grown from cells; it's a sentient animal. Like the trash crab, but bigger. With eyes I can look into. Bile rises in my throat. We are going to kill and eat the animal…

'Sally, twenty-four eggs,' the man calls to his daughter. And then he is among the chickens, turning in circles, choosing a bird. I'm paralysed with horror, silently hoping they all manage to get away. But he grabs one and flips it upside-down, holding it by the legs. It squawks and flaps desperately, feathers flying. Its friends below make horrible confused noises, and it's hard to resist putting my hands over my ears.

'You can do it in there,' he says, nodding towards a barn.

Martha clasps the bird's legs, holding it at arm's length as it continues to struggle, its wings batting against her face. She walks towards the building and I lag behind. I don't want to see what comes next. I really don't.

'Come on, it's your dinner. You've got to help do the deed,' she says.

Inside the building, the bird suddenly calms down, as if resigned to its fate. Or maybe it's the lack of sunshine. The barn is lit by a few bare bulbs and straws of light from outside creep through cracks, but it's still pretty gloomy. There's an air of sadness. Martha sits on the floor.

'Come and hold it down, will you?'

I sit beside her and place my hands on the smooth, fluttering beast, stroking her, feeling her tremble. Tears prick my eyes and I blink them back. With me firmly holding the wings, Martha takes the bird's neck. She pulls and twists it. It struggles, its eyes bulging in panic. She twists again, but it's tough. The bird is suffering. I can't stand the suffering. So I grab its neck and wring it with all my might until there's a crack, and the head flops, still twitching. Hot tears pour down my face.

'Is it still alive?' I splutter.

'No, it's just the nerves, I think. They keep moving.'

Martha is panting. The bird convulses on the floor in front of us.

There is a cough. We look up. The little girl is in the doorway, holding egg boxes. I put my hand to my mouth – how much did she see? If it was bad for me, how did it affect *her,* a child?

'Should have used the axe. It's much quicker,' she says bluntly, putting the boxes down. She takes an axe that is leaning against the wall, and without warning brings it down hard on the chicken's neck. There is blood.

We take the one-chit cart ride home, and I close my eyes and pretend to sleep. In truth, I don't want to talk to anyone or see any more of this place. I'm consumed by loathing. The world I have walked into is barbaric – a place better suited to Kagu Mactua, to stories, to history books. I want to be home, where meat is not ripped from life. Where the air is easy to breathe. Where nothing has ever made my heart hurt like it does now. Maybe Welt was wrong about me. I'm not the ultimate real-life questa after all.

I open my eyes a fraction and look again at the bag on Martha's lap. We've taken the head, to make stock. The chicken's dead eyes and beak are visible through the thin plastic, and the metallic smell of blood finds its way out through the knot. The death we caused is inescapable, but nobody else seems to care. And I know I must do my job quickly and find a way home as soon as possible. I'm too sensitive to be a security operative. Funny, really, as in Star I never felt sensitive enough.

Tonight, I'll take a walk. Cover as much of London Under as I can. Wander the alleys in every direction. Find and check the foundations. See everything there is to see. Walk all night if I have to, so I can build the map and get out of here. Away from this brutal place, where people can smile so quickly after spilling blood.

I thought there was no way I could eat that poor chicken. The guilt of taking her life blocked my throat and stomach like too much potato. But the day has been long and hard, and by the time we get back I'm really hungry. Thinking more rationally, I realise I can't *not* eat the chicken. It would be a waste. Her death would have been for nothing.

Ellie roasts it with salt, pepper and herbs. With every bite I say a silent 'thank you' to the animal for her sacrifice and for her flavour and for being the best meat I've ever eaten. I hate to admit it, but it's true. Better even than Mum's cooking. But Mum works with what she has – and what she has is meat from a Petri dish, bland compared with this. But I've learned now that bland means safe. My taste buds might be alive here, but I do not feel safe.

Ellie has also made a side of mashed potato and pumpkin and greens, smothered with butter. It seems a lot, but she insists that my being here is reason for celebration. Besides, if there's any leftovers, they're placed on a chair out in the street for anyone who needs a little help.

'Not everyone gets a job every day,' Ellie explains.

'Like Danny,' Martha says pityingly. 'Danny has a deformed hand. He misses out on a lot of work.'

'Do you mean he can't pick stuff up?' I ask. I'm shocked by the word 'deformed' in relation to the human body. The only deformed thing I ever saw was a wonky carrot – a farming mistake.

'No, because it takes him ages to do the buttons on his shirt and trousers.'

'Oh!' I laugh, not sure if I should. But Martha is smiling.

'On the bright side, it means he comes here.' She blushes. 'He's sweet.'

'And so long as he compliments my food, he's welcome.' Ellie smiles.

Martha tells her mother about our childish outburst at Sue's Food. The potato joke was funny – I laughed so much, my stomach hurt. In hindsight, I wish there was a way I could have recorded that for myself, for future. Or for uploading, so someone else can have a chance to feel the ecstatic tummy pain of being hopelessly hysterical over the silliest thing. Not even Moles at his best has ever made me feel that way. But I can't upload anything if I don't have my Flip. It's unlinked, and now in pieces somewhere. London Under is so far behind, it would take a hundred years to develop a transfer system remotely close to what's needed. I've seen old phones here – like little bricks and tiles, like they have in the Star museum – but those things don't build a net. This is a civilisation so stuck in the past, I'm amazed it manages to exist.

There's a knock at the door. Ellie wipes her mouth with a napkin and gets up, but three men, including Michael, let themselves in before she has a chance. I notice Ellie's hands clench.

'Are you after roast chicken?' she says, attempting friendliness.

'Why not?' Michael steps forward and pulls out a chair, beckoning the others to do the same. There are no more chairs, so they lean against a wall. 'Looks delicious.' He smiles, wafting the steam towards his face with a cupped hand. 'Is it delicious, Alara?'

'I love potato,' I say, then immediately feel stupid. I feel Martha's knee jig next to mine under the table. I wonder if she's nervous, or if she's about to laugh.

'Potato, eh? Very nice.'

'It is. Especially the butter. We don't have butter. I really like the butter.' I don't know why I'm talking so much. Perhaps it's because silence seems to invite you to fill it. And I'm filling it with rubbish.

'Have you enjoyed your first day in London Under?' Michael crosses his legs and leans back in his chair.

'Yes. I mean, wow, it's amazing. I tried chilli trash crab –'

'That's what she calls litter bugs,' Martha explains.

'She loved it, didn't you, Alara?'

'Yes. And the streets and the people... It's a ... a lovely place.' I feel like Michael needs assurance that his city is great, something to be proud of. Somewhere I could happily start a new life.

'You must be tired after your first day, all your exploring.'

'I am.' I nod. 'And I killed a chicken.' Again, what am I saying? No one flinches.

'So after dinner you'll go right to bed?'

'I think so.'

'You're not going to slip out and go exploring like a little mole?' He laughs, even though it isn't a joke. Of course, the thought had crossed my mind, and I wonder if this is some kind of demonic mindreading. Must keep my cool.

'Absolutely not. I'm shattered. I'll sleep like a log.'

Michael smiles broadly and claps his hands like I'm some great comedy act. I realise once again that I'm a not a guest but a person under suspicion: untrustworthy, a threat. He slaps his thighs and gets to his feet.

'That's excellent news, Alara. We're very happy to have you.'

His mouth smiles. His eyes don't.

He holds his hand out for me to shake, and I take it and shake it strongly, hoping to convey that I'm a good, solid person. No threat at all. Definitely not the kind of person who's planning to go walkabout with a mapping system in her head. Then I feel a prick in the back of my hand.

This is not Martha's house. The room is tiled and bright. Large bulbs dangle from the ceiling, and the smell is vinegary. I lick my lips and blink, letting my eyes adjust to the light. When I turn my head, there's a whitecoat.

Am I back? My heart leaps. Something has gone wrong.

'Don't move. Stay as still as you can.' The whitecoat has a kind face, brown hair swept up into a bun, neat and clinical.

'Where am I?' I croak. I'm wearing a gown. Shivery. My second-skin suit is gone.

'You're in hospital.'

'Medico?'

'My name is Dr Orta,' she continues. 'You can call me Helen. I'm just going to patch you up. You're going to be fine. It'll be sore for a bit, that's all.'

And now I notice a deep throbbing in my arm, occasionally sliced with a sharp, pulsing pain. I fumble to feel what it could be. A plaster over my armpit, where my Sensii chip is. Or was.

'My chip. What have you done with it?'

'Progress brought you here. They said you'd be staying. The first thing we do with London Star defectors is take out the chip. Unders are a bit spooked by Sensii chips. Of course, Advice can't top them up when I'm down here, but I'm sure you can still see why it makes them uneasy. Simpler just to get rid of it. As soon as the dosage runs out, it will be useless anyway.'

I don't understand. But Dr Orta could be reciting the alphabet and I wouldn't understand – the pain makes concentration impossible. It's like nothing I've ever experienced. It's worse than the berserkers' whips in *Warlords*.

'The pain…' I moan.

'Ah yes, sorry. That's not something you're used to. And you'll certainly have a scar,' she says. 'But you're in good hands. We may not have the fancy equipment down here, but I was one of Estrella's best surgeons.'

I prop myself up. 'You're from London Star? But you're called Helen. That's an old name.'

'And I used to be called Honna. I changed it to fit in. Many years ago now.' She smiles efficiently, but her eyes are soft.

'Do you miss it?'

'Of course I do.' She stares at me.

'Are you going back, then?'

'No, that's not what I meant. You always miss what you don't have. But I'd miss this more, despite the hard bits.'

'Hard bits?'

'You know the hard bits. The pain, for a start. Living here isn't an easy choice. But I chose freedom, however hard it might be. Just like you have.'

I nod, still confused, gritting my teeth at the agony running down my arm.

'You were always going to be a runaway,' continues Dr Orta. 'I can tell, just by looking at you.' She checks my wound.

'Right.'

When Dr Orta's back is turned, I peek beneath the cloth strip over my upper arm. There's a line with white stitching, barely visible. I tweak the end stitch, which stretches the wound, and I see a glimpse of the angry flesh beneath.

'Alara!' she scolds, dabbing the wound quickly with a cold, stinging fluid. 'I'll put on a new bandage, but don't touch, okay? Infection – that's another of the hard bits. Something you want to avoid.'

She's kind. She knows how to talk to me, and she thinks she knows my type – a person from Star with a runaway mind. Which I am, although that's not why I'm here. I wonder why she is here.

'Come on, you're all set. Time to get you back home to bed. Every day down here is exhausting, and you never know what's round the corner. Best to be rested and as fit as you can be.'

Chapter 16

Martha is sitting at the bottom of my bed in shorts and a vest top, watching me.

'What the hell?' I moan.

'It's morning.' She squeezes into bed alongside me and flings her arm across my chest. 'Did you sleep well?'

'Didn't have a choice about that,' I say, pushing her away.

The post-operation sedative was like a sledgehammer, and Martha's attention is too much, too early. I'm not happy. I didn't get my night walk, and the countdown continues. Two days left. What's more, I'm beginning to feel like a prisoner, every day tortured with new pieces of horrifying information. *The hard bits.*

'Sorry they keep doing that,' she says. 'I guess they don't trust you yet.'

'Trust me about what?'

'So, do you want breakfast? Mum can make you an

omelette. Or potato, if you like?'

She's trying to be upbeat, but I'm not feeling it. My head aches from whatever drugs they slid into my veins, and my body is sore. My heart, too. I'm sick of the highs and lows. One minute I have flavour, laughter, a feeling of being so alert it hurts; then I see people in pain, the elderly huddling together for warmth, the gruesome death of an animal for the dinner plate. Stitches sticking out of my raw skin. It's too much. It's like a Sensii overload. The bad kind. Good job it's not available for Moles to try. He could really knock himself out with this.

'Come on, Alara. There's plenty more to show you. Hey, what's the matter?'

My shoulders are shaking, then I'm sobbing like a kid. It's the pressure and the pain, welling up together to create the perfect emotional storm. I want to hear my mother's voice. I want Mum.

Just thinking the word brings her into sharp focus. I see her smile, the way she brushes my hair off my face, her excitement at the simplest things I do. Like getting good marks or wearing my hair pretty, or making the finals of StarQuest. She will be missing me. No number of quick cures from Medico will delete her pain. She'll be worried sick. Panic grabs my throat and I struggle to breathe.

Martha leaps up. 'Are you ill? What is it?'

'Just thinking of my parents.' I sniff back the tears. *Pull yourself together.*

'Do you want to go back now?'

'Of course not.' I take Martha's hand, understanding that here it's touch, not a good citizen record, that implies trustworthiness. 'When I left home, I didn't plan it very well, that's all. There wasn't time for goodbyes.'

Martha does what she does – for celebration and commiseration – and pulls me in for a suffocating hug. I struggle to get free and she recoils, hurt.

'Can I even get a wash here?' I gasp.

'Bathroom's round the corner,' Martha says flatly. She moves away from me. 'Water might come out brown at first, but it's fine.'

I've hurt her feelings. But I'm too lost and upset to say sorry.

I'm still wearing the giant hospital gown and I keep it on as I wash, scrubbing myself underneath it with hard soap, then rinsing with a cold wet flannel. I'm going. Decision made. Although I don't know what I'll say to Welt when I return so soon, without a fraction of what's needed in my Gen-Tech chip. But I have to get out of this place. It's like being buried alive. With injections for added discomfort. I'll think of something – say my life was in danger. It probably is; Michael looks like he wants to kill me. I have to go. Create a distraction and run.

Then I remember the tracker on my ankle. It's like a punch to the stomach, like a locked door at the end of an escape route. Rage bubbles inside me. Never felt that before – never felt like I could hit something. Not something that doesn't ask to be hit, like Kagu.

I have *got* to calm down. *Think*. I need Martha on my side if I'm going to get out of here. And that bit is easy. She's so desperate to please, she's malleable. Perhaps she knows how to get the tracker off. It's a good place to start.

Wrapped in a towel, I re-enter the room, apologies ready on the tip of my tongue. She's not to blame for any of this. It was my doing, my risk. I didn't think things out. I didn't think at all. I'm going to explain, confide in her, that I've changed my mind and want to go home. But she's bustling around the room, busy with something, and I keep quiet. There are clothes laid out on the bed. When she sees me, she tucks her hair behind her ears and attempts a smile.

'These are the best jeans I have. This top is the coolest – retro, last century, and the pants and bra are clean. And you can borrow my leather jacket.' She stands back, proud of her donations. 'Get dressed quickly and come downstairs. We're going out. And if Mum asks where we're going, just tell her we're going skating.'

'Skating?'

'We're not. But just say that.'

We're out of the door, carrying a breakfast of bread and butter, and Martha is walking quickly, with determination. She looks too fired up to interrupt, so I don't ask questions in case I annoy her. I need her. We weave through streets and alleys for several minutes, and I think I spot a man following us – craggy face, grey beard. But then I conclude that, as there's nothing to do in this mad place, following people around might be what they do for fun.

We come to a road with one house and a concrete dead end; I turn to see if the man has followed us this far, but he's gone. I'm glad. He was creeping me out.

Martha walks boldly to the door of the house and knocks. She pulls me up alongside her and whispers in my ear. 'I'll do my best.'

There's no time to ask what she's talking about, because a woman opens the door. The first thing I notice is her beautiful dress – light blue with little white flowers, embellished with strips of cream lace – and her wide face and huge blue eyes. I'm guessing she's in her mid-twenties.

'Yes?' she says, unsmiling.

'Is he there?' Martha tries to peer around her.

'What's it about? And who is *she*?' The woman looks me up and down.

'It's a technology problem. Urgent.'

The woman rests her hand on the other side of the doorframe, blocking the way. It doesn't look as if she'll let us in. But then Jay appears at her shoulder. The boy we met in Eat Street. Vim in the flesh.

'Hey, Martha. And Martha's friend.' He nods quickly at the woman, and she slips away, back into the house.

'Hey,' Martha returns. 'We have a favour to ask you.'

'Sure, come on in.' He shows us into a room with old sofas and a table. There are shelves on the wall, holding photographs and books and candles. It's like a home. Not in the way that my home is a home, but like a home for fairy-tale runaways or families of talking mice. Crumbling, modest, well worn. Jay dusts off a sofa and motions for us to sit. He leans against the table by the window and crosses his arms across his chest, waiting for an explanation.

'So, this is Alara.' Martha points.

'You already introduced us. But hello again, Alara.' He smiles.

'And she needs to contact her mother... Alara, why don't you explain?'

'No, I never said I wanted to contact her,' I say, flustered. 'Just that I missed my parents. It's natural, you know, to miss your parents. Even for us in cold, selfish London Star.' I'm laying it on thick, but Martha's genuine concern could genuinely upend me.

'Jay's a good listener. You can trust him.'

Her voice is calm and reassuring. Wondering if Martha can read my mind, I shift in my seat and lean forward. 'I don't know if my dad survived the accident I was in up there. There was no time for goodbyes. But I was just having a moment. Of course I can't contact them. Martha was being a good friend, but it would be too dangerous. Not to mention impossible.'

'Impossible?' Jay says, tilting his head. 'Not impossible.'

'Well, no. No, anyway.' I'm feeling so uncertain. Not sure what's going on. Of course I can't speak to my parents. It's only been a day. They're probably in grief therapy. It'll ruin everything.

'Are you saying that, if Jay managed to sort it out, you wouldn't say something to them?' Martha says, wrinkling her nose.

'No, because of the Advisors. They'll listen in, know I'm alive and come looking for me.'

'Advisors?' Martha wrinkles her nose again.

'They're like … how can I explain them? Teller-offers, but with power,' Jay says quickly. He looks thoughtful. 'Martha, why don't you go to the kitchen and get Dilly to make you a drink? I should probably talk to Alara alone.'

Martha hesitates. 'Okay, but I'm supposed to stay with her –'

'It'll be fine.' Jay motions to the door with his hand.

'Okay, then.' Martha sighs, getting up. 'But Dilly doesn't look like she wants –'

'She's fine. Just slept badly.'

When Martha is gone, Jay stares at me for a long time, and so intensely it takes a while to meet his eyes. How can I look at him and trust myself not to lean forward and butterfly-kiss his cheek, like I used to do with Vim? Or melt on the spot and tell him everything I'm feeling?

'Come with me.'

He takes my hand and folds his fingers over my knuckles. It reminds me of holding hands with Vim. But this isn't Vim. I don't know this person.

We go to another room in the house. It's full of electronic equipment. Ancient, some of it. It's clearly been salvaged from the trashed landscape above. There are screens – old-fashioned solid ones, built into consoles – and physical keyboards, and boxes with flashing lights and thin mouths for discs and cards. Wires everywhere, stuck into generator boxes. Jay is like a vintage computer nerd. A hoarder of tech from yesteryear. He opens a drawer in his desk and pulls out a paper bag. In it is my Flip, peeled apart, disembowelled. He gets a chip from another bag and slots it in, then turns it on and fiddles with the settings. I notice as he works that he has scars up and down his arms. I wonder if he's a fighter, or if he's just wrestled a few chickens in his lifetime. Life down here is bound to leave marks. His fingers are rough but they work deftly, as though they were born to handle tiny computer chips and thread-thin circuits.

'You're the tech guy?' I muse.

'One of them,' he says carefully. 'There are a few of us.'

'And this is your office?'

'This is my hobby. My work is somewhere different. Now, listen – I've disabled video and identification so they won't know it's you. You can call, but be quick, and say nothing. This is just so you can hear their voices.'

'But there's no communications down here. I mean, how can there be?'

'Because I'm a genius.' He flashes a smile and twists a wire and *boom,* my Flip panel is lit.

This can't be happening. I don't want it to happen. I reach for the Flip to disconnect it, but he misunderstands my urgency for enthusiasm. He grabs my wrist and stares so hard at me that the whites of his eyes show all around his irises. 'Say *nothing,* understand?'

And it's too late, he's set it to dial. It purrs. I hope that my parents don't respond.

'Hello, who is this? Hello, is anyone there?'

Dad! He's safe and well, survived the heart palpitations. At least I know that. And his voice is bright, as if it's a normal day, not a day when his daughter might be dead. He's being medicated by Medico, then. Mum and Gavi, too, I suppose.

'Hello? Hello?'

I wish I could prompt him to say something else, but Jay motions for me to end the call. I do, and he quickly takes the Flip back and dismantles it again. Somehow, hearing Dad hasn't made me feel better or settled my unease. All it's done is brought me more misery, and the realisation that I'm alone in London Under, with no connection to anyone or anything.

Jay's face is soft, his eyebrows bunched in concern. It's like he knows I'm hurting.

‘Can you get rid of this thing, too?’ I say, pointing to my ankle.

‘Yes. Technically, I could.’

‘Great. Will you do it?’

‘No.’

‘Well, thanks for nothing,’ I mutter.

‘It’s too dangerous. For you and for me.’

I had said it jokingly, but his reply is unexpectedly serious, and the weight of his attention unbearably heavy. I get up to leave but Jay skips in front of me, blocking the exit with his arms. He is not big, but his presence feels huge.

‘Sit down a second.’ He lowers himself to the floor and pats the area in front of him. I sit, crossing my legs and hugging my knees. He’s not shy when it comes to eye contact. I remember what Martha said about him being a born flirt. He’s probably as sincere as a Sensii hug.

‘You met Diana.’

Is this a question? ‘I’ve met her twice. Oh, and I’ve met David and Michael, head of security. Both of them put me right at ease. What is it with this place and sleep drugs?’

‘Or more to the point, what is it with this place and *you*? You see, Alara, what you need to understand is that no one knows what to do with you.’

‘Why does something have to be done with me?’

‘Because if you go back up there and tell anyone about London Under, this place will cease to exist. That’s what they believe. Until something is settled, everyone is on tenterhooks. They're nervous. *I'm* nervous. We're waiting to see what you'll do.'

'I'm looking for a new life.'

'It's a good line,' Jay says, cocking his head to the side. A smile. It was *him*. 'And saying it certainly saved you from ... more unfriendly measures.'

'And it also happens to be true.'

'Really?' He waggles his eyebrows. 'That's a coincidence.'

I shrug.

He nods and leans back on his hands and I try not to look at his taut arms supporting his weight – the veins, the muscles. Vim had none of those.

'Okay then. How could you possibly know if this is a life you'd exchange everything for when you didn't even know that it existed?'

'People choose death over life sometimes,' I protest. Like Peron. 'If I'd stayed in London Star, that's what I might have chosen, too. There's a reason why I wanted to go tip-turning with my dad. I wanted to get out of the skyscrapers. And when the accident happened, I didn't think. I just took my chance and walked. I would have carried on walking across the Void until I found something else. And if I didn't find something else, then at least I'd be taking my last breath out in the open.' The words are coming out, and I'm even convincing myself, though I yearn to be back in the safety of London Star.

Jay claps his hands slowly. 'Great speech. Maybe it's true, maybe not. But you're unpredictable, Alara, and that makes people afraid. Every time they get afraid, they knock you out for a few hours to buy themselves time. You've created chaos.'

'This whole place is chaos. That's not something I invented.'

He pauses, waits for me to calm down. 'It's not chaos, Alara. It's how we live. You might be "advised" about every aspect of your lives, but we're more old-fashioned, and that's not a bad thing to us. We like the old ways of doing things. The New Anglia Initiative – the group you know of as Advice – told London Star inhabitants to think forward, make up new names, disown the past. But we like the old names and we don't want to disown the past. In fact, we celebrate it. We don't want to be dragged into the future. Not if it looks anything like London Star. But you've just bridged the gap – and that's a problem, for each and every one of us.'

'What does that mean?'

'Up until now we've all lived autonomous lives, really. Each to their own. People go to Diana with problems – she'll investigate unexplained deaths, organise search parties and stuff. She's a kind of troubleshooter. But that's as far as rules and law enforcement go. We live in more of a vigilante society. We sort out our own problems. Individually or in mobs. But this is a different kind of problem that needs a different kind of solution. We weren't expecting you. And you – you affect everyone. So now they've had to form a committee to discuss the "Alara situation". But something has to be decided soon, or some people might take the decision into their own hands.'

'How? Why?'

'Every child down here is taught that London Star is bad. The people there are bad. And that, if London Star found out about London Under, bad things would happen. It's the standard scary story.'

'Is that why Martha's mum is weird around me?'

'Yes, probably. She's got a big heart, Ellie. I know her. I know she would want and *try* to trust you…'

'I am trustworthy.'

'Good. Because if they decide you're not, people are going to panic. As I say, they might take things into their own hands. To stop you going back to Estrella and squealing.'

Swallowing suddenly hurts. All it takes is one person to mistrust me, and my life could be in danger. I remember the bearded man in the shadows.

'Couldn't we tell them that London Star wouldn't hurt them?'

Jay looks at me, shocked. 'No. Because that would be a lie.'

'Why is everyone so paranoid?' I throw my arms in the air, and Jay catches my left arm. He holds it up, staring at the bandage that peeks out beneath my shirt sleeve. He flushes with anger. 'They shouldn't have done that. Not yet.'

'Dr Orta said it's because I'm staying. So people do believe me.'

'No. These particular people were trying to scare you.'

'But Dr Orta seemed so nice.'

'She didn't know... It's not her fault.'

'You mean they cut me up for *fun*?' I think I know who *they* might be.

'Not for fun. To see if you'd run. I told you, some people take things into their own hands. But you have to own it now. Regardless of what you're really thinking, you have to act like you're committed to living in Under. You have to make everyone believe you're staying. Get it?'

There's a cough outside the door. 'That's Dilly,' he whispers. 'Session over.'

'Wait. Please,' I beg.

'Coming, Dilly,' he calls. Then he turns back to me and speaks in a low voice. 'Come to Carnival. Tonight. We can get lost there.'

I nod, although I don't know what Carnival is. We leave the room and head back down the corridor, where Martha is waiting awkwardly with the sulking woman.

'Okay, Alara. Nice to meet you. Glad we could get your tracker loosened. It should be more comfortable now.'

Jay is saying that for the sake of Dilly, who watches me through narrowed eyes as we leave. The door shuts behind us with a gentle click, and Dilly's moon face appears in the adjacent window. She tugs at some pieces of cloth hanging inside the window, pulling them across to shut us out entirely. Their answer to one-way glass, I suppose.

'She's friendly,' I mock.

'Can't blame her for being a little snaky,' Martha says. 'She's worried you'll lead him astray.'

'Why would I do that?'

'Because he's hot!' Martha raises an eyebrow and pretends to fan her face. 'I should tell Dilly she has nothing to worry about. He saw you eating chilli litter bugs. It wasn't a pretty sight.'

'Mmm, chilli litter bugs.' I lick my lips.

Martha laughs long and hard. 'Butter potatoes, chilli bugs, hot tech guys ... I swear you're a London Under girl at heart!'

Chapter 17

After visiting Jay, Martha says we should go skating. It's an alibi, just in case Diana and her crew ask around. And, Martha adds, she wants to see if I'm as boss as I look. She explains that boss means cool. Without my second-skin on, I'm definitely cooler than I was.

The skate place is weird. A huge circular area where the ground has been swept clean down to its original flat, smooth stones, with a second area just beyond, with the earth scooped like a bowl. At first, I think it's another old worship place – the high roof is held up by columns. But then I notice that the ceiling is full of large drill holes – and they aren't columns, but ghostly pillars of natural light funnelled from above. People lounge beneath them, some without tops on. Sun directly touching skin. Either they don't know about UV rays, or they don't care.

Martha sees me looking. 'It's a skate place, and it's also a sunbathing place. There are several around the city. There's vitamin D in eggs, but nothing can beat this. Come on.'

We head down to the skating area, picking our way through the sunbathers. They look half-dead with their closed eyes and half-smiling mouths, and they don't seem disturbed by the racket of slapping boards and wheels and whoops. But then, noise is part of this place. There's always noise.

The skaters are all ages. Some could be forty or sixty – who knows, with this lifestyle? Everyone in this place acts younger but looks older; age is almost irrelevant. They trundle and scoot around on scooters, roller skates, skateboards and old-fashioned bicycles – and there's equipment dumped at the side for anyone to use, it seems.

'Oh yes, we're pretty communal down here,' Martha says, throwing me a skateboard. It's heavy. She steps on the end of another so it flips up into her hand. 'Come on, then!'

She holds the board in front of her and forces it back down to the ground with a foot, leaning forward and launching herself into a roll. With her other foot, she pushes herself along until she picks up speed, then she's away. She turns back and smiles.

'Come on!' she calls.

There's no reason I shouldn't be able to do this. I hoverboard, I air surf; my feet are used to balance-based gaming. But the physical feat of balancing on wheels that have direct contact with the rough ground, uncalibrated, non-standard... Maybe I'm overthinking this. How hard can it be?

I launch myself, just as Martha did, and the board skids out from under my feet. Immediately, I'm on my backside, laughing with embarrassment. Martha slaps her thighs with amusement and manoeuvres her skateboard round, pushing her way back to me.

'Get up.'

'I can't,' I wail, still laughing but feeling pain burn in my calf where I overstretched.

'We learn to skate at five, just about the time you're getting your digital snuggles,' she mocks. 'Advanced race. Yeah, right!' She offers me a hand. 'It's a steep learning curve, so get over the fact that you'll spend a bit of time on your backside and you'll soon catch on.'

I don't catch on soon, and I can't believe it – you know, considering how easily I pick up games and sports. Here, everything lacks lubrication – wheels are stiff, they crunch and skid, my feet catch on uneven ground. Everything is bumpy and irregular.

Eventually I get better at staying upright, and manage to skate the length of the place without falling. I can even shift my weight to make the board turn. Martha is proud of me, she says, and suggests we play 'whip' – it's where she skates ahead of me and reaches for my hand, pulling me with all her strength so I zoom past her, before reaching back and propelling her to the front again. It's such a simple idea, but it's brilliant – until I go wrong and steer my skateboard right into Martha's. She leaps off hers in time, but I end up in a mangled heap on the floor.

A new group of skaters arrive and head for the half-pipe. They have rags tied around their knees, wrists and elbows; some carry graffitied skateboards under their arms. There's hollering and hooting, and within seconds of dumping their bags and jackets, they're skating down the ramps of the bowl, flipping their boards mid-air, grinding the undersides along the edges. Some have roller skates – they look like our air blades – and they leap, tucking their knees in tight to their chest, and land without even wobbling. There is no way I'm showing myself up in front of a cool crowd like that.

Martha isn't fazed. She tries some tricks, and fails time and time again, hitting the floor with thuds that make me cringe. After a hard fall, she skates back to show me her grazes – raw cherry flesh under peeling white rolls of skin. I've seen gore before, in *Warlords*. But that was digital gore, and this is high-definition – painfully sharp, with a metallic, bloody scent. It makes me shudder, but she seems proud of it and hardly bothered that her insides are exposed to dirt. After a quick dust-off, she's rolling back for another go. As I watch her jumping, turning, falling, I realise I'm smiling. One of those smiles you get when you're amused by a good friend; when you feel tenderness towards someone. The way I do when I watch

Moles play his digital guitar, concentrating so hard his nostrils flare. Or when he's trying to slurp up yiros and his eyes roll upwards. In the old days, that is.

My old friend Moles would like my new friend Martha, although I'm not sure if she'd like him. His sarcasm might be too much, his lack of touch too cold. Will they ever be able to meet? Not unless the two worlds collide, somehow – but that's not something London Under is keen on. I'm reminded of that by the arrival of Michael and his sidekick, Mark. They're not here to skate.

Parking themselves on the ground next to me, they laugh along when Martha waves and wobbles. I wish they wouldn't do that. Their camaraderie is fake. And – oh no, the man with the beard is back, too, standing in the shadows behind them. I catch his eye and he ducks back into the darkness. There's a quiet tension between me, the bearded man and the security men: a cat's cradle of tripwires. I mustn't trip up.

'Do you skate, Alara?' Michael looks at me, interested. Mark looks straight ahead.

'No.'

I keep an eye on their hands.

'How long are you going to hang around here?'

'Until Martha gets bored.'

'Are *you* bored?'

'No.'

'You must be bored by now. This' – he gestures at the

skaters – 'is all pretty basic to you. You must be missing all your entertainment.'

Mark laughs and turns away. He gives me a really bad feeling. Michael's sarcastic, but Mark is mean. 'What sort of things do you get up to in London Star?'

'Not much. I don't like games.'

'You don't play games?'

'Not really.'

'But you were in a big competition. A *gaming* competition.'

What? How does he know that? I haven't mentioned it to anyone here. He laughs.

'You talk in your sleep,' he says. 'You say a lot in your sleep.'

My heart thuds. They could be bluffing. Don't trip up. Mustn't trip up.

'Er, yes... There was a gaming competition. But I was only entered into it because my brother put my name down. I had no idea until the semi-finals.'

'Really?' Michael says sarcastically. 'Your brother clearly looks up to you. Your family – you must miss them.'

There's something about Mark's movements that I don't like. He's on the other side of Michael, but he's twitchy, and I see his biceps flex as he adjusts his position. I lean back on my elbows to look at him behind Michael's back and see his coat has risen up, revealing a bulge in his back trouser pocket. A stubby handle sticks out the top.

Michael is still talking. 'You'll have plenty of tales to tell them when you get back!'

'When what?'

'When you get back, I said.'

'I'm not going back,' I declare, as boldly as I can. 'But you know that, right? Because you told Dr Orta to remove my Sensii. Or were you hoping it would scare me into running away?'

Michael stiffens, and Mark leans forward to look at me.

I'm emboldened. 'Well, thank you for anticipating my decision. I am indeed staying, and I'm happy to wear this thing forever if you don't believe me.' I point to the tracker, still clamped around my ankle.

I wave happily at Martha, who has hit the floor hard and is laughing uncontrollably while other skaters leap over her.

Michael taps his bottom lip and looks at me through narrowed eyes. 'Why? That's all I ask. Why?'

'Lots of reasons.' I smile.

'Give me one,' he challenges.

It *is* a challenge. The dirt, the blood, the darkness.

So I call on the one thing I can think of – the one thing that remains constant, no matter what London Under throws at me.

'It's the first time I've ever felt alive.'

Chapter 18

We're sitting in Martha's bedroom. She dabs at her torn skin with a wet piece of cloth. I can hardly bear to look at the sickly pink of diluted blood. After the death of the chicken, I should be immune to it, but I'm not.

She's already asked about Michael and Mark, and I said they were just making a visit to see how I was getting on. In a way, they were.

'I've got something to tell you.'

Martha blinks at me, then slips her arm around my waist. 'I'm all ears.'

'They were going to give me until the end of the week to decide if I wanted to stay or not. And I want you to know that I love it here. I'm staying for good...'

She leaps back as if I've given her an electric shock. 'Seriously?'

I nod, and she punches the air.

Even though I only say it because Jay said so, to

cement my lie, her excitement is infectious. It makes me feel as high as if I'd just secured my own eternal happiness. Martha hollers and whoops, jumping and bouncing on the bed. She looks at me again and shakes her head with awe.

'I cannot believe it. I was so sure you'd change your mind once you saw how we live. And what about your parents?'

I shrug. 'We all have to leave home sometime. I'm sixteen. Not a baby.'

Martha shakes her head. 'I don't dare believe you.'

'Believe it, Martha. I'm staying.'

She stops bouncing and falls quiet. 'I hope so, Alara. I hope that's what's decided.'

Of course. Staying isn't just a case of me not leaving. It's at the discretion – the decision – of others. I remember Jay calling me the 'Alara situation'; I remember he wanted to talk to me more.

'Martha, what's Carnival?'

'Carnival? Oh my goodness, there's one tonight! I nearly forgot,' she says, brightening. 'What perfect timing!'

'*What* is Carnival?'

'It's a big party. It's usually arranged by someone to celebrate something.'

'So what's tonight's celebration?'

'I think it's to celebrate the life of a couple of guys who died last week. They fell down a crevasse when they were out scavenging.'

I put my hand to my mouth. *People die, just walking about?*

'It happens once in a while,' Martha explains. 'When you lot turn the tips up there, the ground gets dangerous – you know, it creates new holes. But let's not talk about that. What is absolutely brilliant is that Carnival coincides with your good news! We are going to celebrate, big-time.'

I want to ask more about the deaths. The kids who vanished into the ground. Their parents. Do they have something to take away that pain here, too? No more questions now. Martha is wild with excitement. She makes us run to the salvage shop to tell Ellie.

'So you're sure you're not going back up?' Ellie asks. I can sense her nervousness. I wonder if she knows what would happen to me if I said otherwise. I get a flashback to the knife handle in Mark's pocket.

'Yep! I'm staying.' I feel like I'm saying it too much, but I can't think of anything else to say. If I did actually mean it, what would I say different? 'I feel like this is my home.'

'It's your potato, I reckon.' Martha laughs. There is a smile at the corner of Ellie's mouth, and I think she's about to relax around me for the first time, but the door opens and a customer comes in.

He stops when he sees me. Hesitates, before browsing Ellie's stock. We stand by silently. He selects an old kettle and a battered skateboard. Ellie charges him three chits. He stops and looks at me again.

'I never seen her before,' he says. 'She the one from up there?'

'She's staying,' Ellie says matter-of-factly. 'She's invited.'

'Invited, yeah?' His shoulders drop with relief and he nods a greeting at me and leaves.

'There aren't so many of us down here,' Ellie explains. 'Around three thousand at last count. When was the last count? Anyway, you get to know all the faces. Yours stands out. And not just because it's new. Your skin – it's so clean, for a start. Like you haven't done a day's work in your whole life.'

'You said I was invited. What's that all about?'

Ellie waves my comment away. 'They'll soon get used to you. You won't be special for long. Now, what shall we have for dinner tonight?'

'There's Carnival, so we'll grab something in Eat Street later.'

'And you have chits for that, do you?'

Martha bats her eyelashes. 'I'll do jobs tomorrow? I'll serf?'

'Here.' Ellie hands over the three chits the customer gave her. 'Don't be too late.'

Back at the house, Martha is getting more and more hyper. She throws me some clothes – jeans that are a bit too tight and a T-shirt that says *Wonder Woman*. It's not my usual style. She giggles as I twirl uncomfortably.

'We don't always get to wear what we want down here. More what's available.'

'It's fine,' I say, undoing the top button of the jeans. 'It's just… I'm starting to think I should steer clear of potato and butter.'

'Maybe. But let's dress up.'

I was thinking we were dressed already, but she opens a drawer and pulls out strings of jewellery and a handful of bronze feathers. They look like the feathers plucked from our chicken.

'We have to express ourselves!' She throws stuff around, telling me to put things on, then take them off again. Thin metal bracelets that tinkle against each other. Necklaces with plastic beads that clink together with a satisfying sound. When I move, I rattle like a viper in *Mexico Alive*. Then Martha plays with my hair, enquiring whether shaved sides is a London Star trend. Just my own, I tell her. She makes two long braids with the rest of my hair, interlaced with the beautiful bronze feathers.

'How is this expressing myself?'

'I don't know!' she shrieks. 'And who cares! You look amazing. Gorgeous!'

I blush. 'Do you want me to do your hair?'

She hangs her head upside-down between her knees and ruffles it. When she's upright, her hair is a messy ball of spikes.

'Done!' She laughs. 'Come on!'

We head out to Eat Street, where Martha makes me

eat some vegetables wrapped in flimsy bread. I'd rather have chilli trash crabs, but she says that's not a good idea before Carnival, and does a fake burp to show why. Then we weave down the tunnelled streets to Bank.

Bank is an old station, she tells me, a bit like the place we caught the cart to chicken man. But Bank goes deep, deep underground. We run down several flights of steps, and we're not the only ones. Throngs of people are alongside us, and we're all headed for a cart train. I try to put aside my bad memories of the previous ride as we climb aboard. The carts fill up quickly, and I lose Martha as people push and shove to get on. They leap on and off carts to find room or sit by friends. When everyone settles, I see that Martha's not in my cart, and I'm suddenly self-conscious, all dressed up without my friend alongside. But worries about my clothes disappear when I see I fit right in. I'm dressed up for a social, London Under-style. And there's no set fashion. Anything goes.

There's denim, leather, loud prints, black lace. Hair up, down, styled and dyed.

Back home, fashion changes all the time, but we usually wear something fitted and stretchy. People like to show off how fit they are – unless they're unfit, in which case they wear baggy sportswear to make you think they're in the process of getting fit. Here, it looks as if no one cares about the body underneath. Slim, big, in between – it just doesn't matter. As the carts pick up speed, all our colourful raggedy tops look like flags flying in the wind.

We career down endless tunnels, lurching to and fro, and I start to feel a fluttering in my stomach again. I don't know if it's the motion or the apprehension. There's a vibe I'm picking up on. A strange sensation that prickles my skin – but it's not fear. It's anticipation. Something big is going to happen. And it's not just me. Everyone seems tense with excitement, like the crowds at an arcade but more joyful. We aren't a chanting mob with money riding on winners; we're a group of adventurers. I grin as people call to each other over the rattle of the cart's wheels, and then I hear shrieks and yells of encouragement. I turn to see a girl two carts down standing up, body swaying. Her arms are out wide and her knees are bent to take in the shakes and trembles of the ride. There's a jolt – something on the tunnel floor? All the carts bump over it, one after the other, and she falls over. There are cheers. Then a boy stands up to take his turn, survives two huge bumps and punches his fists in the air like a victor. The carts swerve around a corner and he tumbles, as his friends jeer. I don't know where Martha is – it's impossible to see – but I think she's somewhere ahead of me. There are about ten people in my cart, and not a single face I recognise. Some look at me oddly. One girl smiles at me like I'm an old friend.

'She's invited,' she says to the others, and a few lean over to pat my leg.

'News travels fast.' I smile, still wondering about the significance of being 'invited'. I know I'm not the first Star citizen to join London Under. Dr Orta came long before me. I wonder if there are others.

'That's because there's not usually much news. You're a hot topic!'

Another girl shakes my hand warmly and pulls me to my feet. Friendly but swaggering. 'Let's see what you're made of!'

I've surfed countless times – I know how to balance, duck and adjust my weight on the hoverboard. Then, I did it for points. But this is pure fun, and I'm grinning ear to ear with the challenge. Keeping my knees loose, I begin to ride the bumps and jerks of the cart as it hurtles through the dark tunnels. I stay up, long after my new companion has fallen, and people begin to notice. The girl in the cart behind gets up again, and one in the cart in front. We're in a spontaneous surfing competition, on the way to a party, and nothing ever, ever felt this good before. My name is fed through the crowds and before long I hear it repeated, over and over again. *Alara, Alara, Alara!* People are on my side. They are *on my side.*

I'm standing, right until the end, when the cart stops with an almighty jolt. I fall, but hands reach for me. As I try to climb out of the cart, somebody slides their arms around my thighs and hoists me up onto their shoulder, and I am carried, horizontal, like a bird in flight. Champion cart-surfer. I spy Martha in the crowd.

'Martha!'

She's looking for me, searching for my voice.

'Martha!'

'Martha!' booms the man whose shoulder I'm on, and she turns and waves.

I thank him, jump off and run towards her. She grabs my hand and grins, and then we wait – fifty, sixty, seventy of us – at the top of another flight of stairs, which leads even deeper underground. A chain of people holding hands blocks us from going further. They grin at us, point out people of interest to each other – crazy outfits, mad make-up. People they like the look of, maybe. Crowds build behind us as we wait. It's my nightmare, but I'm not scared. I'm impatient. I don't want this feeling of excitement to fade.

'What are we waiting for?'

'Patience, girl! They'll give a signal at any moment.'

It's not just me; we're all bouncing on the balls of our feet. Face-painters squeeze through the crowd with pots of glitter. Martha gets a green glitter stripe down her nose. Then the glitter girl stands in front of me, sucking in her cheeks, looking thoughtful.

'Alara, right?' she says. 'Something extra special for you. Welcome to London Under.' She dabs at my cheeks then moves away.

'What has she done?' I ask Martha.

'Given you rays of gold under your eyes. Looks cute.'

All around us, people are sparkling: cheeks glittering,

eyes gleaming. Conversation and laughter are kept low and close by the tunnel walls, and the buzz is comforting. As if we're a friendly swarm, a team.

There's a long screech. Some kind of horn. It echoes through the tunnels below us – an eerie wail, making my hair stand on end. Haunting. It can't be good.

But the chain in front of us breaks and everyone around me cheers – a huge rush of happiness – and we all surge forward. And from deep underground, a drumming starts.

There are stairs in London Star, but nobody takes them – not when a lift can get you anywhere in seconds – and the shock of running down steps at full speed scares and thrills me at the same time. As if keeping up with our feet, the drumming gets faster. It sounds like a hundred drumbeats, but louder, rawer than I've ever heard. It's all way more than everything I've ever experienced before; I have no point of reference. It's magnified, huge, overwhelming.

At the bottom of the steps we follow the sound down the tunnels. Someone hands us a torch – a flaming rag on a stick – and now we're part of a wild procession. It's dangerous – fire and feathers. There are yelps as people accidentally brush against flames. But the tunnel widens and people spread out, and it's here that some start to run. Others wrap their arms around each other and skip, talking and laughing. Martha and I sprint. The drums make my nerves jangle. We get closer and they get louder

– so loud, it's like the beat isn't in my ears but under my skin, my ribs, my hips, my heart. I am a wire stretched tight, vibrating with every sound and movement. I'm so full of sensation, I feel like I might either laugh or vomit.

We break through into a large underground chamber. More tunnels branch away from it, and another staircase leads up and away. Standing on its stairs, twenty drummers – boys and girls, their muscles gleaming with sweat and glitter – beat out the roll and punch. There's no tune, no synthesised strings, piano or bass; it's just drums. Continuous, whirring like a river, purring like an engine.

It stops suddenly, but everyone around me is on the balls of their feet, like they know what's coming next. They're waiting for something. I feel the vibrations of their excitement; I'm excited too. The drummers laugh, seeing us wait, like sprinters waiting for the starting gun. They tease us with their grins.

'Now *this* is Carnival!' Martha shouts, shaking her hands in the air, jogging on the spot.

The silence persists, drawing us all in. We hold our breath.

Bang! The drums start up again. Full volume, full speed. There are whistles. Bleats of high-pitched shrills pierce the air and we're dancing, all of us. I can't stop. It's like I'm a puppet, forced to skip and jump. It's like losing control. It's like nothing a Sensii download has ever done. I'm scared of it. Like it'll eat me up.

And I love it.

The drummers stop for a break and there's an interval act – a few guys who can mimic drumming and all sorts of sounds just using their mouths. They're great, but it doesn't replace the vibe of Carnival drumming. I've lost Martha again. But as I search for her, I see the bearded man – deadpan, unruffled. He hasn't been dancing and he's not looking at the musicians; he's watching the crowds. I don't want to be anywhere near him, so I move to the outside of the throng and into one of the tunnels where other people are heading to cool off and catch their breath. I find a space and slide down a tunnel wall, back flat against the cool concrete, legs outstretched. There is sweat covering my body from head to toe. For someone who used to go nowhere without a second-skin, it feels strangely good.

A bottle of water appears in front of me.

'Here.'

It's Jay. He's wearing jeans and a red T-shirt, kind of threadbare, dark sweat patches on his chest and under his arms. 'Can I join you, Wonder Woman?'

I take the bottle and swig. I had no idea I was this thirsty, and I gulp it again and again, only realising how rude I've been when I've drained the last drop.

'I'm so sorry…' I start, but he has another bottle in his other hand.

'You should be sorry. You didn't do it right.' He drinks half then tips the other half over his head, shaking his hair and spraying me. I shriek. He mimics me, shrieking back. He is so like Vim in this moment.

'Have we met?' I ask.

'I didn't realise I was so easily forgettable.'

'No, that's not what I mean. I mean, I feel like I've seen you before. Before all this.'

He looks into my eyes, unflinching. Then he flutters his eyelashes. 'Maybe you saw me in your dreams!'

I laugh so hard, I surprise myself. And he grins too, like he wasn't expecting himself to be that spontaneous. Or corny.

'If I saw you in my dreams, then that was in *your* dreams!'

He nods maybe.

The drums are starting up again. *Buddum, buddum, brrrrrrr, buddum.*

'Come on, let's dance!' he calls, scrambling to his feet. 'I love Carnival. I don't know how I ever lived without it.'

We head back towards the heart-thumping music. It feels good being with Jay. Natural. He doesn't cling like Martha, but he's not afraid to be playful. My heart feels satisfied and warm, like it's full of buttery potato. We stick close together in the crowd, jumping for what feels like hours. Every now and then the drummers fall silent – a sign they're about to change pace or rhythm – and in those moments, we freeze and grin at each other, drumming our palms on our thighs and hitting each other's hands, waiting for the next burst of noise.

One time, the drums fall silent but the whistles continue – *peep, peep, pip, pip, peeeeep* – and Jay lifts me up so I can see the feather parade: a dancing line of fancy-dress costumes, with show-off headdresses.

'You should be in there,' he says, reaching up and tugging one of my plaits, woven with feathers.

'It's a dead chicken.'

'No one wears a dead chicken like you do,' he shouts happily. 'Come on. The parade takes a while, and once you've seen one feather, you've seen them all. Let's go find somewhere quiet.'

He yanks me out of the crowd and into a side tunnel. But I keep turning to look behind me, my gaze glued to the throng of people, with their colours and their dancing and their drumming. It's just so happy. And I feel different. Something inside me has changed. Recalibrated. Maybe I feel happy, too.

Chapter 19

We pass groups chatting, people play-fighting, eating, scratching words into walls. Kissing. I try not to stare at them, because there's no way they're old enough – not by Estrella's standards – and it makes me feel strange. Jay pulls me further into the tunnel network, cutting through interconnecting alleyways, until we find an empty space. The noise of Carnival is just a pulsing echo from here. Apart from the scuffle of feet and soft laughter in a parallel passage, we are alone and it's quiet.

Jay takes a seat on the cold floor. He pats the space next to him.

'So what do you think of Carnival? Good, right?'

'It's amazing. I've never heard anything like it. *Felt* anything like it…'

He's smiling at me, like I'm a child. I remember his own childish glee as we danced in the crowd, jumping on the balls of our feet, ears full of rhythms. It was almost like it was his first time, too.

'You said … you said you don't know how you ever lived without it. What did you mean?'

Jay hugs his knees and rocks backwards and forwards, thinking. And I push him, rocking him even more, until he plants his hands on the floor. He looks me in the eye and bites his lip. The mood has changed.

'Alara, I was invited.'

'You were invited? *Invited*? Will anyone ever tell me what the hell that means?'

'It means that I came from Estrella.'

Jay tells me everything, from the beginning. That he'd been researching existence outside London Star for a long time. If anyone had checked his Synthia search history, they'd have found reams of queries – from the basic melodramatic stuff like 'is there more to life?' to the more extreme, like how to scale skyscraper walls or make protective wear using products from the home. And someone *had* checked his search history, it turns out. The intelligence guys in London Under. Because, contrary to how London Under functions on a daily basis, the technology it owns is way ahead of itself. There are locked rooms full of technology that would blow the mind of the ordinary London Under citizen.

'They have keywords like "boredom", "explore", "escape". You see, we can hack Synthias. Every time someone types one of those terms into a Synthia, there's an alert down here. When one person starts to set off alerts regularly, they're put on a watch list. We watch them.'

'And they watched you?'

'They watched and they researched. They found out my skills and reckoned that I'd be useful down here. When they were certain that I really wanted to leave London Star, they contacted me via a Synthia infiltration.'

'How could they be sure you'd leave?'

'First, they sent messages that were designed to look like glitches, just to see how I would react. I reacted well, of course. I started to search deeper, ask my Synthia more probing questions.'

'But what if Advice saw all this too?'

'Ah, this is where the Under guys are clever. They infiltrate with a *fake* Synthia browser. The searches I made didn't go through the main system. They were diverted directly to the fake browser. And then they were responsible for every response that Synthia gave back.'

'So it was completely off the radar?'

'Yes. It was very clever. Because I thought it was a glitch, I assumed it was an information leak – stuff that I wasn't allowed to be seeing – so I lapped it up, and of course I asked for more and more information.'

'And that told London Under all they needed to know.'

'Right. When they were sure I'd commit, they revealed who they were.'

And who are they exactly? Jay tells me that the community was established at the time Estrella was built. The founders were a mix of people who, for whatever reasons, didn't want to comply. Some didn't believe the place would be toxic for long; some hated technology; and others rebelled on principle, thinking the catastrophe wasn't an accident at all, but an excuse to impose a new world order. And so, as most survivors boarded ships to take them to quarantine islands in the North Sea while London Star was being constructed, they went underground. Since then, they've led primitive lives – they still do – but they needed medical expertise and technical help. A team known as Progress recruits skilled London Star dissenters. Dissenters like Jay. And now Jay helps with the recruiting.

He has recruited plenty of people. Doctors, scientists, farmers. At this, I find myself tearing up. To think of the people that went missing, presumed dead, and the families and friends mourning them. I am momentarily angry for them. I think of Moles and his sorrow. And then I mention Moles, because maybe... But Jay says he never knew a Nate in London Star. He lived in South-West 63.

I'm disappointed. But still, in SW63 there is a family who has lost a son. Who knows? Maybe they watch their refuse teams returning from work through binoculars, waiting for news of a body, like I do.

If I'd been invited like they had ... if I was going for

good, I'd have found a way to prepare my family in some way, to let them know they needn't worry. But I haven't been invited, and I realise that I'm not comfortable with that. Although it's more than discomfort, now. It's envy. I feel like a hanger-on at a party.

'If I'd been on your watch list, would you have invited me?'

Jay laughs a little. 'No.'

'Why not?'

He smiles at me sweetly. 'Because what use would you be?'

'Thanks a bunch.'

'Come on, don't be like that. You're not a doctor, a communications expert, a farmer. You're good at games. And down here, we don't have games. Don't take it personally.' He nudges me playfully. 'But who needs an invitation when you're Alara the Unstoppable? I've heard the news, by the way. Everyone's talking about it. Be honest with me. Are you really staying?'

'If I said no, what would you do?'

'I don't know. But I'd advise you not to say no – not any place someone might hear you, anyway.'

'Or what? They'd kill me?' I laugh. But Jay doesn't answer, and I remember the bearded man and the lovely Mark, and briefly imagine finding myself down a dark tunnel at the business end of a blade...

Jay's eyes flicker, as if he's picturing that, too.

'I said I'd stay,' I say again, nodding.

'I believe you. Let's hope *they* believe you.'

'What will it take?'

'I don't know. Tonight is a good start, though. They'll have spies out. They'll see how much you enjoy Carnival.' He takes my hand. Runs his finger up the inside of my arm and stops just before my bandaged armpit. He chuckles. 'Imagine the money you could make if you'd uploaded Carnival...'

'So much money!' I laugh.

'Can you imagine never experiencing it again?'

That winds me unexpectedly. Imagine going back to a life without Carnival. Imagine sitting at my window in London Star, knowing that I would be missing out on the best fun I've had in my entire life. But imagine *not* going back. Never being around to tease Gavi, or beg Moles for a morsel of his friendship, or feel Mum's hugs or hear Dad calling me Banana.

Live with a crazy bunch of strangers – or be at home, safe and loved. What a choice.

Jay clicks his fingers in front of my face. 'Hey, what are you doing tomorrow?'

'I don't know. I think Ellie said we had to serf.'

He thinks for a minute. 'Before you go, there's something I want to show you.'

'What?'

'You'll see. Come on, we'd better get back.' He pulls me to my feet and we walk in silence through the maze of tunnels.

After the noise and the exercise, my head has suddenly starting hurting and my legs feel tight and sore. Jay gets out a torch and flicks it up and over the tunnel walls, illuminating graffiti from centuries back. *Kaz luvs Gupta. Hang Parliament. Stink City.*

'Remember doing Old London in Civilisation?' he says, breaking the silence. 'This was their underground train system. Trains criss-crossed the city for miles and miles. Freedom of movement. Cheap. We're still excavating it all.'

'What about the foundations – of the skyscrapers? I haven't seen any down here. Do you ever hit one of them by mistake?'

'No way. And you won't see them, because they're protected – encased in concrete that's metres thick.' He regards me out of the corner of his eye. 'Weird thing to be interested in.'

'Just wondering, that's all. I guess if you hit one by mistake, then Star would know you're here.'

'We know the exact location of every scraper's foot. Like I say, each one is encased. Each excavation is planned. We have no desire to wake up Advice. Besides, we've got tunnels that go beyond the boundary of Estrella anyway. There's no reason for us to dig anywhere near the towers ever again.'

'Where are you digging to, then?'

'Just out. Further and further out until we get to the sea.'

‘I’d like to get to the sea,’ I whisper.

He reaches out and we hold hands. My palm, pressed against his, burns as if I’m holding hot coals. The heat spreads along my arm and into my body, and my stomach flips like a pancake. I think I know what this is. If I was connected to Sensii, it would alert Advice. I’m only sixteen … this shouldn’t be happening. It’s not normal. But it feels right.

We join up with a group making their way back to Carnival from another tunnel, and Jay drops my hand, running to catch up with them. Mark is in the crowd, too; he’s watching me. And behind him, the man with the beard.

People who see right through me.

I run as fast as I can back to Carnival.

Chapter 20

A sign says *Spitalfields Market,* but Martha calls it the workplace. We are here to serf, along with others of all ages waiting to find out what's on offer. Serfing is work, I know that much, but it's work by choice, and there is laughter as we wait. A small group strum their guitars and bang on crates and boxes to make a beat; it's a song I don't know, but people sing along. A young boy, not missing an opportunity for business, walks between us with freshly baked bread rolls. Their smothering, doughy scent is irresistible. I reach for one, but Martha snatches my hand back. We are here to earn chits, not give them away, she chides. And she reminds me that Ellie made me mashed pumpkin for breakfast, which I had with butter and salt. It was sweet and filling, but I'm so tired after Carnival that I need to eat to stay awake.

I don't know what time we went to bed, but it was probably morning. There is no colour-changing sky to give us a clue to the time down here. My legs had turned to lead by the time we made our way up and out of the deeper tunnels, and my eyes snapped shut as soon as my head hit the pillow. I didn't stir until Martha shook me awake. Another night without expanding my map. And today is – what? – day three. I'm expected home tomorrow. I feel sick at the thought. It's my last chance to gather information. But it's not just that. It's my last day of feeling my pulse racing, of experiencing new things in the vibrant quest that even Burbeck wouldn't be able to conjure up in his dark, decrepit mind.

The crowd quietens and forms into loose groups, based on their skills. Martha shuffles left and pulls me with her.

'Where are we going?' I whisper.

'Cleaning.'

'Cleaning?'

'Yes. Something tells me you're not up for hard physical labour today, or anything that requires brain power.'

She has a point. We join Cleaning with several others, some of whom change their minds when they see friends elsewhere or spot too much competition. All the serf groups morph and mingle, and across the square a line of people waits for us to settle.

'Who are they?'

'People who need serfs, of course!' Martha shakes her head at me. 'Definitely not up for brain power…'

One by one, the employers approach groups and quote the jobs that need doing. The jobs are varied: wall-building, sweeping, childminding, cooking. The serfs put their hands up and are selected, one by one. Those who aren't chosen from one group move into another. Three left over from the Odd Jobs category next to us move into Cleaning, and some of the Cleaning serfs tut. It means there's now a higher chance of rejects in our group, although Martha explains that it's all for show – no one goes without. There are always things that can be done for food and drink, and there are kind people like Ellie who provide, regardless. Everyone will get their three square meals.

I notice the serfs offering hard labour disappear fast; hard labour is in demand because of the ongoing excavation. I suddenly remember that's why I'm here: to check where they're excavating. Cleaning is going to be such a waste of time. It's not going to add anything to the map – and, worse than that, the dirt and dust down here are never-ending; the thought of a day down a filthy tunnel makes my spirit crumple. I realise I'm craving light.

'Where's the salvaging group?' I ask Martha. 'Shouldn't we be doing that? Then we can earn and find stuff for the salvage shop…'

'It's called raiding, and raiding is a night job, stupid. No one is allowed up there during daylight. Not so close to the Spikes.' She points to the roof above our heads.

When our time comes, we put our hands up for every job: cleaning houses, scrubbing carts, washing clothes. We're picked together for laundry duty, and the lady says she'll pay us four chits each for the day, and feed us. It doesn't sound bad, but Martha informs me that laundry gives you blisters on your fingers. But with chit jobs running out, we don't have much choice. We fall in line with three others, shuffling slowly out of Spitalfields for our day's work.

Then we stop. I can't see properly above the others' heads, but our employer is talking to someone. She motions for me and Martha to stand aside, and chooses others to take our place. Why? I hope it's not Michael. I hope it's nothing to do with me. Other girls jostle in front of us, ready to offer themselves for work, and Martha starts to complain. But then I see the cause of the disruption. Silently, Jay points his finger at us and beckons. We follow without saying a word until we're away from the crowds.

'What was that about?' Martha snaps. 'We were about to make eight chits between us!'

'I need you.'

'And what will you pay?'

'That is irrelevant, as you know,' Jay says sternly. 'But since you ask, I'll pay you ten each.'

Martha's mouth drops open. 'Ten! What do we have to do for that? Kiss your feet?'

Jay smirks. 'While my feet could do with kissing,

there isn't time. Martha, you'll be in the tech building, doing whatever the guys there tell you to do – making drinks, sorting through wires, labelling chips. Alara, you're coming with me.'

Martha shoots me a look I can't decipher. Suspicion, or jealousy perhaps? But she doesn't say anything. She just peels away, leaving Jay and me to continue, walking apart in silence, until we get to a stairway that goes down. It's a travel tunnel. I'm disappointed. I hoped we'd be going up. I am desperate for sun. If I saw some, I'd probably run and cluck in its rays like one of the crazed chickens.

'Stay here. I'll be back in ten minutes. Here.' Jay passes me a bread roll, no longer warm but still soft, its insides damp with melted butter.

I sit at the top of the stairs and sink my teeth into the bread. Kids on bikes shoot past me, ricocheting down the stairs as they set off on bot-brained adventures. Other kids walk past, playing a hand-slapping game – slapping too hard sometimes. There are screams and laughs. Pushing, shoving. Adults usher them on; they're late for woodcraft. These kids will learn to make things; at the end of the day they'll find splinters embedded in their skin, and they will hammer their fingers and cry. That doesn't happen in London Star. In London Star, everything is made for you by printing machines or people in other countries. It's an easy life.

'Alara, I'd like you to meet Freddie.'

Jay's back, and there is a child hiding behind his legs. Jay pulls him out and places his hands on the boy's shoulders. Freddie smiles. It's an unusual smile. His eyes, too, are different. Pink-rimmed and shaped like almonds. The boy puts his fist in his mouth. I look up at Jay, then back at Freddie, unsure what to do.

'What do you say, Freddie?'

'How choo,' the boy slurs around the knuckles still in his mouth.

'Hi, Freddie.' I shrug at Jay, but Jay ignores my confusion and motions for us to go down the stairs.

He tells the driver we are going to the end of the line, and we board a cart with another couple. Freddie sits on the floor and plays with the laces on Jay's shoe, and Jay avoids my eyes. I don't want to be caught looking at him, or staring at the strange child, so I look straight ahead. I had been hoping – even aching – to see Jay again, but not in this way, not with me confused and him refusing to explain anything. Annoyed, I cross my arms and shut my eyes. I doze, catching up on some of the sleep Carnival stole.

When I wake, I realise my head is in Jay's lap. I start.

'It's about time you woke up, sleepyhead. You're missing the view.'

'Ha,' I mutter, rubbing my eyes.

'Okay, you haven't missed anything. Do you feel better?'

'Not yet.'

'You will. You will. Come on, Freddie.' Jay nudges the boy, and he holds on to Jay's knees and pulls himself up. 'We're nearly there. But shhhh!' Jay holds his fingers to his lips. 'Don't tell Alara where we're going.'

Freddie grins his lopsided grin. He points to my nose and leans forward, trying to touch it. I stiffen. Jay gently moves his hand away.

'You can't go touching people's noses without asking first,' he explains. He's way too young to be a dad, but he's good and kind. But I still don't get what's wrong with his child, and he's made it clear I can't ask.

The other couple in the cart smile along; they also look at Freddie as if he's different. There's a softness in their eyes, and an understanding. I could do with some of that. They get off a stop before the end, and I watch them head up a tunnel to street level. I don't know where we are, but I know we're far from the centre of London Under.

'Some people choose solitude,' Jay says, reading my mind. 'They hire labour, excavate themselves a hidden corner, live their lives peacefully. Nice, don't you think?'

I don't have time to answer. The battery-powered buggy at the front stops. The tunnel is walled off. There's nowhere else to go. We're literally at the end of the line. I imagine the mapping going on in my head. Surely, I've gone above and beyond for Star now? I wonder if they'll give me a special honour.

'Come on, daydreamer. This is our stop.'

Jay leaps off the cart and helps Freddie down, then me. The cart driver unhooks his buggy and drives it to the last cart, ready to take it all the way back to where we came from.

'Right, come here.' Jay pulls me towards him and turns me round. I get to see those eyes again, and I want to hold his hand again, too. But there's Dilly. I have questions.

'Jay, can I –'

'Stop talking.'

He ties a blindfold around my eyes. Although I'm tired of being blinded, sedated, kept in the dark, I can tell by his gentleness that this isn't for ugly reasons. Although what reason could there be to hide our surroundings? Apart from the chicken farm, everything's been the same. Dirty buildings and red clay.

We walk into a passage. I can touch the walls on either side without even stretching my arms. They are uneven, rough, crumbling. I raise my hand and find a low ceiling, and the feeling of being trapped starts to grip me again. My breathing becomes heavy and laboured.

'Breathe in through your nose for seven, then out through your mouth for eight. In for seven, out for eight. It'll help.'

Gripping Jay's shirt and counting and breathing, my heart begins to slow to a more comfortable thud. Up ahead I can hear Freddie skipping and stumbling, and Jay's encouraging words, warm and fatherly. My mind is screaming with curiosity about Jay and his private life, but I focus on regulating my breathing.

After a while, I notice there's more pressure on my thighs, my ankles… We are walking uphill. I can hear Jay pushing Freddie along, grunting with effort. My strides become short and awkward. What could be worth this journey?

We come to a stop, and I hear Jay fiddling with something – something metal – the latch of a door, perhaps. Then his hand wraps around mine. He pulls me forward onto wide, earth steps, and we climb up and up.

Finally, fresh air hits my face. We're outside. We're *outside*! We're on the surface! My hands fly to the blindfold.

'Alara, do it slowly. Take your time.' Jay's voice is amused, warm.

I slowly pull the cloth downwards. Bright light sears my eyelids, and I blink as patches of colour come into focus. Soft colours. Space. Swathes of light and emptiness. We are above ground, but where are the rubbish dumps of London Star? Where is the Void?

We are in a field of swaying grass, light green, shot with gold, surrounded by forest. Everywhere I look, there are various shades of green, illuminated by the mid-morning sun. *Green. Real green.* I gasp, as if the colour is climbing down my throat and filling my heart too fast, too full.

'Oh, my gosh … it's green! It's green, Jay!'

'Green, s'green, Jay!' Freddie says.

'Come on, then – dive in!' Jay calls, gathering Freddie in his arms. They run ahead, Freddie laughing as the long grasses tickle his arms.

This is the opposite of Carnival, with its thumping underground sounds that strummed my nerves, but it's just as visceral. It sings under my skin. The breeze runs through my veins and makes my lips tingle, the colours seep through my every pore, and I am smiling, drunk on joy. It feels right, as if this is where I belong – where we all belong, with nature, colour, the wind, rain and sun. And it's not an ambience screen. It's real. Real.

We run – Jay, Freddie and me – across the field and into the forest, where the trees soak up the wind. The air here is still but thick with a presence, as if the trees have eyes and creatures lurk behind every trunk. I reach for Jay's hand, like I do with Vim exploring *Wilderness,* because this is the wilderness, and we walk on the soft forest floor, which is covered in pine needles, damp and springy underfoot.

'Where are we going?'

He doesn't answer. We walk along a well-trodden path towards a hut hidden deep in the trees.

Chapter 21

'It's not much, but it's mine,' Jay says.

Rough built, like everything outside London Star, it looks as if it might house an animal. Outside, tools, buckets, nets and logs are stacked against the walls, and large stones circle a mound of ash, where a fire has been lit. It's straight out of *Wilderness*.

Jay pushes hard against the warped door, which sticks in its frame.

Inside the cabin, there isn't much: a bed, a table, two chairs. Beneath the single window there's a sink, and beneath that a tank of water; cupboards on either side contain pots and pans. Jay gets some of them out, along with wooden spoons, and gives them to Freddie, who bashes them like drums.

'Come on.' Jay leads me back outside and shuts the door, bolting it with a wooden plank. He clocks my expression. 'Left to his own devices, he'll play orchestra for hours. It's perfectly safe. He'll be okay for a few minutes.' He grabs one of the buckets. 'Let's go fetch some fish.'

On the other side of the cabin, a path winds through the forest and down to a grass bank. Below it is a pebbled beach, and on the beach are tubular fishing nets – fine mesh stretched over a wooden ring – for snaring trout. Jay wants to explain them to me, but I'm drawn to the river just beyond, which oozes past us, lazy with summer and the lack of rain. I crouch and dip my hand in the water. Despite the weather, the river is ice cold, like the water from the pump. I keep my hand submerged until my fingers go numb. Jay paddles past me, wading into the water, stumbling over hidden stones. He places nets in the centre of the river, wedging them into position with flat river rocks. Large-winged insects flit above the sparkling water, their bodies bright green and yellow. They don't stay still long enough for me to inspect – they're too fast, dancing like glitter on the wind.

'Dragonflies,' Jay says. 'Beautiful, aren't they? You can see them close up in midsummer, when the river is even slower. So much happens here. I'll never get bored of it.' He lowers his cupped hands into the river and fills them with water, which he tosses back at me. I gasp at the cold.

'Feel that? Can you *feel* it? It's real, Alara. This is all real. No Sensii trip can give you the shock of fresh spring water. Or the taste. Drink. Drink it.' He slurps a handful and lets out a big sigh. 'No chemicals, no cleaning process, no added goodness. Just pure H2O.'

I reach forward, but Jay is in front of me, cupped hands already full of water. He tips it into my mouth. It pours in, freezing and refreshing. Rather than gulp it, I let it slide down the back of my throat.

'Good, right?'

My head is fresh and light, as if it's a room that has been cleaned of junk and had the windows thrown open. I look around me, at the fields the other side of the river and at the forest behind, at the layered shades of green under the open sky. Jay stands behind me and puts his arms around my waist. If I hadn't got so used to Martha's constant touching, I would have flinched. But this simple, unexpected gesture of friendship feels okay. More than okay. I sense tenderness. And something else, perhaps, but I don't know what. I've never felt it before. Not with Moles. Not even with Vim, and I felt I could do or say anything with him. Maybe I can with Jay.

'Jay, who *is* Freddie? Is he yours?'

He doesn't let go of me as I expected, but rests his chin on my shoulder.

'Freddie is Dilly's, but not mine and Dilly's. Just Dilly's. She's a dressmaker, so I look after him when she has to work.'

'He's a bit ... strange...'

'He has a chromosome disorder.'

'But his face is...'

Jay breaks away from me and points into the distance. 'They don't have syndromes over there in London Star. They don't have syndromes or disorders or disabilities –' He sees my confusion. 'But that's just life. It's not Freddie who's not normal. It's us. *We* are not normal. You and I – we are *not normal*.' Jay pauses. He's breathing heavily, as if he's frustrated. 'We're modified. Our genes are twisted, manipulated, selected like food from a menu. You, me. We're free of disease and the genetic problems of our ancestors – free of natural eye colour, even.' Jay spits the words, as if they taste bad. 'We're so unnatural, it's ridiculous we even call ourselves human.' He punches his chest. 'No heart problems here.' His stomach. 'Guts in perfect working order.' Taps his head. 'And they almost got my brain. Almost.' His eyes are flaring. 'So next time you wonder what is or isn't advised, wonder this: in Estrella, is it advisable to be human at all?'

I don't know what to say. I'm not even sure what he's talking about. His mood has changed. He is not Vim, after all.

Jay stands, staring at the horizon, his hands on his hips. I chew over his words and try to make them mean something. Of course, I know about gene therapy and gene 'washing', which is what they do in the embryo clinics. But it's for the greater good, and eradicating human imperfections means progressing as a species. Gene manipulation is just a cure, like the old-time vaccinations, but on a larger scale and less invasive. All the curing happens before we have a chance to go wrong. And isn't it human nature to want to make bad things better, to self-improve? That's what I've always thought.

But Jay's words are like ink in water, discolouring everything that I thought had been so clear. And then his voice is back again, softer, kinder.

'We're different, Alara. The embryo therapy didn't quite work with us, did it?'

'What do you mean?'

'They didn't factor in the rogue genes that might make us less … compliant.'

'Rogue genes? My parents aren't rogue.' I laugh. 'In fact, they're pretty compliant, if you want to use that word.'

'Ah, but they add extra genes – they make babies in clinics using three parents. You just don't get to meet the donor. You wouldn't know that, of course.'

I am stunned.

He nods seriously. 'And *our* donors – yours and mine – must have had different kinds of make-up. They weren't content to be content. Think about it. Our attention spans aren't curbed enough. Our senses not dulled enough. Sensii is an annoyance, not an experience, am I right? They use it to control our every mood, but it doesn't command us like it does the others.'

Dulled. He was dulled? 'You, too?'

'Yes – there are lots of us.'

I've always known that I wasn't like the others, but I

don't understand what Jay is saying. The eugenics centre and Medico used extra donors? Who are they? Does that make me a freak? Although I've always known I was. After all, what other teenager likes to sit in the Botanical Gardens?

I step into the freezing water and wade up to my knees just to remind myself of the feeling. But my silly feet aren't used to walking on a stony riverbed, and I slip.

'Alara!' Jay runs towards me, his serious mood vanished into the sky. He's trying to help me, but I keep rocking and sliding like a beginner on *Tightrope Trials* and he gives in, watching me flail in the water. 'I'm sorry! I'm sorry!' he keeps calling, before falling to his knees, crying with laughter.

Finally, I drag myself out. Freezing. The breeze turns cruel as it plays over my skin, making me sting all over, and there's a clicking sound. I realise it's made by my chattering teeth.

'Here.' Jay strips off his long-sleeved shirt. 'I won't look,' he says, turning away. I strip off my shirt and pull on his. 'The rest of you will dry in the air. Let's get back to Freddie.'

Jay drags out a net containing a couple of trout, and puts the angry, flipping fish in the bucket with some river water. We walk in silence up the bank. I think how I've never experienced cold like this. How everything in London Star is temperate. Even the swimming pools don't drop below twenty-five degrees, and the changing rooms are blasted with warm air. I'd welcome some of that now.

Comfort. Is that the best we can hope for in life?

I think of the old couple in London Under, huddled together in the cart. Are genetic programming, technology and safety really so bad, when the alternatives are illness, discomfort and imperfection? But then there's this, isn't there? There's green. There's Carnival. There's feeling.

And love. Did Advice control that, too? Was Martha's teenage crush normal? Is that the fizz I feel now – the flutter that feels like the tickle of a thousand feathers? Am I acting *normal*? In Star, were our human instincts delayed on purpose? And does that mean that Jay – my real-life Vim – is already taken?

'Is Dilly your girlfriend?'

Jay doesn't answer immediately. He stops and scratches his head. 'People think she is,' he says. He waits. 'And we want people to think that.'

'But you're not?'

'When I arrived here three years ago, I was just fourteen. I was put with Dilly's family until I found my feet. It turns out it wasn't just a nice gesture – they wanted me to serf because Dilly was heavily pregnant and couldn't work. And whoever the father was, he had gone missing. Her parents weren't that understanding and the mood was weird and angry, so I found a place of my own as soon as I could. I said to Dilly that if things ever got too much, she could move in. Freddie was born and as he grew, it become clear that he had a syndrome. Dilly was picked on, teased by idiots with nothing better to do.'

'Why did they tease her? I thought you said it was normal for humans to be born with differences?'

'And it's normal for some humans to be born cruel and stupid. Anyway, Dilly was scared and alone, and I wanted to protect her. By then, I'd gained a good position in London Under; I knew people who could look out for her. I care about her, and Freddie, a great deal.'

'But you're just friends?'

'More like brother and sister. I know people gossip about the age gap. About such a young teenager being a dad. It doesn't bother me what they think. What's important is that you are willing to stand up for people, even if they're not your own.'

'What?' My heart stops.

'You have to stand up for people.'

That's what Vim said. My mind is too cold to process this.

Back at the hut, Freddie is asleep on the floor next to a saucepan. Jay lifts him into the bed and pulls the blankets up over him. Then he takes some clothes out of a cupboard and throws them at me.

'They won't fit, but at least they're not wet.'

Oversized trousers, warm socks, a jumper. I climb into them, knotting everything tight so it doesn't fall off. Invigorated by the low temperatures, but no longer suffering, I feel suddenly, wonderfully energetic, like I've picked up a boost pack in a Sensii game. I run my fingers through my damp hair, tugging at the knots woven by the river. I see Jay watching me, and raise an eyebrow. He blushes, as if he's been caught out.

'How do you like trees?' he says. To break the tension, I guess.

'I love trees. The Botanical Gardens is my favourite place.'

He takes my hand and leads me back outside, where he points to a nearby fir with a thousand branches. Just looking at the top makes me dizzy.

'I've chopped away some of the sprigs so it's easy to climb. Just follow me.'

I've climbed before – virtual climbing, like in *Scar Face*. I've felt the blunt Sensii pressures on my hands and fingertips, but as I start the ascent, I realise that nothing can prepare you for real life. This is raw wood, rough with spikes that push into my skin and under my nails, and a sharp pine-needle scent fills my nostrils. Stupidly, I look down and immediately feel a stab of fear: a fall here won't be punished by 'game over' or a dent to my pride. I'll be battered by branches, cut, bruised. I could die.

Jay climbs fast but checks regularly to make sure I'm okay, and I return a smile that says 'I'm totally fine'. But I'm not. The branches start to thin out near the top; we are dizzyingly far from the ground. He stops and pulls me up alongside him. 'You go ahead of me, just to the next level. Tell me what you see on the other side.'

I do as he says, awkwardly moving past him. I carefully edge my way up to the next branches, finding firm ones for my feet and using the trunk's burls and knots as handholds. On the other side, branches have been cut away to reveal the view.

The view is so vast, I have to hold my breath and close my eyes to stop myself being overwhelmed. I lock my arms around a skinny branch for safety. I only open them again when I'm sure I won't let go.

The tessellated treescape stretches ahead of me, the pointed tips of the tallest evergreens poking through the canopy. Birds dive in and burst out, insect swarms cluster. Then, in the distance, I see them. The skyscrapers of London Star.

They look so small from here, like needles huddled tightly in a pincushion. But it takes my breath away. Not the magnificence, but the lack of it. Our entire society is encapsulated in those few constructions; we are like specimens in test tubes. The smooth white floors, one-way glass, the people, the SpyLogs, the entertainment systems that keep us looking in and not out...

'Alara, are you okay?'

I'm not okay. I'm sobbing and shaking. Jay wraps his hand around my ankle.

'Come down, now. Come down. I've got you.'

I take a last quick look and start to descend. We don't say a word all the way down. I try hard to concentrate on footholds and handholds through my tear-blurred vision and distracting thoughts. Jay stays just below me. He reaches up to tap my foot, to bring my concentration into focus or to show me a good branch to step down onto. A couple of times I catch his eye when I'm looking down. His cocky expression is gone. His face says he understands. And when my feet finally touch the forest floor, I fall into his arms. I don't know what it is. I don't know why I feel so miserable.

'I look at Estrella at least twice a week,' he says. 'To remember what and who I left, and to remind me why.'

'You brought me here to torment me?'

'I'm sorry,' he says. 'But how could I not show you this?'

His words don't help. Because I'm neither here nor there. I'm in limbo – afraid to stay, and now frightened to return. The only place I feel safe is by his side.

'Say you'll stay,' he says.

'I did.'

'Not for them. For me. Say you'll stay.'

This is unfair. Jay has laid out my wildest dreams before me, like some kind of magician. He's taken a sterile life and filled it with trees and grass, rivers and breezes. He's coloured it with sensations I didn't know existed – a freezing splash, a warmth that goes deeper than skin.

So now I have a head full of maps and a heart full of new feelings, and no time left to work through them. What Jay said about Advice – I have no reason to disbelieve him. The control they exert over us, the life they program for us – it makes sense now. But it's my home. And it's only a matter of hours before my family is shattered by men in suits shaking their heads sadly, saying they did all they could. I can't do that to my family. I can't. And I need to shelve my selfish wants and plan my return before Advice knocks on their door. I need to go. Now. Before I'm bewitched any more.

As I gaze at Jay, I fill with sadness.

He is playing with Freddie. He plays with his fingers and toes, counting them over and over again. He occasionally catches my eye and gives a sad smile. He knows that, despite his efforts, I won't stay. My silence said it all. Outside the window, the sunlight dissolves into the forest, and Jay mentions making our way back. I'd almost forgotten about London Under and Ellie and Martha. Hypnotised by the landscape, I'd forgotten everything but what I have right here, right now.

Outside the hut, Jay guts the fish. Freddie whinges. He doesn't want to go back down. Neither do I. The swish of branches in the breeze, the musky smell of sun-warmed leaves – it's so sensual, it's painful. Jay wraps his arms around my waist and rests his head on my shoulder again.

'Okay?'

'Not really.'

He waits for me to explain, but how can I? He doesn't know why I'm really here – or why I really can't stay. The blue sky is yellowing and pinking, and the silhouettes of birds create lines and then paragraphs as they flock to roost in the forest. It's so beautiful, I can't bear it.

I've never felt this way before. And how many times have I said that now? I think of what Jay said: *they use it to control our every mood.* Did he mean that Sensii isn't just used for games, but is designed to control our mood, all day, every day? It can't be. Yet that would explain why down here, without it, my feelings have arrived – some happy, some razor-sharp.

'Is it me?'

'No. Not you, Jay. There are things you don't understand.'

'I want you to stay. But I want you to be happy...'

'I'm not going to be happy, whatever I do. There is no happy ending.'

'Then choose an unhappy ending with me,' he tries, with a weak smile.

I step back. I must stop it before it goes too far and I ruin everything. I'm here on a mission, not a date. They chose me – Advice chose *me* – because I am rational, intelligent, questing. I have to go now, before I compromise everything.

'I need to go home now. Please don't ask questions. But if you like me as much as you say, you won't try to stop me.'

It's a risk. He could tell Mark and Michael. He could seal my fate. But – and maybe I'm just being fooled by the memory of Vim – I feel like he wouldn't betray me.

Not after this perfect day.

Jay's face hardens. He's tried to woo me and it hasn't worked. His pride is hurt.

His sudden cooling-off stabs my heart, but I must stay determined.

'There's a small problem,' he says quietly, pointing at my foot. 'How are you going to get home?'

The question stumps me. I always thought I'd just leave when the time was right. Sneak off, disappear. Walk out. But now I remember there's the tracker, and everywhere eyes are watching me, waiting for a sign of betrayal. Some even wanting it.

We walk back down the tunnel in silence. Even Freddie seems to recognise the change in mood. He sobs all the way, and Jay is too numb to comfort him. I'm numb, too. It's another feeling I haven't had before – not brain-numb, but heart-numb. No sensations, but a flutter of dread in the pit of my stomach.

I'm going to have to make a run for it. Across the Void, tracked and vulnerable. And if I'm caught, will I be dragged back as a trophy or sent tumbling, lacerated and bleeding, into a chasm to be tip-turned? I have no choice. Tonight, in the dead of night, I will go.

We don't say a word in the hour we wait for the cart to come back for us. And then we have a huge journey ahead – miles and miles of rickety cart ride back into London Under.

On board, Jay leans back and shuts his eyes, not even

changing position when, further down the line, people board. I try to play with Freddie, who sits on the floor at our feet with his hand in the bucket, trying to stroke the dead fish. I'm not sure if I should let him, but he seems mesmerised by their slippery sheen. When he picks one up and tries to put it in his mouth, I reach out to stop him, but Freddie is strong and insistent and I end up struggling with him until he relents. He gets upset and shouts, 'Mamma! Mamma!' and I try to cuddle him, but he fights me; passengers in the adjacent cart look concerned. Jay opens his eyes and leans forward to scoop Freddie onto his lap.

'I-I'm sorry,' I say nervously. 'He was –'

'Doesn't matter. Doesn't matter,' Jay murmurs, turning away.

I don't know if he's saying it to me or Freddie, but my cheeks are hot. When we get off the carts and head back up to street level, Jay turns to me with red eyes. 'Take the fish and these chits to Ellie. If anyone asks, say you childminded Freddie while I mended nets.' Jay places the chits in my hand.

I run, aware that it's late – although the darkness down here makes time irrelevant. As I turn a corner, I am hit by the smells of Eat Street. They excited me before, but now I find them stifling and smothering. I long to be above ground again, in the breeze, with the sun on my skin, in a light so bright it forces me to blink. But I can't think of that. Because whatever happens, I won't be there again. If I get back to London Star I will be sealed in once more, and if I'm caught trying to get back there, I might be sent still deeper underground.

I shudder and run through back streets, criss-crossing into new lanes and paths I haven't yet taken. Building the map in my head. If nothing else makes sense to me, the mission does at least. And if I do that well, I've achieved something.

'Alara?'

I stop and turn. It's Mark. His face is set, his brow heavy.

'What are you doing out on your own?'

'I've been serfing,' I reply.

'Really getting into the way of life here, aren't you?'

I nod and try to smile. He walks towards me with his hands in his pockets. I can't take my eyes off them.

'Trouble is,' he continues, 'I don't think I believe you.'

'Don't you?' I gulp, edging backwards. He pulls his right hand from his pocket. The blade glints like a flame under the dull glow of the ceiling lights. 'Mark. I promise you, I –'

'You're London Star scum,' he hisses. 'Your promises don't mean anything to me.' He turns the blade one way then the other, holding it at neck height, stepping closer. 'Stay, go, stay, go,' he mocks. 'It might be easier for everyone if you vanished.'

So it ends here. Prematurely. I put down the bucket of fish and hold up my hands, prepared to deflect the weapon and fight to the death. *Think of him as Kagu. Rip his throat out.* But I'm not as brave as I thought. I'm trembling.

'What is this, Mark?' A deep voice stops his advance. It's the man with the beard. I'm in trouble now. There's two of them and no one else around. Nowhere to go. I think weakly about how Moles calls me Alara Tripp-up – and here I am: tripped right up. The man is striding towards me. But instead of grabbing me, he pushes me aside and stands off against my would-be attacker. 'Why are you holding a knife to that girl's throat?'

Mark steps back, looking at me worriedly. No, he's pleading. I could make things easy for myself, maybe, if I get him a little more onside.

'Well?' The bearded man is losing patience.

'Mark was showing me the best tool for gutting fish,' I stammer, picking up my bucket of trout. 'He said it would be easier to gut with a smaller blade in future. I made a mess of these, see?'

Mark looks at his feet. The man searches my face.

'So long as that's all it was,' he says cautiously. 'Alara, I'm John. If you have any problems, come and find me. Now hop home and take care.'

Without looking again at Mark or John, I run, water thumping against the sides of the bucket, gasping for air like a dying fish. I head for the main streets, where I won't be alone, but my senses are on overdrive: I pick out the smell of laundry soap seeping from the doorways of washer shops, of oil from mechanics and bread from bakers. I hear cries, arguments, laughter. My skin feels tight and my eyes sting with dust and tears. It's like a thousand Sensii trips at once, and I can't take much more – not even Ellie's concern or Martha's playfulness. When I get back to the house, I hope the bucket of fish will distract them from asking too many questions.

'There she is!' Ellie cries as I walk through the door. 'Where have you been?'

'Childminding,' I pant, heaving the bucket onto the table. 'And I brought fish.'

Martha clatters down the stairs and emerges, frowning, clearly trying to shake herself free of a bad mood.

'Hi, Alara.'

'Hi … I got fish.'

'Fishing? Is that what you two were doing?'

'Well, I was babysitting.'

'That kid of his? Have you got childminding experience?'

I pause. 'Yes,' I lie. 'What have you been doing?'

'Nothing worth talking about. I had to untangle wires *all* day. I was so bored I could cry.'

'I'm sorry,' I say.

'That's okay. You can make up for it tonight!' She grins and flies towards me, wrapping her arms around my neck, and again I am subjected to the tiring pull of emotions.

'Oh, right. How?'

‘I don’t know. Maybe we could grab a bite in Eat Street, see if there’s any live music going on. Alright, I’ll be honest. Danny and his friends are going to be at the skate park with guitars and tambourines. I have a little thing for Danny, and I was hoping you might get a little thing with one of his friends. They’re cute, just saying…’ She waggles her eyebrows at me and I make myself smile.

But I all I can think about is running, and how fast I can go.

Chapter 22

Ellie cooks the fish. It's a harsh reality, trading a life for a plate of food, but the trout is moist and flavoursome. No tissue lab could produce this, no matter how many chemicals and additives they injected. On the table is mashed potato, too – a big steaming bowl of it, a crater in the middle cradling chunks of butter. Ellie is disappointed when I only eat a little. Feeding me gives her great pleasure, I note – probably because I wolf down even the lowliest of meals. But I'm on edge, my stomach churned by cart rides and emotions, death threats and fear.

'Do you girls have any plans tonight?' Ellie says, clearing the plates.

'Just going for a walk, nothing much.' Martha winks at me.

'Oh, I see…' Ellie tuts. 'Walking and gawking at boys, perhaps?'

Martha blushes. 'No! Just walking.'

'Well, if you find there's nothing to look at on your walk, you can come back here. I got bored at the shop today so I made a new deck of cards. I'll teach you how to play rummy.'

Martha rolls her eyes. 'Sounds like a heap of fun.'

There's a banging at the door. Ellie throws us her *what now?* look. 'Who is it?'

'Progress.'

Not again. Not again… I try not to show any emotion as my heart drops.

Martha groans and opens the door. The boy outside is probably eighteen years old, but his face is heavily pockmarked. His hair is greasy.

'What is it?'

'Raiding. Your daughter and the other girl are required.'

Ellie steps forward. 'This is late notice,' she says, softly but firmly. 'The girls have made plans. Can't you ask someone else?'

'We're running low on electrics, and there's been a new tip-turn. We need small serfs. We meet at the market square in fifteen minutes.'

Ellie sighs and nods, and shuts the door after him. 'Sorry, girls. But you could do me a favour and keep your eyes peeled for new stock while you're up there. I'm running low.'

'What sort of stuff do you need?' I ask. I wipe my

clammy hands on my trousers as I try to calm myself down. This can't be happening. Not tonight.

'Pots and pans. Anything quirky or interesting for the curio shelf. We can't rely on serf income alone.'

'It's not fair,' says Martha, and Ellie nods sadly. 'I was going to introduce Alara to the music boys. She was looking forward to it.'

Hardly. It would have felt awkward for me, pretending to melt into the culture and custom of London Under, while all the time I was trying to work out when and how to escape. But at least pretending to listen to music would have given me time to think – about what exit to take, and what to do back on the Void. Now there's no time at all – and worse still, the darkest night hours, best for escaping, will be reduced by the raiding expedition. My mission failure is imminent. And what happens if I turn up after four days?

If you're not back in three days, you'll be dead. There it is. It won't be allowed to happen.

'Why do they need small people?' I ask, quickly rejoining the conversation.

'To slip into the new cracks. We're lighter, too. Tip-turn raids are super-dangerous. People get swallowed up all the time. Not us.' Martha laughs, rubbing my arm reassuringly. 'You'll be fine. You're new, so they won't get you to do any of the tricky stuff, and I am an expert.'

'There's no such thing as an expert,' Ellie scolds. 'Take every step as if you were a beginner.'

We dress in what Martha calls scavenger gear. Thick trousers – proper denim, she tells me – and tough leather boots. She makes me layer up, with several T-shirts, then jumpers, one on top of another. She says it's for protection. I'm confused.

'This won't protect against the toxins, will it?'

'What toxins? There's only dust.' Martha laughs. I remember when I was stripped of my hazard suit, when I saw that my captors weren't wearing them either. How Freddie, Jay and I wandered through a forest, breathing just fine. Had Advice become so accustomed to taking precautions that they'd never checked to see if there was still a need? Or did they know the poison had gone?

'What's scavenger gear for, then, if there's no poison?'

'It's for if you get cut on the trash. You could bleed to death. Or your cut could get badly infected. Here, put on another one. And these gloves.'

I feel swaddled, double my size, and wonder how I'll qualify to be small and nimble for the kind of work they want us to do. And how long will it take? It could be hours, Martha tells me. 'Hours' takes us till morning. No plan and no chance, I realise, as I struggle to pull a sock over my tracker. Where are my quick thinking and resourcefulness now?

Martha smiles pityingly. 'Aw, Alara – scared of hard work!' She laughs, throwing me a backpack. 'It's actually fun. If you like being scared, that is. I won't lie. It can completely shake you up. But we'll stay close to some of the experts. Mum's wrong, by the way; there *are* experts. We'll be fine.'

Wearing empty rucksacks on our backs, we walk towards Spitalfields. It's late, and the usual noises of life underground have quietened. There is an occasional cough, but the only other sound is our feet, scuffing. The strings of lights still twinkle from the ceiling. If it weren't for the habits of mankind, there would be no night and day down here. As we get close, I spot others walking silently in the same direction.

'We're nearly there,' Martha whispers. 'So here are a couple of rules. Stay low. You mustn't risk being seen, and also that way your centre of gravity will be lower and you'll be less likely to fall and impale yourself.'

'Nice.' I sniff.

'And test every step before you put your full weight on it. Don't lift anything too heavy because it'll throw you off balance. By the way, if you see any small items for Mum's shop, grab them, but don't let anyone see you. We're raiding for electrics – we're not supposed to fill our own pockets at the same time.'

When all the raiders are gathered, I count thirty, which seems a lot. Martha explains that while there is safety in numbers, it can also be dangerous. It's competitive. With so many people, it's easy to get away with murder. Not literally, she laughs. But she swallows her good mood when we're approached by a tall girl with blonde braids wrapped around her head like a crown.

'Who are you?' She looks me up and down as if I'm a thing.

'This is Alara,' Martha says.

'Is she the one from the Spikes?' The girl peers at me and Martha hesitates. 'So she *is* from up top.'

'She's one of us now. This is her first trip.' Martha turns to me. She's shaking a little. 'This is Rana. She raids full-time. Every night.'

'Every night?' I try to join in. 'That must be hard.'

'Best job in London Under,' says Rana. 'When I was little, I wanted to be a pirate when I grew up. So in a way I'm living the dream.'

'A pirate?'

'I live for the love of looting!' Rana rubs her thumb and fingers together. 'You can always find a little bit of treasure if you look hard enough.'

In London Star there is no treasure, only money, and you can't touch that. It passes in and out of unseen accounts with the scan of a Flip. Out there in the grey Void, I have no idea what they think of as treasure. There's nothing but scraps, bricks, dust-covered boulders. If we can find them, pots and pans would be practical, but they're hardly precious.

Rana must sense my confusion, because she raises a trouser leg to show me an ankle-chain made of gold.

'Hey,' Martha says, frowning. 'That's got to go in.'

'I already put gold in. Plenty. I'm like a gold magnet.'

'But gold is electrics. It's the rules –'

'If they run out, then I'll give it up, okay?' she snaps. Rana rolls her eyes at me playfully, nodding at Martha. 'She is such a good girl. Always follows the rules.'

I just smile, not wanting to be rude to anyone. A group from Progress approaches. There's the boy who knocked on the door, and two other men. One of them is John, the bearded guy; the other one is Jay.

I don't know what's going on. He never mentioned this before. But making a fuss won't do me any favours. Not with the toughest bunch of London Under kids I've seen, who would gladly see London Star dwellers fall down a crack. Jay doesn't look at me, even though I stare at him for some kind of reaction. The rejection hurts so much, I imagine running a blade through him like I did with Vim.

Could I do it? He's acting like I already did.

'Okay, gang,' John says in his deep voice. He claps his hands together in a friendly manner. 'Jay here is in the middle of upgrading our systems, and we're running low on supplies. So tonight we want you to source wires, motherboards, chips and raw materials – that means copper, silver and gold...'

I see Rana shift slightly, but her chin is lifted and defiant.

'Titanium, if you can get it. Ha!' He laughs, as if he knows that's impossible. 'Bonuses for good finds. Take anything you think we might be able to make use of. Jay has pinpointed a tip-turn to the south, so we'll be heading there. We need to get as much done as we can before dawn, so work fast and work safe. As you know, it'll be dangerous. So here are the rules. You'll work in twos or threes. If you investigate a pit, then go down one at a time. You need a spotter on the surface to raise the alarm if something happens. You do not use your high beams unless you absolutely have to – those times being in the case of falling, or searching for the fallen. Low beams only. No raiding for personal use permitted. Time is precious. And we're paying you thirty chits for an exclusive trip. I repeat: do not pick and mix your salvages. Do you understand?'

We nod, and then we're on the move in a ragged crocodile, back across the square and through the streets. Back up the tunnel that I was probably dragged down three nights ago. It feels longer than that. I feel like a different person.

When we're close to the top, fresh air starts to filter down. People knot shirts over their mouths to protect them from the dust. Martha motions to the top of one of my jumpers – a rollneck. I roll it up over my face until only my eyes are visible, and she gives me a thumbs up. Then Rana squeezes past us, turning to wave a bottle of clear liquid in front of my face.

'Want some Dutch courage?'

I shrug and reach for it, but Martha knocks it from my lips and the liquid sloshes onto my top. It smells sharp.

'Hey, that's not water,' Martha hisses. 'It's brew. You

shouldn't be drinking that before a raid. It'll make you dozy.'

Rana just laughs at her and hands the bottle back to me. 'Are you going to believe Martha the martyr here, or me, who's been successfully raiding since I was ten?'

'Don't be stupid, Rana,' Martha retorts. 'It'll knock her out. She probably hasn't had brew before of any kind. Have you?'

'Just once or twice. Not really.' If they're talking about alcohol, I've had a glass with my parents on special occasions, but that's about it. Moles once downloaded an illegal Sensii trip that made you feel super drunk, and it didn't sound like the kind of thing I'd enjoy. Alcohol makes you stupid and inert. In London Star I never needed more of that.

'Oh yeah, that's right. Spikies don't have fun.' Rana nods wisely, condescendingly.

'Is she from the Spikes?' A previously quiet boy leans in. 'Is she really? Wow. So what are your special skills? Why did they choose –'

Martha pulls me away. I feel rude for not letting the boy finish his sentence, but I can sense she's uncomfortable with this crowd. We walk briskly past them.

'They seem fun,' I try. Martha grunts, and I guess there's a story behind it.

'We watch each other's backs out there,' she says suddenly. 'But we all collect for different reasons, and that creates issues. Some collect for their own businesses, like me and Mum. Rana is a maverick. She collects whatever she thinks she can sell. Sometimes there are clashes. Like one time, I found an amazing old bicycle frame – proper vintage. She tripped me up on the way home and stole it. Didn't even help me up off the ground.' Martha shows me a jagged scar behind her ear. I pull a face. 'Yeah, exactly. So just watch out for people like her.'

Torches flick to low beam as we file out onto the surface. I think of the lights I saw through my binoculars, and it clicks: they were raiders. All this time, I've been seeing humans, not animals. I want to find Jay, but I can't risk raising my torch, so I flick it at the boots of the people walking by me, but there's no way for me to tell them apart. I haven't seen him since the market square, and I kick myself for being distracted by Rana and Martha. I should have kept him in my sights so I could read his expression, try to work out what he's thinking. People do funny things when they're hurt. I briefly imagined blading him, so it isn't impossible that he considered telling Michael or Mark I was a fake.

I guess now all I can do is keep my cool and play along with everyone and try to work out a plan. And there's an opportunity now. Not the best, with all these people. But at least Mark isn't here. And I won't get another chance.

We've surfaced, facing south, somewhere in the middle of the row. The vertical lights of London Star twinkle far above our heads. Close up, the scrapers are no longer pins in a pincushion, but metal monsters. No one stops to gaze in awe, like I do. They pick their way south, silent apart from the odd curse when someone slips or tips a boulder. Martha stays by my side and insists on taking my hand, although I'd feel much safer if she didn't. How will I ever get away?

The tower legs are dark, their thick basement doors shut, impenetrable. I don't have my Flip with Dad's downloaded rotas, so I have no idea where or when the next refuse trip will be, or which leg will open next. If I can detach myself from the group and remain out here until morning, Advice's lookouts will see me. That's what Welt promised.

That's easier said than done. I can detach myself, but I can't detach the bloody tracker. If I get separated from the raiders, my location will be picked up in no time. I'll be found, dragged back underground, and who knows – proven right, Mark might get his chance to fillet me, after all.

'What's up?' Martha whispers.

'What do you mean?'

'You sighed.'

'Did I?'

'Probably wishing she was rid of you so she could have a drink,' Rana nags as she walks past us. I notice there's already something in her backpack.

After an hour, the group walking in front of us halt and tell us to stop. We do the same to the group behind. We wait for instructions. Jay steps towards us. There's silence but for the chittering of trash crabs scuttling in the dark.

'The tip-turn is up ahead. It's a total mess.'

'That's a good thing,' Martha whispers.

'Wait here, and you'll be sorted into teams for safety.'

'But we're sorted – Alara's with me. I'm looking after her.'

'Just wait for orders. You'll be sorted into teams,' he repeats.

We shuffle into the best orderly line we can manage, while the Progress team consults paper maps, using their low beams, crouched down behind a trash pile. They return and pick raiders out one by one to form small groups; each group is given a direction to go. Then they come to us. Martha is pulled away from me.

'See you when the shift's over, Alara. We'll go for chilli litter bugs on the way home, okay? My treat!'

'Sounds good,' I say to the darkness. I hear her shuffle away with Rana and one other person to explore the freshly turned ground. Like pirate treasure on the seabed, the good stuff must sink down eventually.

I'm the last to get selected. Not surprising. Who wants a total beginner on their team when there are incentives for quick work and bonuses for lack of injury? A hand grabs my elbow and drags me backwards. Keeping my mouth shut and my alarm packed deep in my gut, I let myself be led. We are heading in the opposite direction to the raiders; their low beams dance further away, flickering against the rusting piles. Suddenly I want to be back with them, part of the gang, working hard for the promise of Eat Street food at the end of it.

Lips press against my ear and I hear Jay's voice, low and calm. 'It's now or never,' he says. 'North-East – there's a refuse team on their way back. You can beat them if you leave now.' Suddenly his hands are round my ankle. The tracker rubs against my skin as he works at the locking system, the torch between his teeth, his head awkwardly positioned to point the light at the right angle.

'What will happen to it?' I whisper.

'It'll fall down a crevasse. And the story will be that you did too. Now, strip and get into this.' Jay holds out a hazard suit. 'You might need it.' He holds my arm to steady me as I peel off some of the layers Martha gave me. I climb into the suit.

'I don't think this is mine,' I whisper.

'Of course it isn't. If that went missing from our stores, that would be way too obvious. It's one I picked up on a raid. I thought it might come in useful one day.'

He knocks on the visor section of my hood and holds out his hand for me to shake. Although our goodbye seems too fast and too formal, my apprehension about the escape eclipses everything. And, despite his lack of warmth right now, I realise that Jay is risking his own skin to help me.

'Jay. I'm sorry.'

'It's fine. If this life is not for you, there's nothing more I can say.'

'It is for me.' I should have left it, turned and gone. But I want Jay to know that it's not him, it's not even me. It's bigger. And a sudden need to tell him the truth is blooming inside me. 'I want to be here. But I can't. I can't. I'm on a mission.'

There, I said it.

'Advice sent me. To scan the layout.'

He flashes the torch in my face and I wince.

'I knew it. *Shit.*'

'I should have … I'm sorry.'

'What was your mission? Tell me, fast.'

'To look around and check that the tower foundations are safe. That's all. They're safe, so it's good. But I'm sorry. I should have –'

He lets out a groan and stamps his foot in frustration, then pushes my shoulder, hard. 'Just go. *Go.*'

He ducks into the darkness and I'm left alone, reeling. I've done something bad.

Part Three

–

The Drop

Chapter 23

The suit is in good condition, considering it's been salvaged from the tips. And although I now know there isn't any toxicity down here, it'll stop me worrying about getting cuts. Even after my new experiences of blood and pain, the human body still shocks me; the vulnerability of it. But the suit isn't really to prevent me seeing my own blood. It's for my reintegration. A citizen of Estrella couldn't possibly waltz in from the Void in baggy jeans and T-shirt without ringing alarm bells.

But why? Why? The questions return.

The Void is safe. So Advice is either stupid – or Welt and his officials are all lying. And I don't think they're stupid. Maybe they say the Void is toxic as a precaution, to stop people wondering what it's like to be out in the open and finding a way down, only to get their soft skin shredded to strips on the sharps and daggers of century-old trash. And then there's infection; even the Unders worry about infection.

I suppose that makes sense. Not that anyone would consider leaving the comfort of the scrapers to 'see what it's like' outside. London Star isn't exactly jumping with curious minds. Of course, that's why they had to have the whole charade of StarQuest – to weed out the few of us who did possess some daring. I guess I'll have to sign something to say I'll never talk about the Void. If there was a way, they'd probably wipe my memories of it… But what if they do have a way? Then Jay, Martha, Carnival … all would be lost. My stomach twists with a pain like indigestion, and I push the worry to the back of my mind and keep walking.

The going is slow. The ground is particularly uneven here, mounds of trash like mountain ranges groaning and squeaking as they shift and collapse. I shudder, despite the regular temperature inside the hazard suit. It's a reaction to loneliness, not cold, and the feeling of belonging nowhere, neither up nor down. When I think of warmth now, it's London Under, claustrophobic and germ-riddled though it is, that comes to mind. It's the cosiest place I've ever known, warmer even than my pristine, temperate bedroom back in London Star.

Too late. No point in chewing it over. The mission needs to be completed. I didn't have time to explain it to Jay – that it was only an innocent structural survey. There wasn't time for anything but a quick change and escape. But his reaction when I told him the bare bones replays in my head. He was shocked, desperate, as if he thought I'd brought impossible danger to his doorstep. Or maybe I was imagining that.

Distracted, I slip. Got to stop overthinking everything. Need to find a safe place to bed down. I scrabble through the rubble, spotting trinkets and wires and thinking how they'd be of use to Jay and Ellie, until, finally, I find somewhere that doesn't look too perilous. It's an old train carriage, and it's right next to a tower.

NE20. The address is painted in letters fifty feet high on the base of the scraper and the sight crushes my spirit. It's such an industrial address. Practical. Not characterful, like Chadwick Street, Dobbins Road and Spitalfields Market. But this is a practical place to stop. A good place to be spotted at dawn, when I'll be visible to anyone looking through high-powered binoculars. Then they'll come and get me. Until then, it's a waiting game. Just me and the trash crabs and all my worries, which roll in like a storm.

Jay's mysterious insights, Advice's lies, what they'll say about my missing Sensii, and the Gen-Tech chip in my head. I'll be going straight to that weirdo Burbeck's lab for extraction, and then what will happen to me? Another mission, or will I be retired? It's all guesswork. I'll find out soon enough, so there's no point in driving myself mad. Instead, I force myself to picture the faces of Mum, Dad and Gavi. Their Alara Banana Tripp back in their lives. And Moles, too. Did he miss me? Did he even know I was gone?

I don't know how I fell asleep, but I did. The sun is already halfway up the sky when the sound of grinding and crunching reaches my ears. Blinking in the bright light, I see sweepers – a row of them trundling along. I stretch my limbs and fight to find the right mindset. I have been stranded in the Void, and I am desperate to be saved. A miracle! I stand and wave and yell.

It takes them an age to reach me, and then they have questions. Am I okay? Can I walk? They have to get me back as soon as possible for checks and quarantine. No one has spent so long out in the open in just a suit.

They're either playing along with me – or, as I suspect, they have no idea about the Void or what's underneath. They've been fed the same line over and over. Dad, too – he always talks about the need for hazard suits, and what the poison could do to skin and lungs if it seeps in because of a careless mistake. Dad has no idea.

They call ahead to let Advice know I've been picked up. A refuse worker sits in the back of the sweeper pod with me, nodding at me constantly – wanting me to nod back that I'm okay. No one is talking to me, though, about what happened and where I've been. Perhaps they've been told not to. Fine by me. As we head back towards the middle of Estrella, I press my visor against the pod window and stare out at the open space, watching the concrete breaking under the wheels of the adjacent sweepers and the blooms of dust that billow in the air. As well as concrete dust, I have the grime and dirt of London Under in my pores, my eyes, up my nose – molecules of another civilisation buried under my skin. Decontamination will ensure that not a speck of it remains. It will all come off with hygiene scrubs. But what about my memories? Will they be as easy to erase?

I don't even know if Advice has amnesia therapy, but I have to face the truth now, because it's coming at me fast. They'll want me to forget all that I've seen. But I won't – ever. My subconscious will throw up details at night in my dreams. Perhaps Gen-Tech will, too. Short of having my brain sliced up, there's no way I could wipe out London Under, or the journey I took out into the countryside, with its green fields and cold river. And Jay.

Jay. I whisper his name, and my heart implodes as I remember his smile, his expressive eyes, his kindness. He was my Vim. My real-life Vim, only better.

Being a security operative isn't going to be easy. That's something Welt said to me. And I thought that any pain was worth the safety of Estrella.

But I don't think he told me the full story. He was hiding pieces of it from me.

I was told there was danger to Estrella, but I didn't see any. The excavations around the towers were all done years ago, it looked like, and carefully. And Martha said there had been no tremors. And isn't that what it was about – tremors that signified a threat to our foundations? The new digs were way out from the boundaries of the Void, tunnelling towards the open countryside, and what was the harm in that? Maybe it's not my job to know. I was conscripted to carry out work, not analyse the data, and I suppose the Gen-Tech chip might reveal details that passed me by while I was busy living and blending in.

Living. Blending into Under. That was the biggest mission of all.

I am so deep in thought, in the sorrow of it all, I don't realise we've stopped until the man next to me gently shakes my shoulder. We're at a sweeper station. A giant door at the foot of the tower slides up and the sweepers take turns to file inside. Once in, we all get out and gather by the lift that will take us up to the dressing and decontamination rooms.

'You okay there, Alara?' The man finally speaks as we wait for the lift.

I nod.

'Good job someone spotted you out there. I know your dad. He's a good man. He'll be relieved that you've been found safe.'

His breath steams up his visor as he talks. Everyone is still wearing their suits; they believe it. Even the people who go out there every day. But it's all a lie. *What else is a lie?*

There's a clank and a whirr as the platform lift makes

its way down the shaft to collect us. Sharp sounds, metallic and unfeeling. We shuffle in. The journey up takes forever. I watch the endless stream of greasy streaks on the shaft walls, keeping my thoughts packed inside my chest, trying not to hyperventilate. Anxiety gnaws at my gut. Home is somehow alien, as if it's mutated in my absence and might spit me out at any moment.

The lift slows at the changing-room floor. Hazard suits from the previous expedition hang like dead men from their hooks, dripping with cleaning fluid. The milky, dusty water channels into drains. We strip, leaving our suits on the floor so they can be hosed down and hung up, and move on to the next process.

The next level is decontamination. I already know, from Dad's stories, how this goes: strip naked, walk into room, stand on the turning circle, get rotated through washer brushes, then get steamed like a dumpling in hot antibac mist. I'm told to hang back and go last in case I feel nervous about exposing myself with so many people around. But I'm not shy. Ever since Burbeck stuck that thing in my head, my body hasn't been my own; over the last few days it's been prodded, tortured, cut open and stretched. Not to mention exposed to a zillion germs. But I don't want any questions if someone sees the wound in my armpit, so I hang back. And part of me hopes it goes unnoticed in my medical, too. I don't know why, but what Jay said down by the river, about being human, it plays on my mind. I don't want my Sensii replaced. Not yet.

In a side room, I wait. They give me a vial to drink – an internal cleanser to zap any uglies I might have ingested. From inside the decontamination room I hear the men chat and chuckle as the brushes probe every part of them. They do this, day in, day out. You'd think they'd be immune.

By the time I've been through it myself, overseen by someone in a hazard suit, the workers have gone. A soft robe is waiting for me, and a voice through a speaker tells me to zip myself into the quarantine bag, which I guess is the plastic body suit hanging alongside it.

On the other side of the doors, people are waiting to meet me. Whitecoats. And Welt. His smile is big and warm as the sunshine, and he opens his arms and takes me in a fatherly bear hug. My quarantine suit crinkles and rustles. I feel like a chicken in a bag.

'You did it,' he says. 'You actually did it.'

'It wasn't that hard,' I say through the plastic, my voice muffled, although yeah, it was. If it wasn't for Jay and John, who knows what might have happened?

'We're not going to be able to keep the refuse team quiet. They know your dad, and they'll be keen to tell him you've been found. You'll be keen to see your family, too, I'm sure. But we won't be allowing visitors into quarantine just yet. You'll need some time to adjust and relax.' He pauses. 'And get your story straight.'

Welt steps back and I'm taken away. Not home, but to the clinic. Apparently, I'll stay here until they're sure

I'm not contaminated. Do they believe this charade? I think they do. I think only a couple of people know about the lies – and the truth. Trouble is, I'm not sure who they are. And worst of all, I don't know why they have to tell lies in the first place.

What happens next is a series of mind-numbing procedures as they check me head to toe, including my armpit. There are murmurs, phone calls. The Sensii is going to be replaced, of course. Medico says they'll reinstall my birthright immediately, so I don't feel abandoned. So I can be part of society again. 'So you can get started playing those games right away,' they say, and laugh. Then they turn back to their prodding. Moving bits of my body without asking, as if I were nothing but an empty second-skin suit. I shut myself off from their small talk, and Jay's words return: *We're so unnatural, it's ridiculous we even call ourselves human.*

I wake then. On those words. Like a kick to the head. If I'm not human, I'm a robot. And robots are controlled. Without my Sensii, I can't be controlled. *That's* what this is all about. The gaming? It's just a distraction.

But there's nothing I can do. Nothing.

It's a painless procedure this time – the opening and closing of my skin nothing more than a strange tugging sensation. Star's got a superior approach to surgery, I'll give it that. As they work on implanting a new Sensii, Jay's impassioned words scrabble to the surface of my mind, along with other bits and pieces that didn't make sense at the time. *As soon as the dosage runs out, it will be useless,* Dr Orta said. So that's it? Now I'm being dosed again? To feel no pain and no love; to sleep when they say so; to behave how they want; programmed to be content…

The whitecoats show me how blemish-free my operation has left me. There's nothing there – not even the marks of Dr Orta's stitches. It's weird, but I suddenly want to see them. It may not be a normal choice of souvenir, but my stitches showed that I was there and what I went through. Battle scars, as they say in *Warlord*. Although I was in good hands there, however roughly they handled me.

A fat tear rolls down my cheek. Then another. This is crying. Will I do it ever again? My tears are about to miraculously dry up, I bet – I see the whitecoats at a panel, fiddling with buttons and levels, sliding their gaze towards me. Dosing.

I'm more resistant than most, but within seconds I can feel myself slowing down. It feels like quick-hardening cement has been pumped into my veins. Can't fight it. Too tired to try.

'Sleep now, Miss Tripp.'

In my waking moments, my mind is empty, and I'm almost pleased to see Welt standing by the bed, his hand on my leg like a concerned relative. His sparkling blue eyes gaze at me, interested.

'Morning, Alara.'

'M-morning.' I stretch and prop myself up.

'Are you awake enough to talk a little?' He pulls up a chair and slides into it, crossing his legs neatly.

'Yeah, yeah, I'm fine.' Actually, I feel good, fresh. No sore muscles.

He lifts my hand and gently strokes my forearm, and I notice I have a new Flip, to replace my lost one. But this one is implanted, not worn. Fixed into my skin, like an exoskeleton. I lean back, close my eyes, grit my teeth hard.

'Call it an upgrade,' Welt says, all friendly. 'It's the least we could do. We're making it mandatory soon, anyway. Then we'll all be instantly connected. Safer, together.'

I notice he doesn't have an implanted Flip. He sees me looking and smiles broadly. 'We certainly didn't make a mistake choosing you, did we?'

Is that a statement or a question?

I smile. 'It wasn't so bad. I'm sure anyone could have done it.'

'I don't think that's true at all. So tell me, what was it like down there? Indulge me, tell me everything. I've never been,' he reminds me. But what do I say – that I liked it? Would that be treason? I wonder if my heart is being monitored for lies.

'It was dark and claustrophobic. I struggled to breathe sometimes.'

'And the people?'

'Basic, dirty. They were kind to me, though.'

'Kind? They took your Flip.'

'I lost it.'

'They cut your Sensii out.'

'Yes. No. I hurt myself on waste in the Void. I slipped. They checked me over. They thought it was a shard of metal, I think.'

That's not good enough. I'm not prepared enough for this. Welt leans back, smiling, but his eyes have narrowed. 'Well, you're safe, and that's all the matters.'

'Thank you. It's good to be home.'

'Did you meet anyone interesting?'

'A girl called Martha was nice to me. And her mum.'

He waits.

'I didn't see anything dangerous,' I add. 'They weren't excavating anywhere near the skyscrapers. It was further out in the countryside.'

'You went to the countryside? Beyond the Void?'

Say nothing.

'Without your hazard suit?' he presses. Gently.

Say nothing. I yawn to fill in the gap.

'How did you get out in the end?'

'I waited until night. No one was around.'

'And life down there – do they have any technology you're aware of? Any defence systems?'

'I don't know.'

'Not to worry. When we download the tech, we'll

be able to make a proper assessment. We hope your info will fill in some missing pieces, complete our picture of the threats to Estrella. We'll do it first thing tomorrow. Right now, I imagine you'll want to see your parents. Tell me what you'll say.'

'I'll tell them that I banged my head when the sweeper lurched, and when I woke up, I got out and just started walking. I was dazed.'

'And where did you walk to?'

'Nowhere specific. I was dizzy. I just found a place to lie down in the trash, and waited to be found. I went in and out of consciousness.'

'Excellent. Any other questions, just say you don't remember. Or tell them to come and see me. Don't attempt to explain. If you do…'

He leaves it hanging – a kind of threat. It's like we're playing hide and seek. It's as though he is suspicious of me and I of him. Suspicions are there, alright, but they're not precise. All I know is that things aren't quite how I thought they were, both above and below. But it doesn't matter, because all my mapping will prove is that London Under isn't about to damage Estrella, that there is no problem with their digging. They'll find that out and then everyone can take a big breath and relax. As for Sensii and the manipulation that's been going on – maybe that's something I can write about. *A new perspective, Mr Leppito.* If I dare.

'Do you want someone to escort you home?'

'No, I'll walk, if that's okay.' I attempt a smile.

He leaves, and I get dressed as quickly as I can. I have to get out. The clinic feels frightening, with its blinding white lights and sterile shine. And to think I was craving cleanliness a few days ago, scared of dirt and an earthen floor.

Chapter 24

Through the windows of the pedestrian tube the sky is blue, but everything below and beyond is the grey of powdered concrete. And below that dull, dusty layer is an abundance of colour. A carnival of it. Dig beneath the surface, and there's life.

My face is calm as I walk, purposely so. But in reality I want to scream my lungs out. At the tubes and travel tunnels that don't lead to grassy plains. At the body hijack – the Sensii implant now reinserted and the Flip buried in my skin. I have to use all my willpower to stop myself from digging my nails in and prising it out. I couldn't do that anyway, not without damaging my veins. It would hurt, wouldn't it? Even with Sensii's numbing, it would have to hurt. Now that I've felt pain, I find I can conjure the memory of it easily... That's another world.

I'm home now.

The polished floor squeaks beneath my shoes. Even

outside the clinic everything is pristine, glazed with a self-cleaning, germ-repellent veneer that smells kind of lemony. I hadn't noticed that before. It gets up my nose, irritates me more than the dusty, smoky streets I just came from. How is that possible? My new shoes and the rock-hard surface are hurting my feet, so at the next travel hub I grab a train. Welt was right about getting the publicity over and done with. No one takes any notice of me on the train. When I get down to the Quarters, there are regular greetings, but nothing more. No curiosity. After being stared at in Under, it's weird. I feel like a ghost.

My apartment is dark. I had prepared myself for noise, but there's nothing but the blink of standby lights from the appliances. Where is everyone? This feels like a frozen moment, a background scene, paused while life loads. I'm kind of grateful for the breathing space and the time to remember what normality is and how Alara Tripp is expected to behave.

Leaving the lights off, I turn the air purification to full and stand next to the vent, just to feel a breeze in my hair again. I want to get cold, to have goosebumps. I want to be reminded that my body is vulnerable. After a few seconds, the thermostat kicks in powerfully, as if disgusted that I could let the apartment get so cold. Its job is to ensure the apartment doesn't drop to a subnormal temperature, because that would be *dangerous*. Huh. They don't know what dangerous is.

I walk slowly through the rooms. It's home, just as I remember it. But somehow it's soulless – missing something. Noise, perhaps. It's unnaturally quiet. And not just my apartment, but all of London Star: a soundproof capsule in a world of noise. It drives me mad, because I know that outside the thick glass, there is creaking debris and crashing trash heaps and skittering crabs and singing birds. And below that, there's the hubbub of London Under. Children screaming, kids whizzing through tunnels on bikes with squeaky wheels, hungry raiders down on Eat Street after their shift, laughing raucously over meat and vegetable stews, mocking each other. I wonder if it will be different today. Perhaps a few people won't be as loud as normal. The new girl, the one from London Star who slipped into a deep crevasse – she couldn't possibly have survived the fall. Some will say they tried to rescue me, but it was too dangerous, the rubble too unstable, and there was no response when they called my name, not even a cry or a moan. Jay will say it was all his fault; he should never have allowed me, a total beginner, to come on such an expedition.

I press my nose against the window and look down. Haven't I always done that? Haven't I always wondered about the Void? I felt drawn to it. Now I feel like I belong to it.

In three days down there – in just three days – I felt more vital than I have in sixteen years up here. The hard bits, the cruel bits, the incredible, heart-thumping bits that made my face ache with smiling. For a short while, that was my life. My filthy, electric life.

Now, I'm suffering a power cut.

Lights suddenly blaze around me and there's a burst of excited chatter. My family is back from wherever they've been, hooting like the baboons in *Build a Zoo*. There's the clank of bottles in bags. Half of me is distracted by their joy-filled arrival, and curious – where have they been? – and the other half is trapped in my other life, the one I'm starting to think is the real one.

'Alara? Are you home?'

Hooking a smile back on my face, I walk towards the kitchen area to see them. They squeal and squeeze me and squeeze again, in case they didn't manage to love-crush me enough first time. They feel every part of my body in case something's fallen off, and only when they've counted my fingers do they relax.

That is, relaxing in the way that my parents do – not chilling the hell out, but peppering me with questions. I roll out stock replies to their questions. Slept in the wasteland, hit my head, don't remember much, it's not Dad's fault. Just one of those things. Everything's going to be okay. All's well that ends well.

There's more hugging, a lot of 'thank God Advice never gave up searching', although they don't look as if they've been suffering. Of course not; they were *dosed*. It's unsettling how easily they've accepted and rejected the worry of losing their child. As if I was only gone for a split second. And now they want to tell me where they've been all morning.

'You'll never guess, darling,' Mum says, her eyes glittering.

'Then I won't even try.' I shrug, trying to act cute and curious. 'Go on.'

'Checking out our new apartment – on Level 70.'

'What? Seriously?'

Dad hugs me. 'This is how Advice is apologising for not finding you sooner. Not bad, right?'

'We're moving up?'

It's been Mum's dream for longer than I can remember, but I'm now outraged that we would so easily give up the friendliness of the Quarters for a dollop more luxury. For what? For making our lives slip by more easily?

Shiny floors. Sliding doors. Where's the friction that makes you *feel* stuff? Where is it? My heart starts racing. Mum picks it up on her Flip, and reaches out to stroke my knee. She nods slowly to tell me everything is going to be alright. I'm safe.

'It's got a massive Ent room, Alara,' Gavi squeals. 'Preloaded with the best games.'

'You two are going to lose days in there,' Dad says.

Gavi tugs my arm. 'And guess what? There's Vim. They said you lost him, but they've reinstalled him just for you. Do you know how much Pixels *cost*?'

Vim? If you'd told me that a week ago, my heart

would have partied. But Vim is a downmarket Jay. Nothing more than a pretty shell.

'Champagne!' Mum calls, pulling a frosted bottle from a shopping bag.

Dad pops the cork, sloshing the fizz into tall glasses. 'To having Alara safely home.'

'To a happy day,' says Mum.

Gavi is in our faces with the Echo-Pen, recording holograms of the moment, and Dad runs off to blow up some balloons to make it a real party. My face aches from smiling so hard. Whenever Mum isn't gazing at me like I'm a miracle, I stare out of the window. They notice, but I don't care. Couldn't hide it even if I tried. We're going up. Further away from the ground. So far up, I won't be able to see it. At the thought of being more and more detached from the land, my heart spirals into darkness. The fussing. The noise. The excitement. All for something that's not *real*. I can't bear it. And Gavi's cooing over my inbuilt Flip, wishing he could have one too.

Eventually, I have to tell them that I feel strange about it all, and need time to adjust. Need to be alone for a bit. They're concerned, but of course, of course, I've been through hell, they say with smiles that are heavenly happy. They back off, quickly distracted by looking at new furnishings for our new apartment. A new apartment, hey? Well. Welt certainly fulfilled my conditions, and then some. But did I fulfil his?

I slip to my room. My stomach is churning with

worry, although I can't put my finger on why. *Why?* My mission has been accomplished. I'm home in one piece. So where's the problem? There were lies here and there, things that came as a shock, but at the end of the day, Advice lies to keep its people safe. To help humankind progress.

No, there's more to it than that.

Jay's reaction when I was honest with him… He had looked at me as if I'd endangered his home and shattered his world. His expression. How different it was from the way he'd looked at me down by the river. My heart twists at the memory; the dosing hasn't erased that bit yet. Love; I think it was love. But what good is love to me here? What good is it at all, if it can change in an instant from joy to pain, and cut both ways? I suppose over time I'll become numb or have my heart decommissioned by a heavy dose of Sensii. I'll end up in a correction clinic, one way or another. Reprogrammed like a robot. Because while I'm in Star, that's all I am. Isn't it?

But Jay isn't. He's forced to live on, thinking he made a mistake about me. Or perhaps he feels I've made a fool of him. If I could just speak to him one more time, explain…

Instinctively, I look at my bedroom screen. And my Synthia icon. As if I could just call him up, like any Star resident. But maybe I could...

He created a ghost version of Synthia to invite skilled people. He watches and waits for search terms and trigger words. If Jay is at work now, there's a chance he'll see me. He might also ignore me. But I have to try.

'Synthia, search the term "trouble".'

You want to search the term 'trouble'. Trouble suggests dangers–

'Don't repeat. List.'

Danger.

'Next.'

Threat.

'Search "outside Estrella".'

There is no outside Estrella. There is the Void.

'Next.' I need her to keep saying potential trigger words.

Being outside Estrella is not possible.

'Next.'

There are no reasons to be outside Estrella.

'Search 'life in danger'.'

You want to search 'life in danger'. A life in danger is one that is threatened by its environment. Search stopped. Call coming in. Caller unidentified.'

My heart stops as a grainy image emerges on the air screen. I can't see the face properly, just a fuzzy outline. He whispers low and fast.

'What is it, Alara? What are you doing?'

John. Jay's confidant.

'John, I need to speak to Jay.'

'Why?'

'I just have to.'

'Alara, these messages have to be quick. Is this about your mission?'

'I need to explain it to him. It isn't bad, I promise.'

'First, tell me. The complete story. In bullet points.'

This wasn't what I had expected to happen. But there's nothing to lose. And perhaps, if I tell him the truth, I'll salvage some respect.

'Okay. They put a chip in my head – some new PlayBeck gaming technology. It's just for mapping London Under. They want to be sure the foundations of the towers are all okay. They're going to download the information tomorrow –'

The line goes dead. I can't believe it. Did I put my foot in it? What if John isn't Jay's right-hand man, after all? Did I get that wrong? Agony tears through my chest. I've just made things worse.

Then Synthia wakes. *Call coming in. Caller ID unknown. Audio only.*

'Alara, it's Jay.' His voice is low, a whisper.

'Jay, I'm so sorry I didn't tell you. About the chip. I was told not to trust anyone.'

'It's not the best news.'

'It's just mapping.'

'No, Alara. It isn't just mapping. It's way more complicated. Do me a huge favour – delay your download as long as possible. Say you feel ill, have a headache, anything. Put them off. I'll sort something out. Don't call me again.'

'What? Why?'

'It's too dangerous.'

'But I want to talk to you.' I hiccup. 'I can't never talk to you again.'

'When you've been downloaded, they'll wipe you. You won't remember all this – or me. Perhaps that's for the best. If you forget, you'll be safe.'

I know the price of safety. It hits me like a bowling ball between my eyes.

'But I don't want to be here.' It's as true as hunger, as the horror of blood. It's real. 'I have to get out.'

'Do you mean that?'

I think about my parents – their warmth, their love, their silly nicknames for me. Of how living in London Under would take years off my life. But then I remember, while I still can, the swathes of green, Carnival, my body vibrating like an instrument.

'Jay, I have never been more certain of anything. But how do I get down? What do I do?'

'Say you're sure. One last time. Because it can't be reversed.'

'I'm sure.'

'I can't tell you how glad I am you said that. I'll send someone. It has to be today. Be ready.'

It's so fast. So immediate. 'Now? Who?'

'My contact in London Star. Pack a bag. No electronics.'

'Jay. My Flip. They implanted it.'

'Oh God.' There's a pause, a cough. 'We'll figure it out, we'll figure it out,' he mutters. 'Be ready for the contact.'

'How will I know it's him? I don't –'

'You'll know.'

Jay's voice fizzes and disappears. I wonder what I'm doing. Not just to me, but my family. I can't leave without explaining. I take out a pen and paper and write.

Dear Mum and Dad
As you probably realise, I am in trouble. I have done nothing wrong. I am going somewhere, and I won't be back for a while. I will be safe. But if you tell anyone or try to find me, I will no longer be safe. You will have many questions, and I hope that one day I'll be able to answer them. But for now, all I can do is assure you that I'm alive and okay.
I will miss you more than words can say. I love you. Please tell Gavi I've gone travelling. In a way, I have.
Love, Alara (always Banana)

What am I doing? *What am I doing?*

My wrists ache from clenching my fists. My brain hurts. My stupid brain with its chip, mapping out a disaster I don't even understand. It still hasn't been explained. From start to finish, I've been no more than a machine carrying out a task. A good little robot. I thought robots were banned long ago in Star. But maybe we just replaced them. Time for a malfunction.

I hear the intercom buzz. I'm not ready, but I have no choice. There is no pause button now. This is it. I go to take a last look at my brother – he's in the Ent, playing *Kapow.* I don't disturb him; seeing his sweet face, I'd either give in or give something away.

My parents have let someone in; they're in the kitchen. Voices float down the hallway, low and concerned-sounding. I take a big breath, compose myself, and go to greet the visitor.

'Darling, Moles is here to see you.' Mum smiles.

Oh no! Of all the times to turn up...

There he is, hands in pockets, looking moody again. This really is the last thing I need. Another obstacle to escape, another person to feel bad about.

'Hi. This is a bad time,' I say hurriedly.

'I'd like to talk to you.'

'What for?'

'To see if you're okay, of course. I was worried about you.'

'Not now, Moles. You look like you need a good lie-down anyhow – overdosing on Sensii again, eh?' I try to laugh and keep it casual. Believable.

'It'll only take a minute,' he insists, his feet fixed firmly. He's not going anywhere.

'Okay.' I sigh.

'Your room's this way, right?' He marches off towards it.

Mum rubs my shoulder as I follow him. 'He cares about you, darling.'

Moles' face turns thunderous as soon as I shut the door behind us. But his unpredictable moods are the least of my problems.

'What is it, Nate?' I don't feel it's the time for pet names.

He shuts his eyes and breathes deeply in through his nose, out through his mouth. In for seven, out for eight. *In for seven, out for eight.* He opens his eyes. 'Before we go any further, I just want to say that I'm heartbroken.' He digs his fingertips into his eyes aggressively before rolling his shoulders and looking at me in the eye.

'Moles, I don't know what –'

'I'm here to get you out.'

'What are you talking about?'

'I'm the contact, and I'm here to get you out.'

Is this a joke? 'You? *You?*'

'So, listen to me. I am going to go out of the room. I'm going to tell your parents that I'm taking you to a social hub. I'll say the change in environment might help you relax and get back to normal. Basically, everyone will agree that would be a very good idea. And then I'll tell them you gave me the slip and disappeared.' Moles looks at the note on my bed. 'That's not a good idea,' he says, grabbing it. He stuffs it in his pocket.

Stunned, I nod. He nods. It's time. Jay said it would be quick.

'No time to pack, Alara. We need to go.'

'I'll be out in a minute.'

Moles looks at me warily, but leaves. I'm alone and I only have a second to process everything. A last chance to decide something for myself. I scribble another note and leave it under my pillow, because I can't do this to them. I can't just abandon them. Although that's exactly what I'm doing: removing their daughter and replacing her with a million questions. At the very least, I could leave them with the answer to one: I'm not dead.

Moles is waiting outside my room. He narrows his eyes, but doesn't go into my room to check on his suspicions. Instead, he takes my hand and we go to talk to my parents. Every one of my words sticks like a thorn in my throat. In the end, Moles does the talking. Just as he said, they agree that getting back to normal is a great idea. As we turn to leave, I see Mum and Dad hug each other tightly, as if they're standing on a precipice. While they're not looking, I take the Echo-Pen and slip it into my pocket. It's full of family scenes.

Although holograms could never replace the people I love.

Chapter 25

We don't talk. In the lift up to the travel hub, the train round to North, the corridor to the social hub, he is silent. This is new to me. Moles can be moody, but I can usually break him free with sarcasm, cajoling. Or I can tell him he's being a jerk and walk away. None of those options is open to me right now. I'm relying on him. He's Jay's contact.

My head spins. How does he know Jay? How on earth could Moles have become his contact, considering how he feels about the Void? And now he's actually *helping* me down there?

'I'll answer your questions when it's safe to talk,' Moles says. I click my tongue with impatience as we queue for snacks. 'Don't do that,' he says. 'You'll draw attention.'

We take smoothies to a quiet table. Moles sits first and I go to sit opposite, but he pats the bench next to him.

'Scooch in here,' he says with a smile, acting. He puts his arm around me and whispers in my ear. 'Okay, so here it is. Jay is my brother. He's Peron. Shhh, don't react. But I don't want to talk about Peron. And the moment you leave, I'll never want to talk about you either.'

Oh, God. I'm just another person abandoning him. 'Moles, I'm sorry –'

'I knew this day would come. Peron's been messaging me for a while, asking who you are. Your Synthia searches ... you never gave up asking questions. I guess that's what makes you a questa. Jay didn't need you, of course. But apparently fate had other plans.'

I am kind of crushed by his words. I know I'm worthless but still, it hurts to know that. And worse, that I'm an irritant. To everyone, it seems.

'So if I'm so worthless, why are they bothering?'

'Because of your mission for Advice. You're a human grenade. Advice don't want to check on tunnels and structural safety. They want to kill everyone in Under. They want a map so they can work out which tunnels to block to trap everyone in, and maybe release some foul chemicals and choke the lot of them to death.'

The words come like wrecking balls, knocking my breath away. But my brain kicks in. Who can I trust? Michael and Mark, who would probably kill everyone in Estrella in an instant if they could, or Welt, with his warm fatherly smile? And Moles? How can I trust anyone who has been so distant, barely registering on the friendship scale? And what if London Under only wants me back so they can kill me?

I lean back and look at Moles, his cold expression, and wonder if he's capable of murder. Because that might be what this is about. Here I am expecting an elaborate escape plan, but what if I'm going to be killed and shoved down a rubbish chute? I edge away, but he yanks me back viciously.

'Don't be stupid, Alara,' he hisses.

'Alright. If London Star wants Under gone so badly, then why don't they just head on down there with an army? There's only a handful of them.'

'Keep your bloody voice down or you'll get us killed. I'll tell you why. Because if they charge in there, Under will have time to damage the towers. Mutual threat and trading – that's what's kept the two civilisations civil, up to now.'

'Trading? Trading what?'

Moles grinds his teeth and covers his face with his hands.

'Tell me, Moles. Why does Advice want to move in on them now?'

Moles looks up, shaking his head, like he doesn't believe the words he's going to say. 'It's because of Peron. He was a Star operator, Alara.'

'No, he was invited.'

'Right, well, no. He told you that because he didn't want to tell you the truth – that he was originally sent to spy and to harvest. Perhaps he's made himself forget that.'

'What do you mean, *harvest*? Harvest what?'

'People. To replenish Estrella's gene pool. For all the brilliance of our laboratories and scientists, they can't create new DNA from nothing.'

'What the hell am I hearing? Jay *harvested* people from Under? How did he do it? Cut them down like plants? Package them up like steak?'

Moles slaps my thigh under the table. We're having a dangerous conversation in a public place.

'He took bodies of the deceased to the surface, to meeting points, so their DNA could be used here. That's the truth. It's been going on for years. Advice has been planting people in Under from the very start. When one retires, another takes over. The current one is Jay.'

Bile rises in my throat, and I retch.

'You're going to have to get over this, Alara. Get over it. He didn't do anything bad – and anyway, he's on Under's side now, and Advice is mad. The harvesting – the DNA supply – has stopped, and now Star experts are defecting. Advice has no idea what my brother's been up to, what systems he's been building or whether he's developed weapons. Advice is paranoid. They think he's building a society that will rival Star in strength. One day it might. And they want to kill him first.'

'Why doesn't Advice just tell everyone about Under so it doesn't stay this spooky underground threat? If it comes out in the open, it'll be more transparent.'

'And what will all the people in the skyscrapers do when they find out they've been lied to for a century – about the Void, about their genes, about their Sensii chips? There'll be riots. Advice will lose control.'

All of us stuck in test tubes like brainless organisms. My parents. My brother. Babies concocted in labs using bits and pieces of Under people… I can't digest the details now or I'll go into a spin.

'So if I stay, I'll be responsible for the death of Jay and London Under. But if Under think I'm a spy…' I draw a line across my throat.

'No one knows about what's in your head but Per– *Jay*. And he seems to have taken a shine to you. He took a shine to you long ago. He won't let anything happen to you.'

I can't tell if it's his brother's new name or his affection for me that sticks in Mole's throat. Is that why he's become so distant?

'Why don't you come, too?'

'Someone's got to stay and be the contact. Stay there and don't move,' Moles commands. 'And for God's sake, try to look normal.' He walks away and joins the smoothie queue. I see him casually checking his Flip. Then the walls and ceilings. He's sussing out the CCTV, the security. Then he's making a call. Who is he calling? He looks back at me, once, twice, and something feels wrong. No one else in Estrella knows about all this, apart from the baddies. Is he with them? Has this all been a quick info-dump before I'm whizzed off for brain-scrambling?

He returns with two more smoothies, but orders me not to drink mine. I need to keep light, and I'm not going to have time for a wee... Someone is coming to pick us up. When they do, we'll have to be fast.

'Who, Moles? Who the hell is *collecting* me?' I'm shaking, examining his face for betrayal. Does he work for Advice? I can't believe I'm thinking these things, but for someone with the best upgrade in London Star, I'm very much in the dark.

A shadow falls over our table.

'Yes, do tell.' Landi peels back her glasses. Her Flip is flashing. 'Can I sit with you two a while and chinwag?'

Her? Moles shakes his head.

'Not a good time, Landi,' I mutter.

'But the other day you were so keen to get to know me. It was almost as if you want to make friends, yet now...'

'She's not feeling great. Back off.' Moles leans across me to make a point.

'She looks fine to me. Come on, be social. You are in a social hub, after all. Unless... unless you're *hiding* something. Where exactly is it you're off to?'

'I'm not hiding anything. I'm just tired and want to spend some time with my friend.'

'She's feeling out of sorts. We've called her parents

and it's all in hand. So if you could run along and disappear, we'd be most grateful.'

I didn't know Landi had a smile, but there it is, slowly stretching across her face. 'There's something about you, Alara. I can't put my finger on it. But not to worry, I'll run some queries past my aunt. She works in Advice, quite high up. Knows Welt Eldon. A journalist should always have her book of contacts, right?'

'Right.'

We watch her saunter towards the exit, flicking her digipad. But she doesn't leave. She hangs around in the doorway, watching us.

'*Shit.*' Moles looks around desperately. 'We can't wait for pick-up. Too dangerous. Let's go.'

'Where are we going?'

'Burbeck's lab. He says you have the password.'

'Yes, I do.' He was very keen to get me to visit, I recall. 'But there's no way I'm going back there.'

'Don't be stupid. He's going to wipe your chip and get you out.'

Moles grips my hand with a strength I didn't know he had. We walk slowly but boldly towards the opposite exit, away from Landi. Before we leave, I look back at her. She is calling someone. Her aunt? Medico? Bloody hell, that girl can chase a story.

We head through tunnels and by train, as quick as we can, towards PlayBeck Laboratories. I've given up struggling. If Moles is lying, I'm stuffed. Let's face it, I'm stuffed either way. Landi, Advice, Burbeck... I'm running around Test-Tube City like a rat in a glass box. There's nowhere to hide. There's no way out of this.

'We're nearly there,' Moles says. He's dragging me, and I hardly have time to register the numbers on the towers, levels, travel tubes. Then we stop as Moles checks his Flip for an incoming message. He drops my hand.

'What is it?'

His face falls and he starts to run back the way we came, beckoning me. 'We have to go back. Run, Alara. Run!'

Without asking why, I do. Side by side, we sprint into the nearest pedestrian tube as fast as we can, knocking people aside, too fast for citizens' arrests. We'll be logged but not stopped, if we just keep going.

At the other end of the tube, Moles pulls me into a social hub, then into a private talking booth, where gossipers go to share juicy details. We wait for the door to close. Moles is dripping with sweat, his eyes wild, his hair plastered to his head.

'Advice is at Burbeck's door right now. We can't...' His voice breaks and he doubles over, sobbing. 'Alara. We can't.'

We can't make it. We're trapped. I'm dead meat. London Under is dead meat. I failed the moral quest spectacularly. He raises his eyes, weary as someone after a week-long Sensii trip. My Flip buzzes. So this is it. I hold out my arm. I don't want to see it – the red Advice alert. The gotcha. Moles turns my wrist, his sweaty fingers slipping on my skin.

'It's Hoppi!'

Hoppi is there, flickering on the screen. I look around at the walls of the cubicle, with its digital menus for 'room service' and social media screens, and think how strange it is to have this cantankerous old man in here with us. His voice is calm, authoritative.

'I can't help you in the way I'd like, Alara. You're going to have to do this on your own. I'll explain how, but I have to be quick. My technicians are holding them up – faulty door.' He winks a baggy eye. I smile weakly. 'Get to South-East 50, Level 100. You'll go down the food refuse chute. It's narrow enough for you to crab your way down. We have found a weakness in the system there, and can manipulate the door controls. Your Flip will emit low-frequency radio waves, so when you get to the Void, Peron will try to track you before it runs out. It's not efficient, but it's the best we can do. Your Flip can be picked up by radar equipment anywhere, so get away from here as quickly as you can. Good luck, Alara. I hope I won't see you again.'

I look intensely at Moles. 'Can this actually work?'

He gulps. 'Of course. How else do you think we get people down?' He's talking about the Invited. I'm not the first person Moles has helped, of course. That reassures me about the plan, but not about my ability to make it. I hold out my hand. It trembles.

'Don't think about it,' Moles chides, knocking my hand aside. 'Act normal.'

It's too much. It's all too much. It's based on crazy opportunities and me not failing – and I feel so drained and emotional, I can't see how I can do it.

'Let's walk and talk. Act like we've just enjoyed social time.'

We leave the booth and take the lift down to the travel hub, where we get the train towards South-East 50. We can't talk because it's full, so we do what everyone else does – look at our Flips. Moles and I get messages from Hoppi:

> In precisely two hours, we'll trigger a release of rubbish onto the Void. Get down and make for the door ASAP. We'll open again ten minutes later. There's a chance it could set off a fault alarm, so be fast. Get out and stay low. There are refuse teams out there. You must not be seen.

My sweat has cooled and I'm suddenly freezing. Moles, too. We stare at each other, shivering, half scared, half knowing. Our Sensiis can't adapt fast enough for this real-life excitement. The next train is nearly empty. As we whizz towards our final destination, he reaches for my hand and leans towards me. I think he's going to say something sentimental. If there's a time, it's now.

'When you get down, follow the numbers on the doors of the towers. Walk due north-north-east to reach

East 50. Then walk in a direct line to North-East 50, then north-north-west to North 50. Peron will be following the same route in reverse. It will be dangerous because the refuse teams have been tip-turning around there, but that will make it easier to stay hidden.'

'Moles, if they've just tip-turned, won't there be gases? Is it safe?'

'They don't do it to release gases, Alara.' Moles leans toward me and knocks my shoulder with his forehead. 'Don't you see? Nature always takes hold. But not if you keep interrupting it.'

'No green.'

'No green,' he confirms.

So Advice deliberately keeps nature away. Stops us seeing natural green, to make us forget it. Moles knew this. He knew it and accepted it. I guess I'll never understand him.

The train arrives at South-East and we take the SE–NW Compass train down to skyscraper 50. We are so close to our destination now that neither of us can talk. I squeeze Moles' hand and pull it onto my lap. He flinches, but he doesn't pull it away. His face is emotionless, as if life has drained from his body.

'Are you okay?' I whisper.

He nods.

'Moles, I'm sorry. I'm so sorry.'

He taps into his Flip and I get a message. *I'm going to miss you.*

I tap on mine. *I'm going to miss you, too.*

He writes, *I'm not prepared for this.* He taps his heart.

There is no Sensii trip that prepares you for this, I write.

I should have been a better friend.

I look at him and nod. Yes, you should have been.

Our train pulls in and we take the lift down to Level 100. We are the only ones there.

'This has to be quick. You ready?'

'I think so.'

'Okay.' Moles lifts up the chute hatch then hands me a pill. 'I was keeping this for me, to help me keep going after you left. But you take it. It's a gym pill. It'll give you energy. Put it somewhere easy to reach.' I take it and place it in my top pocket.

He nods. 'Now, go slowly. You might hit a greasy patch. It's dark. You won't be able to see. And remember to gauge how tired you are. Take the pill when you think it's time. I don't know what's in that thing, but it's better than death. Now, come on. Hop up.' He pats the edge of the chute, but I can't. Not without saying goodbye.

I wrap my arms around his neck. He tries to pull me away, but not with much conviction, and eventually he hugs me back.

'Why don't you come, too?'

He laughs, sad. 'Fragile me in Dirt City? I'd perish!'

'No, I mean it, Moles. Come too. Get away from this place. There is so much out there. It's thrilling. So much more thrilling than –'

Moles shuts me up with a kiss. His lips press hard against mine, but it doesn't feel right. It's not passion. It's desperation, sadness. He pulls away. 'Sorry,' he mutters.

I pull him to me and hold him tight. What will he do when I'm gone? I think of all the trips he'll take to block out the pain. What will become of him? Perhaps he could have a Pixel to mould. A Vim. A PlayBeck creation. Suddenly, it dawns on me.

'Moles, Vim wasn't a coincidence, was he?'

'Burbeck helped Peron to get out. He made a replacement of him for me, complete with some of his sayings. I hated it.' He clocks my expression. There's so much I didn't know. 'Hoppi would do anything for Peron. Peron was his prodigy, see? So at least one of us had a father figure who cared, right?'

Oh, Moles…

'So he's a good guy. I wouldn't have guessed it when I met him.'

'Burbeck suspected they were using you for something, but he didn't know what. That's all.'

'And now I'm leaving with the prototype of his best invention yet,' I say, tapping my head. 'He must hate me.'

'Advice would never let it get to market, anyway. They're paranoid that Gen-Tech could be used to tap into the subconscious – the buried cell memories of past generations. It might give people dangerous dreams of a new life.'

'Totally paranoid!'

'Well, that *was* Hoppi's intention, to be fair.' He grins.

We stare at each other a while. Years of scoffing yiros and mocking each other, getting pissy over missed meet-ups, and unspoken tenderness are playing out between us.

'No more, now. Go. Go!' he croaks.

I sit on the edge of the chute and place my feet flat on the wall below me. This first bit is precarious. I need to lean forward and place both hands on the wall opposite – that's the tricky bit. If I slip, if my upper body strength isn't up to it, I'll fall immediately. *Five thousand feet.* My breath is shaky. Moles strokes the small of my back, telling me it will be okay. I breathe in deeply and let it out slowly, regulating my heart as I know how. And then I push out and forward.

My palms touch the wall opposite. They slip a little, but I manage to keep enough tension by pushing more weight onto them. I move one hand around so I'm in a starfish shape – it's a stronger pose, less prone to tilting and rocking, with less pressure on my wrists.

'I've got it,' I say.

'You have just under two hours before the door is opened at the bottom. Ten minutes until the outside door opens after that.' And then Moles shuts the chute hatch, and I am in darkness. A mile in darkness.

I start my descent. It's rocky at first, and my heart leaps into my throat with every move, bringing up bile and smoothie. I spit it down the chute, along with my fear, and tell myself that this is like *Sky Jump* or *Caver* – just another game that requires me to keep calm and keep steady. I count – I *have* to count, with two hours and no watch – and begin to coordinate my movements with every other second.

One. Two. Shift hand. Three. Four. Move other hand. Five. Six. Move foot. Seven. Eight. Move other foot.

The physical part is okay. The fear comes in waves – every time my hand slips or my foot doesn't grip as well as it should. But total darkness is my friend. I can't see the abyss below me. And when my rhythm is good, I feel enveloped and safe. It's the emotional impact that puts me most at risk. Because when I think of reality, I wobble. I mustn't think of what I've left, and I can't think of the future either. Not of Jay, with his raw excitement and his cabin in the woods... Because if I think of him, I think of Nate, his brother, now abandoned by two people he loves. So I force myself not to think, but just to count.

Fighting the interruptions means I lose track of time. I find myself going over the same numbers. How long have I been doing this? Will I make it? I'm tired – not tired enough for the gym pill, but I know it's a fine line, because if I wait too long, then I won't have the strength to hold myself with one arm while I retrieve the pill with the other hand. I judge that now is probably the time.

I force my hands and feet against the chute, shuffling to accommodate the uneven spread of my weight as I release one hand. I rock, and push my hand back again quickly. Then I shift, pushing with every muscle until it burns, and I grab the pill and put it in my mouth, then quickly slam my hand back against the wall.

Then there's a rushing noise above me. Swishing. Getting louder. *Rubbish!* I brace myself. Feeling the gym pill kick in, I am able to lock myself across the chute space – just in time. The trash hits me. This is the food chute, so the garbage is soft and rotten. Wet, too, and I make a mental note that the walls might be slimy from here on. Must be careful. I begin the descent again, counting from the beginning. One, two, shift. One, two, shift...

There's another rush of air above me and a second bag of rubbish smacks me on the head. I wobble, my hand slips, and I can't recover. My weight is thrown off and I lurch forward. I can't correct it. Yet another bag hits me, this time on the back of my knees, and I lose my grip. I'm tumbling down the Drop, trying to grab at the walls to stop my fall. I make connections, temporary bridges – but I can't hold my weight and I ricochet, a scream lodged in my throat, down and down...

I land in rubbish. Stinking, putrid. But I'm alive. I must have been closer to the bottom than I thought. The fall must have been two levels – four at most. But I made it. I crawl to the edge of the rubbish pile and flatten myself against the wall to avoid being hit again. I wish I could call up to Moles. He wouldn't hear me, not from down here, but I want him to know that I'm safe. That so far, the plan has worked. Instead, I stay quiet and wait.

I wait twenty minutes, perhaps, worrying that I've missed my slot, then lights flicker on in the ceiling above. I can see I'm in a room within a room – a large scoop inside the foot of the skyscraper, designed to be ejected through the door and on to the surface. It's piled high with revolting, pungent trash. I have ten minutes to get to the door, but it's harder than I thought. My feet sink into the rotting muck and every step is an effort; each leg feels as if it weighs a ton. I'm glad I took the pill. I certainly have more energy than before, but I'm still too far away when the chute door slides open, releasing the landslide of rubbish. I surf on top of it, running and tripping over the last gush, racing to reach the door before it closes again. There is still a little light outside – dusky blue fast turning navy – and I run for it, pushing past the rubbish, slipping with every step. Then I start to skate – not lifting my feet, but pushing them forward and outwards across the gunge, sometimes skidding and falling, but making progress. The door is fully open and I can see outside. I can tell by the single row of scrapers in front of me and the way the rows on either side branch away that the doors opened facing South-East, away from Central. I have my bearings now. I just need to get out. But the door is only open for seconds before it begins to close again. *No!* I cry tears of frustration as I push my way through the mulch. I must ignore the building sense of hopelessness, or it will bring me down. I have to keep going. Even if it means running under the door at the last minute, being crushed into pulp like everything around me. Gritting my teeth, I plough on, but it's futile. I watch, chest heaving with stress, as the door closes. It clanks against the concrete floor, like doom.

I crawl across the remaining trash to the closed door and push my tired body against it. Its metal is cool against my hot face. Then I slide down it like a rag doll and sit on the floor. I want to bang my fists and wail, but I have to be rational and calm. I don't want to die here.

How much rubbish is here? There are around five hundred apartments in a tower; if each apartment chucks one bag a day, that's five hundred bags. If I can count a proportion of the bags here, then estimate the total, I'll know how many days' worth there is – and therefore when the door will open next to empty the chute. Was it once a week or twice a week? I can't remember...

It's hopeless, anyway. The ceiling lights flicker and fade and I'm in the dark.

Can't count bags in the dark; can't even find a ray of hope.

Then the door behind me shudders. I shuffle forward and turn round, feeling the cool evening air pour in and lick my ankles. I don't wait to see if there's anyone on the other side; I am not missing this chance. I roll out as the door rises, then shakily stand up outside. I stretch my arms and legs, letting myself stand for a moment, enjoying the breeze that wraps itself around my face and body. Then I go.

Chapter 26

The walk between the towers takes longer than I thought. The distance between the rows this far out along the line is immense, but as evening sets in and lights turn on, I start to notice a pattern – where the windows are placed, and how they are spaced. They all angle inwards; not one looks out beyond the city limits to the fields of green. From the moment they built this city, they've been actively deterring our connection with nature.

And innocent people are helping them, blind to reality. Like Dad, tip-turning. Of course, if plants were allowed to take root, there would soon be trees. A rapidly expanding patch of green, growing out and up. Animals would come to feed or nest. They'd make burrows among the roots. There would be colour and life and promise – and inside London Star everyone would grow restless, watching creatures roam free, not poisoned. They would feel trapped, and lied to. What would happen then? Could Sensii dosing and gene-washing suppress the powerful rebellious surges created by injustice? The discovery that you're not free from a diseased life, but instead being deprived of living a perfectly normal one? That you're like a laboratory monkey? That could blow up all kinds of trouble. *Mr Leppito, I present to you 'A New Perspective'.*

And then I wonder if anything is real at all. Like: is New Europe really polluted? Is break-away Scotland sick with CO2? Are they really all making Flip cities to be like us, or are they really wondering what the hell's going on in New Anglia? Feeling sorry for us?

My theories keep me company as I plough on through the rubble. Those, and the trash crabs. I say hello to them as I go, promising each and every one that I won't eat its brother or sister, but knowing, as I remember the taste of the sweet meat in that fiery sauce, it's not a promise I can keep. They scuttle and leap on me, attracted by the scraps of food from the rubbish chute, but I don't shake them off, except when they crawl on my hands when I'm trying to negotiate a trash pile, or they tickle my face as they clamber too high. I am glad to be alongside other living things. I've learned to love the contact.

I don't have protection this time, but my fingers know how to feel for glass that might easily shatter and sheet plastic that doesn't. My feet adjust and balance on broken masonry and breeze blocks. I skid a couple of times, and chasms open up below me, created by shifting piles of rubbish, like tectonic plates, but it's as if the last few hours have primed my body to react quickly to changes. I skip out of danger and move quickly across the newly turned surface.

Dark falls too quickly. Only a small amount of milky moonlight. I take a piece of broken mirror glass, thinking I might be able to use the moon's reflection to light my path, but then I remember how I saw lights down here before – and how tonight there might be others watching for the same thing. The scrapers are lit up and their light is enough for me to see by, just. So long as I have any of the ring of 50s in my sights, I have something to aim for. That, and Jay.

Peron, Nate's older brother. Now there's a twist in the tale. They're so different – Moles' sharp wit and reclusive existence, Jay's soft manner and broad horizons. They are opposites, yet they are two sides of something perfect. I will miss Moles. But perhaps not as much as I look forward to seeing Jay.

The sound of motors snatches my attention. Refuse teams returning home. I peer over a mound and see the leaping headlights of sweepers rolling over the lumpy surface. Some headlights are pointed in my direction. They're nowhere near me yet, but the sweepers are faster than I am on foot, and if they get within range of my Flip, there's a chance they'll pick me up. Trash crabs scuttle with the vibrations, and I have to go too. To escape the beams, I run sharp east, knowing that the longer it takes me to get round to the North arm, the more likely it is that Jay will give up, presuming that my escape failed.

I walk for hours. I'm tired. My knees buckle and I fall more easily. I slice my elbows; a rusty cord whips across my face. I have deep cuts across my shins that I dare not touch, in case they're worse than I imagine. Trash crabs cling to them, which isn't a good sign, but I can't worry about blood or infection now.

As soon as the sweepers' lights disappear, I curve back round to continue walking, but I'm lost. I can no longer pinpoint tower 50. I can't see the numbers on the doors or work out where it would be in the row ahead; it's impossible to count forwards or backwards down the row because of the distance, although I can guess at the middle. But what's the point of heading in a direction if it might be the wrong one? Jay and I could miss each other; I could end up walking forever until the light comes and I'm discovered by refuse teams or a search party. Dad would certainly be out there at first light, if he isn't already...

I need to rest. Just an hour or two to regain my strength, and to prevent an accident like the one London Under thinks I had. After a nap, I'll think about what to do. I'll work it out.

I curl up behind a burnt-out carcass of a vehicle and shut my eyes. I'm so tired, it feels as if my body is melting into the rusty metal. So tired I know this will be longer than a nap, but I can't help it. Can't stop it.

'Alara!'

I blink open my eyes. It's still dark, but I can tell by my leaden limbs and muddy brain that I've been asleep a while. Longer than a quick nap. I could sleep forever. But something woke me. A voice.

'Alara, wake up!'

'Jay?' I reach out to touch him.

He grabs my hand and pulls me up. 'We have to go. Come on.'

'Jay, I'm so tired.'

'We have to go now.' He's pulling me, but my body is floppy and unresponsive. After the sleep, my muscles hurt more than ever. They have been torn and strained from descending the Drop.

'Get up!' he hisses, yanking painfully at my arm. 'Get to your feet and put your arm around my waist.'

We limp along slowly, stumbling and falling. Ahead, day breaks on the horizon. Jay stops every now and then to consult his compass and map. We walk in silence for hours. Then he stops and takes me by the shoulders. In the low light, his eyes are shiny, his smile lopsided. His voice is croaky with emotion. 'You know something? You really are Wonder Woman. You did the Drop. You're amazing.' He laughs and shakes his head.

'I had an energy pill, so I should be disqualified,' I slur, weak and tired. 'Besides, I'm hardly a pioneer. It's how all the Inviteds get down.'

'No, it isn't. Usually we have more time to prepare

these things – we disrupt security systems, sneak people out around refuse team movements. We have months to design an escape and work on it. But your descent was down to determination and strength of mind alone… That's never been done. We never thought it could be.'

'But Moles said…' Moles said what he did to stop me chickening out. In a way, I was a sacrifice. I shake off the thought of what might have happened if I hadn't believed it was possible. 'So, now I've made it this far, how are you going to get me back in? We can't walk in like this.'

'Good point. Thanks for reminding me. Stop a minute.' He squats by my feet and retrieves my old tracker from his bag and presses some buttons until it beeps. Activated. 'Told them I thought I picked up a signal, registered it moving,' he says, attaching it to my ankle. 'Congratulations – you survived your fall.'

'And how did I do that?'

'You knocked yourself out when you fell. When you came to, you slowly began to climb back up. You're pretty beat up, but you made it back.'

'But I'm not that beaten up.'

He motions up and down my body. 'Alara, are you not aware that your face is cut, your arms are torn, and your legs are covered in blood?'

I look down to see the bottom half of my left leg, so thick with sticky blood it looks like beetroot flesh. Then the pain starts to register. Pain like I've never felt. Like boiling oil bubbling through my veins.

'We'll need to rough you up a bit more, though,' Jay says. 'But we can do that with dust. We'll have to improvise.'

'What about my clothes? I'm not wearing the same ones I went missing in.'

'I brought a change with me. We'll say your old clothes were so torn, they were indecent. Get those ones off.'

He's thought of everything. I find a flat surface to sit on, and Jay helps me to peel off my trousers, slowly and carefully so he doesn't disturb my wounds. The touch of his hand on my thigh makes me freeze, and my heart thumps out of control. It's not the anticipation of being hurt, but a sudden painful shyness; my cheeks are hot with embarrassment. They didn't have time to dose me properly before I left. In a way I wish they had, as I don't know what to do with this feeling. I try to push his hands away but he shushes me gently, like a nurse, thinking I'm scared. His fingers tug at my trousers again but the stuck cloth of my second-skin tears at the crust of blood, and it rips – cold and sharp, exposing new skin and a fresh flow of blood. I gasp. I'm kind of grateful. It brings my focus sharply back to reality, to being hurt and exposed in the Void. I'm not safe yet.

'Now, give me your top.'

I do as I'm told, and I wrap my arms around myself as he tears a strip off my top and binds it tightly around my leg.

'Better?'

I nod.

He grabs a handful of rubble dust and rubs it into my hair and over my face. 'Now you look like you've been lost for days in a crevasse. No one will know.'

'What about my head? The chip?'

'It'll have to stay there. No one needs to know about that.'

'And this?' I hold my wrist up to show him the Flip, buried in my skin like a leech.

Jay gulps. 'That's not great. Argh.'

He turns in a circle, struggling with a solution, but there is only one. My eyes are stinging as I think of it. Crying as I say what has to be done. 'You have to rip it out.'

He is rigid, but he nods. There's no other way. He fetches a pocketknife from his bag and flicks open the tiny blade.

I turn my head away. He grips my arm and twists it, so I can't move. I'm grateful for whatever dose of compliance potion is still in my body, because if I'd thought too long about what was coming, I wouldn't have agreed. As soon as he starts to cut, the pain is unbearable. My skin rips, splits; I hiss with agony as the nerve endings shred. He does it as quickly as he can, and it's too quick and not quick enough. The sensitive flesh beneath suddenly meets elements it was never meant to encounter. The breeze feels like whips against my raw flesh, and the dust settles on it like pins. I faint, but he catches me.

'We need to get you to Dr Orta now. Right now.'

'I'm going to … I can't…'

'You're doing brilliantly.' He wraps another strip of cloth tightly round my wrist, and I scream again. I am raw meat, singing with pain.

'You'll be fine. Fine. Alara, I'm sorry. We should have thought of another way.'

'But now, no one will know now, right? No one will know what I did?'

'One day they might, but not now. Now, you look like you've been through hell.'

'One day?'

'Every action has a consequence. But quiet now – we need to move.'

The sun comes up fast, but while it's still low in the sky we shuffle between the towering heaps and hide in pockets of shadow. It's exhausting, but Jay doesn't offer me his water. He says I need to look in a bad way. How could I look worse? My tongue sticks to my mouth; it blocks my throat and makes me gasp for air. I inhale the dust he rubbed into my face. Eventually, somewhere north, we stop. Jay pulls aside a sheet of metal, ordinary-looking. Behind it is a tunnel leading down into the earth.

And everything goes black.

Chapter 27

Jay stands in the doorway, watching as Dr Orta removes a needle from my arm. It takes both of them to help me off the bench and to my feet. I yelp. I've been washed and cleaned, but my feet sting the moment they touch the floor, as if I'm treading on glass. It's my muscles cramping.

'I can't,' I whine.

'Come on, Hopalong, you only have to get as far as there.' Jay points to the doorway, to a wheelchair. 'Your chariot awaits.'

A tear escapes unexpectedly, and Dr Orta wipes it away with her thumb. 'Better to feel something than nothing at all,' she says, giving me a big hug. She turns away to clean her equipment. 'I'll need to see you again in a few days, to check the stitches. Oh, and welcome back, Alara.'

She winks and puts a finger to her lips. She won't

say a word. Of course, she knows. I feel for the stitches where my new Sensii chip was removed, and notice the bracelet of rough stitching where the Flip was implanted, yellowed with iodine solution.

'If anyone asks, you had deep lacerations from the fall,' she adds, wrapping a clean bandage round my wrist. She makes a neat knot, then reaches behind her for a bag of pills, which she puts in my lap. 'Painkillers. You're going to need them.'

'More pain. Great,' I say, and smile sarcastically.

Jay pushes me away from the surgery room, singing.

'What are you so happy about?' I wince.

'Nothing,' he says mischievously. 'Nothing at all.'

The tunnel outside is warm and light. Steam from cooking floats in through the windows. I breathe in deeply and my tummy growls. I don't know if it's day or night, but I know I'm hungry.

'Jay, I'm starving. Can we go to Eat Street?'

'Nope. We've got a date and we can't be late.'

'Oh, Jay, please,' I beg, laying an arm across my stomach. It's started to growl.

He pulls up outside his house and raps on the door. Dilly answers, and takes me into the living room. Jay disappears then, leaving us together.

'Sorry about last time,' she says, shutting the door. 'I know you must have thought I was rude.' I shake my head, but she smiles. 'I'm a bit wary of strangers.'

'Jay explained. I understand.'

'Did he also explain that he's terrified Advice will send someone to assassinate him?' She looks at me. 'I know everything about him and his past, Alara. And I know he took a big chance on you. I wasn't quite so sure.'

'I would never hurt him.' I gulp.

'I know that, now. Well, let's get you dressed.' She turns to a large box and starts to pull out clothes. They are colourful: some have ribbons and lace, other have panels of floaty fabrics.

'Did you make all these?'

She nods and drags the box to me. 'Tell you what, why don't you choose something yourself? You should be able to choose your own wardrobe.'

'Seriously? I get to have some of these?'

'Don't get me wrong – I'm not stupidly generous. These are the items I didn't manage to sell. They've been sitting around for ages. I should be tearing them up and recycling them. But seeing as Jay is generous with his chits, I can afford to let you have a few pieces.'

'Okay,' I say meekly, picking through the garments. 'Thank you.'

'Start by passing me the ones you like the look of, and then we can whittle them down.'

I pass her the exciting clothes – the bright reds and the royal blues, the ones with buttons and flyaway threads, simply because they catch my eye. Comfortable-looking clothes, too. I pass them all to her, grinning. Then I see something that takes my breath away. It's simple, but it's perfect. I hold it up. A halter-neck top made of green materials, some silky and some rough; a patchwork of my favourite colour, with a high neckline and a low backline. She nods approvingly.

'It'll go beautifully with your skin.' She sighs, looking at the top and then back at me. 'I have some raggy white trousers you could wear with it. They're soft and roomy, so they won't rub against your sore leg. Try them.'

She helps me put them on. I do a painful twirl so she can see what needs adjusting.

'We don't have time for proper alterations,' she says. Instead, she clips the top in place with pins.

Freddie runs in and stops dead in front of me. 'Lara girl,' he says.

'Yes, it's me, Alara,' I say. 'Hi, Freddie.'

'Wow, you almost look human.' Jay laughs, returning with a big bag slung over his shoulder.

'How long will you be gone?' Dilly looks serious as she strokes Freddie's hair.

'Two or three days. Maybe more. I can take Freddie, if you like.'

'No, I'd rather he stayed with me. And you should have some space.'

'Where are you going?' The words burst from me, rude and abrupt. Jay can't be leaving me already?

He doesn't look at me. He takes Dilly's hand. 'Don't worry about a thing. John will come later and he'll stay with you until I'm back. I promise, nobody will mess with you. Got to go,' he says, kissing her on the cheek. He gives her a wink and she smiles. I don't know what's going on. I feel queasy. Jay lifts Freddie and swings him round. 'Look after your mummy, Freddie, okay?'

'Where are we going now?' I ask. I'm tired.

'Will you stop asking questions!' he scolds. He wheels me back onto the street, zigzagging across London Under, and then we go down. He bounces the wheelchair awkwardly down the steps; I'm half crying, half laughing. At the bottom he wheels me through the tunnels and down more stairs. We must be well underground. And it's dark. He slows down until we're barely moving, and I'm impatient with hunger and anticipation.

'Jay. Come on!' I shout.

He doesn't answer.

I turn around in the chair and feel for him, but he's gone. 'Jay!' I can't see a thing and I don't know where I am. 'Bloody hell!'

Suddenly flames appear – one after the other, flickering against the clay walls of the room we're in. They take hold and burn brighter, illuminating a table laid out for a meal. Then I see Martha with her might-be boyfriend, Danny, and Ellie, Diana, Michael, David. Others, too. John, who smiles a welcome. Lots of people I don't know, but who are introduced to me as 'pillars of the community'. They cheer and whistle.

The welcome, the food. Things I craved so much. In my mind, there's a buffer of unbearable sadness, but it pushes the relief and joy to the front, and I'm crying. Then I'm apologising for crying. Eventually Jay steps in.

'To the table!' He wheels me to the head of the table and everyone else takes their seats. Then they take it in turns to come and talk to me.

Mark is the first. He shakes my hand firmly. I'm not quite sure what to say, and I feel everyone in the room tense. 'Welcome back, Alara.'

I breathe a sigh of relief so loud that everyone laughs, which makes me think they weren't sure about Mark's intentions, either. Then the others come – all warm, familial, even. Especially Ellie, who clutches me to her like a daughter, without the tinge of nervousness I used to detect. Martha bounces on her toes, waiting her turn.

'Alara, I'm so glad you're back!' She wraps her arms tightly around me and rocks me back and forth. 'I'm never letting you go!'

I have to peel her off me, just to breathe.

'Watch her stitches, Martha!' Ellie scolds.

Martha grabs a space at the end of the bench seating closest to me, forcing a 'pillar of the community' I recognise as the librarian to shift further down. Jay catches my eye.

Serfs, hired especially for the occasion, file in carrying fragrant trays of hot vegetables, breads, and a roast chicken I say a quiet 'thank you' to. A huge bowl of mashed potato swimming in butter is placed right in front of me.

'Speech!' someone calls. 'Alara, say something.'

I shake my head. I can't. I don't want to. I'm overwhelmed, exhausted and hungry. Jay notices and nods. He scoops out a spoonful of mash and hands it to me to eat.

'But I would like to say a few words, if you don't mind.'

He turns to me. I stop spooning the creamy potato into my mouth, embarrassed.

'Alara, as soon as we picked up your signal, I cannot tell you how relieved we all were. And then, to find you alive... It's a miracle.' He winks. 'And, seeing as only the toughest raiders have ever survived a fall, I think it proves you're made of strong enough stuff to live in London Under.'

There are murmurs of agreement, and I look around and see smiles.

'This meal – this *event* – is our way of saying thanks for choosing life, and thanks for choosing to live it with us. To Alara!'

Serfs circle the table, pouring clear liquid into our glasses.

'It's brew,' Martha whispers. 'Okay on special occasions. Drink it in one go, though, because it's disgusting.'

We all hold up our glasses and knock back the thick liquid. It's bitter and syrupy. There is coughing and laughing, and although it tastes terrible, like mouldy lemon, I feel a warmth spreading out from my stomach, flooding my body. I grin, involuntarily.

'Food! Food!' someone shouts.

Ellie leans over from further down the table. 'How's the potato, Alara?'

'Not as good as yours!' Although, to be honest, I can't tell the difference. It's all so good. 'What about the litter bugs?' I ask, wiping away butter with the back of my hand.

'Litter bugs for a dinner party?' Diana says. I stop and look at her, still fearful of her authority. 'Save those for your dirty treats in Eat Street, Alara. I have a pretty good idea I'll know where to find you if I need you.'

We eat and chat about my miracle rescue, and they sing along as Danny strums his guitar late into the night – or maybe it's morning. I don't know, and I don't care. People start to drift away, stumbling after the brew, heading for bed.

'Time to go,' Jay says, wiping his mouth. I dreaded this: him going wherever he's going. I look at him, panicked, but he smiles. 'Michael?'

Michael steps forward and kneels at my feet. He removes the tracker and throws it to one side.

'Say goodbye to everyone, Alara,' Jay says, positioning himself behind my wheelchair.

My heart leaps. Wherever he's going, I'm going too.

Chapter 28

The day after my return to London Under, I wake up to birdsong. Not one or two birds, but thousands, like an orchestra warming up. My head hurts a little. Something tells me it's the brew. But it's also my Sensii dose disappearing, making me feel *more* of everything. I shrug off my blanket and step outside the cabin door into the forest. Through the canopy I can see that the sky is bright blue again, and I know where Jay will be. I hobble on sore legs down towards the river.

Just before the stony bank, I stop and watch him work. He examines a net then drags it into the river. He slips on a rock, losing his balance – his arms fly up and he drops the net, which floats just out of reach into the middle of the stream. He's forced to pick his way across to it using stepping stones, calling the net all kinds of bad names. He grabs it and turns. That's when he sees me. Embarrassed, he does a little bow.

'Enjoyed the show, I hope,' he says.

'If that's a show, I want my money back.' I laugh.

We swim. I shouldn't be getting wet, not with my stitches, not while my tortured skin struggles to heal. But I can't resist the water. It's freezing and vital. Afterwards, we dry off on the rocks, lying on our backs watching the clouds overhead morph and divide. It's no ambience screen. That blue above – it goes on forever and ever. It's a simple pleasure denied to everyone without a penthouse dome in Estrella, which is practically everyone. And it makes me angry. We should all be able to sit under a sky like this, feeling part of the world.

I sit up, suddenly cross. 'We should do something. We need to tell everyone in Estrella all about this.' I gesture at the scene around us. 'They would all want to live like us, given the choice.'

Jay shakes his head. 'You're wrong.'

'What do you mean, I'm wrong?'

'A lot of people wouldn't be happy here at all. Although they may not have a choice now that you've shaken the ground.'

'What do you mean?'

'You've shaken the ground. You've defied Advice. Like I said, all actions have consequences. Something will happen. I don't know when, but it's on the horizon.'

'If you're trying to scare me, it's working.'

Jay smiles. 'We're all scared of the future. But who knows? Maybe it will have a good outcome.'

'If it means your brother gets to come down here and join us, that'll be a good outcome.'

'My brother wouldn't be happy here.'

I know straight away that he's right. 'Why? Why is he that way?'

'He'd never admit it, but he needs the support of Star. Life down here would be too much for him. Besides, can you imagine him swimming in a river?'

I puff out my cheeks and shake my head. This is not Moles' scene at all.

'Why did you not tell me you were his brother?'

'I couldn't, without then explaining a lot more. As if things weren't complicated enough...' he says, raising an eyebrow.

There are plenty of other complicated things I need to ask him about, but not right now. Not at this moment.

'London Star is not a bad place, you know,' he continues. 'If it's a government's job to keep its people safe, then that's what they're doing. Their people are safe from every enemy imaginable, from the big to the very, very small. An antibacterial palace. No illness at all. Can you imagine going back two hundred years to a London ravaged by cancer and killer bugs, and telling people that one day they will have a citadel where everyone will live well, eat well, be entertained, employed, and never have to worry about early death or a disease we can't find a cure for? For the majority of folk, that would be a dream.'

But the spies, the paranoia, the harvesting? I wonder

if I should say something about the DNA supply, but not now. After all, Jay was used and manipulated, just like I was. Lured by the glory of doing something for the good of Estrella, and the chance to escape the dullness of life inside it.

'Every ruler in every civilisation since the dawn of time has done dodgy stuff. The important thing for me is that Nate is safe – for now – and I've got good people looking out for him.'

He's right, in a way. In Test-Tube City, it's a fine life for some. For people who like luxuries, like Mum. My chest tightens. It's as if Jay knows what I'm thinking, because he sits up and takes me in his arms to comfort me.

'They'll be grieving, Jay,' I say, feeling a burn in my throat and eyes.

'Shhh.' He kisses the top of my head.

'They'll be heartbroken. Blaming themselves.'

'It's okay.'

'It's not okay. It's not.'

I think back to what Dr Orta said. About making choices. But this seems an unfairly high price for someone else to pay for the choice I made.

'What if I *promised* you it's going to be okay?' Jay says cautiously.

I throw a rock into the river, angry.

'Alara. It *is* going to be okay. I *promise*.' The way he stresses 'promise', it almost makes me believe him. I wonder what else he's not telling me.

'Come on, let's go back.'

'Under?' I don't want to go back under, not yet. Not when the sun is still shining.

'I was thinking we could go back to the cabin, actually. Cook some fish, forage for greens, go for a walk. Just hang out for a few days.'

'Really?'

'Yeah, really. We've got a load to work out before you join the community.'

I smile, raising my face to the sun, feeling my tears dry to salt flakes on my cheeks. 'What do we need to work out exactly?'

'Oh, you know. Things like where you're going to live – although Martha and Ellie are keen to have you. And what we're going to do about your potato addiction.'

Jay and I go back to the cabin, where we cook trout on hot embers and drink tea made with river water. He teaches me card games. We walk in the forest, collecting leaves and berries for later, for dinner. I spot wild deer. Jay says he'll hunt one for me one day, or get John to. Venison is good meat, he says. I suggest we find juniper berries and visit the dairy farm for cream, to make a perfect sauce. And before bed, we climb the viewing tree.

I'm nervous about looking. *You've shaken the ground. Something is on the horizon.* But if there's trouble brewing, I can't see it from here.

London Star glows in the dusk, lit up by its hubs, arcades and screens – a society plugged into electronic dreams. But I know now that I want more than dreams. I want pain, dirt, purpose and love. I want real life.

And real life is down here, beneath my feet and under my skin.

Acknowledgements

Many thanks to all those who have read my books and continue to support me: to my dear friends, who cry and cheer with me through all the highs and lows; to my family, who put up with a hell of a lot; to everyone in the writing community, which is always there for me (it would be a lonely road without you). And to my mother, Anni Delahaye, who reads and reads and reads.

Being an undisciplined plotter, I am hugely grateful to those who have given their time to troubleshoot my manuscripts – Sinéad O'Hart, Jamie Russell, Darren Simpson, Gabriel Dylan, Liam James, Martin Howard, Tom Easton and Stu Atkinson, to name just a few. And thank you to those whose enthusiasm for Electric Life kept me buoyant, including Clare and Ian Harvey, Hannah Fazakerly, Sadie Toghill, Mimi Thebo, Katie Preedy, Matilda Johnson and Maja Varadinek.

Big thanks to the talented Anna Morrison, who designed

the cover, and to my patient and eagle-eyed editor, Jane Hammett, who helped me wrangle the book into shape.

Special thanks to Joanna Nadin, who allowed me to borrow a detail from her wonderful book, No Man's Land.

Huge thanks to my wonderful agent, Alice Williams.

And endless thanks to Troika – for their belief in my writing and for putting this book out into the world.

About the Author

Rachel Delahaye was born in Australia and now lives in Bath, UK. She has written children's fiction for Egmont, Stripes (the Mort the Meek series and an animal adventure series) and Piccadilly Press (the Jim Reaper series). Rachel also writes fiction and poetry for accelerated reading schemes, to help children gain confidence in reading. Electric Life is her second book for Troika.

Find out more at her website: www.racheldelahaye.com

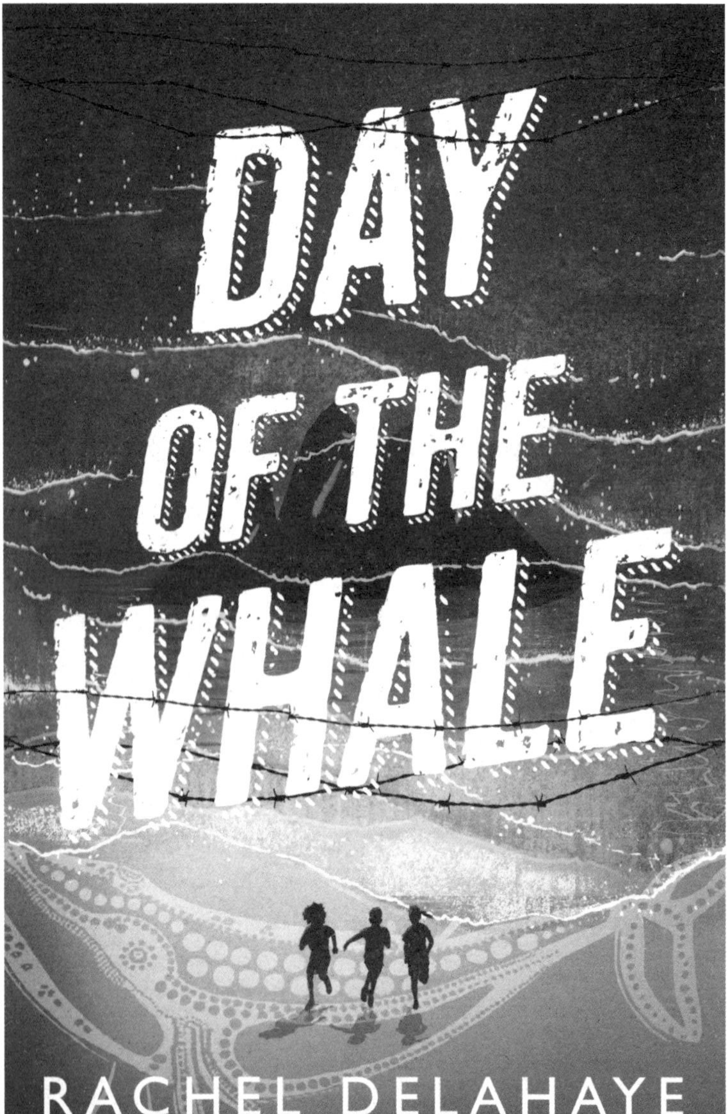
DAY OF THE WHALE
RACHEL DELAHAYE

DAY OF THE WHALE

RACHEL DELAHAYE

On an island ruled by whales, one boy is searching for his missing father, another refuses to forget the past, and a girl is on the run. Together, they embark on an adventure of discovery that could anger the whales and crack their community apart.

'In a story filled with danger, adventure, determination, daring and immense courage, Delahaye explores topical issues like climate change, truth, history and freedom as the three curious youngsters unravel some dark secrets. Gripping and moving in equal measure.'
Pam Norfolk, Lancashire Post

'I raced through this book. The story is scarily believable and the characters so well developed. When I read that Rachel

had written Cam, Banjo and Petra to represent truth, history and freedom, I shouted YES!! That is EXACTLY what these characters bring to this story: it is steeped in these very themes. I urge anyone and everyone to dive into this dystopian adventure.'
Claire Menzies

'Day of the Whale is a brilliantly written and captivating story set in a future dystopian world. It addresses the impact of human greed and control on the natural world. Full of intrigue, secrets and lies, and with powerful environmental and societal messages, this is a great book.'
Kevin Cobane

'Day of the Whale is a mesmerising, thought-provoking tale set in a dystopian world that feels alarmingly realistic. Delahaye cleverly weaves in environmental and political themes throughout as Cam embarks on a perilous emotional journey in his quest to find the truth. Superb characterisation meets atmospheric storytelling in this thrilling adventure.'
Book lover Jo

'Learning who to trust, which messages to believe, and how to think independently all form the plot of this story. I would love to read the first few chapters of this story and leave it open to discussion among students. Do we need to believe all we are told? At what point is it braver to believe the truth than listen to the lies? Who would the students trust

at various points in the story? What makes that character so believable?'
Erin Hamilton, Just Imagine

'This is a gorgeous story about secrets and truth, about authority and corruption of power, about our relationships with nature and the wild and the people around us, about our responsibilities and our memories. Day of the Whale is beautiful and exciting, a rich tapestry of a novel.'
Liam James, BookWormHole